FFS:
Politically
Correct

Pride and Politics-Book 1

GIA STONE

FFS: Politically Correct

Pride and Politics – Book 1

Copyright © 2025 Gia Stone

All Rights Reserved.

ISBN:(e-book) 979-8-9993475-1-0

ISBN: (print) 979-8-9993475-0-3

DEDICATION

To Schatzi, who never left my side and always pulled me up from the depths of my despair

Chapter One

"There are many possibilities, but only one truth."

I've never been a fan of bad lighting. Dim and not delightful would be the best way to describe this setting. The kind of dull overhead that forces unnecessary shadows on your face and ages a person to the point where cemetery decisions are considered. Even worse, we're crammed into the back room of a restaurant. The sounds of fajitas sizzling and bubbling enchiladas drift in and out as people join the meeting. The crowd is diverse with every seasonal color palette being represented. One bulb keeps flickering, creating a weird visual over a woman leaning against the wall with a cane. She keeps eyeing the clock above the door. I think it was hung specifically for our group. Beside her, a teen with braids secured with rainbow-colored beads taps her screen and laughs. With an air of assumed importance, a man in a blazer, tie, and starched pants marches past them to sign in. He already has a name tag. Most likely a judicial candidate. Lawyers begin with enough money to afford their own professional name tags. I, on the other hand made mine by sliding a business card, designed by yours truly into a plastic card holder. The kind you would get from a trade show. Our backgrounds range from middle class to barely making it. I fall into the latter. But we are all here for the same reason. Democracy.

I make one more glance around the room and shift my feet. *Steady*. There is only a brief moment in between speakers. I am one of the last. It's obvious from the toe-tapping and clock-watching that people only have so much patience for democracy on a Tuesday night. I take a deep breath. Saliva floods the back of my mouth. My blood prickles at the base of my neck and tingles near my ears. I press my eyelids shut for a less than half a second. Hopefully, no one notices. This is the part I hate about this whole thing. Being in front of the crowd. Public speaking has never been my forte. But it's part of the job. Not that anyone would consider this a job, as in, it's unpaid. At least this part is.

Maybe if we had a podium, I would be more comfortable. I could use it like a life vest of security to hold on to. But instead, it's just me in my heels and a microphone. I raise the wireless device to my face. "People often ask me why I decided to run for public office. What made me have the courage? Why would I want to put my name on the ballot and a target on my back?"

The crowd laughs. I make eye contact with the woman with the cane. She taps it on the ground and nods at me.

"This is the part that isn't funny." I let my eyes focus on a woman holding a swaddled baby. "This is the part I don't like to talk about." My lips rub together as if they are going to start a fire.

Nerves. I tap my fingers on the side of my legs. I can do this. "Rape insurance."

The crowd gasps. The teen with the braids drops her phone.

"What is rape insurance you might ask, if you hadn't heard of it." I shrug my shoulders. As if anyone could shrug off something so horrendous.

The whites of people's eyes have expanded. They haven't heard of it. Most people hadn't. It's one of those bills that goes undetected among the thousands of others that may or may not make it to the House and Senate Floor in the Texas Capitol.

"This was a bill that actually made it to the House Floor." I nod to assure the crowd how horrific it is. "Yes, it had a lively debate. About the concept of women needing to have supplemental insurance in addition to their health insurance that would cover any costs associated with being raped." I am silent. It is imperative to take a pause and let them take this in.

The women in the crowd are shaking their heads. The men appear to be confused. I get this. Most of the women understand that these types of draconian bills and policies do exist and are written. Yet most men do not consider this to even be possible, as they haven't personally experienced anything like this to be able to contemplate that it is a reality.

I raise the microphone. "To me ... this was egregious. To me, this was barbaric. To me, it's sick, just like Dick Mikelson. We don't need rape insurance. We need access to affordable healthcare and education on consent. Texas House District 193 is ready to flip-and I'm here to do it." I step back and nod.

The woman near the wall raises her cane and shouts "Yes!" The teen with the braids dropped her phone again but is clapping. The mother has covered up her baby's ears and is shouting "Let's go!"

Mr. Starched Suit is clapping and eyeing the room. It is probably his time to speak. Not exactly a good moment for him to try and grab the microphone.

"Let's do this! Please come sign up to join my campaign and let's flip this seat together. I'll be right over there." I point to the table to the side where my flyers and clipboard are. I hand the microphone to the suit guy. My face is warm. This is the kind of energy that feeds me. This is the kind of energy that I have to rely on when I am out knocking on doors of potential voters in one-hundred-degree weather. Got to love the hot Texas sun as it beats down against my head as I pound the pavement.

I sit back down at my table. The Starched Suit is up, and is indeed a judicial candidate. I'm new to this scene. I didn't really have a lot of friends who were politically engaged before putting my name on the ballot. But now, it's like this club. The candidate club. Some of us only have one actual political or neighborhood type of club to go to like this one, whereas others that are seeking to represent a larger area have to go to many clubs. Going to clubs has three purposes: speaking to voters, trying to grab some new volunteers, and hopefully adding a donation to our campaigns here and there.

A light tap on my back draws my attention back to the present. A woman with a wispy silver bob and creases from an active life line her face. She hands me a white folded paper. "Here, hun, take this and take him out."

I'm sure it's a donation. The sides of my mouth pull up. "Thank you, I appreciate your support. Please sign here to join the campaign."

She fills out the sheet and leaves the room just as the last candidate finishes. Mary, the club president, takes the mic.

"We want to thank all the candidates that came to speak with us tonight. Be sure to sign up to help them or go to their website and kick into their campaign. Remember everyone here has an option to help, whether you knock on doors or dig into your wallet. Please consider donating your time or your treasure." Mary claps her hands.

"Or both," I shout.

The woman with the cane laughs. Thankfully, some people will do both, but most do not. Most people are not motivated to help political candidates. Studies have found that it is extremely difficult to run as a woman as well. But this does not discourage me.

"Good job tonight—I didn't know about rape insurance. Who wrote that bill?" Debbie asks. She is a congressional candidate. Her stump speech is about being a lawyer and the problematic laws that keep being delivered by the incumbent, who isn't a lawyer. You don't have to be a lawyer to be a legislator. Some people might think it's a good idea, and those people are mostly lawyers. I think it's good to have a legislative body that reflects the people they represent.

"Thank you, you too. Um, it was a guy from Amarillo."

She rolls her eyes. "Of course, not that it matters … all those guys voted for it, right?"

"Yep, they did." I shake my head.

"All the more reason for us to get elected." She pats the table and stands.

I follow as we make our way through the restaurant. People at tables gawk at us. You can tell they are bothered by our meeting. This just goes along with the territory. We are not exactly in a friendly district. It's almost comical how much people get bothered by a conversation with the opposing party or even if a political group shows up to volunteer for a non-political event. The looks of disgust while in the process of servitude while participating in building beds for children in need or working at a soup kitchen. It goes along with the whole concept of "I don't do politics" right. Except politics does you every single day. This district has been a hard red seat for almost longer than I have been alive. Sometimes I wake up with the thought of *Mia ... are you sure about this?* But then I quickly remind myself that if I don't try I won't be able to sleep at night. On the scales, the sleep factor always wins. And I have to stay true to my blue self.

"Indeed ... Hey, are you block-walking with us this weekend?" I push the door open.

"Yes, every weekend, I'll be there. Have a good night." Debbie waves as we split ways in the parking lot.

There is only one person I want to talk to right now. We have our name for our friendship but most would just refer to her as my best friend. I hit Ginger's number as soon as I hop in my car.

"Mia Verita Health and Hotness Hotline, how can I be of assistance today?" Ginger's voice is like a big, pearly white grin surrounded by red-covered lips.

"Ha, well, I think my health is okay ... as long as I can get through this non-insured moment without any major ailments." I laugh. "Oh, speaking of, I mentioned the rape insurance … do you think that was okay?" I sigh. "I know sometimes people get put off by that."

Ginger snarls. "Put off by the mention of it? Ha, they should be put off by the *facts* of it. Or the facts of sexual assault. Cry me a river of hypocrisy if anyone is bothered that you mentioned it."

I smile. "I know, I mean, it was a friendly crowd, but I really want people to know about this. No one is paying attention to what is going on under the pink dome."

Ginger sighs. "Exactly, babe, that's why you have to mention it. Friendly crowd or not, you have got to educate these people, scratch that, these voters on what is at stake."

"I know, but maybe I should go with public education needing more funding, or teachers not having a cost of living adjustment in over twenty years."

I glance at the time. It's almost nine o'clock.

"Yes, public education is good for families and teacher money talk is good for that crowd, but you have to hit them where it matters most to them—their wallet. You know most people will only show up to vote or kick into the campaign when something affects them directly.

This is how you get more people donating to you and signing up to volunteer."

"Good point. Real quick, is it too late for a quick drink?" I am hopeful she is not already in bed or has an early surgery or something in the morning.

"You are in luck. I just got a bottle of red that you would die for. Wait, don't die for it, just drive on over, and let's have it."

"On my way, and I will arrive alive." I laugh as I end the call. Ginger and I live in the same district. Except my abode is vastly different from hers. I drive down a more discreet road that signals "quiet luxury" to get to her place.

I click the code to get into her gated community. One of the many difficulties of canvassing is when a neighborhood is secured by a gate and I can't get in to knock on the doors. Legally knocking on doors is not a form of solicitation and is protected by the Constitution, but that doesn't mean people are not bothered when you show up.

They say things like, "I'm not into politics." This is one of my favorite statements, as I respond with, "Whether you are into politics or not, politics is into you every single day in a multitude of ways, how much time do you have?"

Chapter Two

"The sands of time are slower when watched."

It's a ticking time bomb, the calendar. There are no actual detonators attached to it. It's a simple paper calendar. The pictures are in color but low quality. I got it at the Dollar Store. No real visions of an explosion in Hiroshima exist in it. The images are all picturesque views of Italy. This month's picture is a place I hope to visit someday, Venice to be exact. The picture probably doesn't do it justice, with its worn bricks and a pale turquoise shade of water. The sunset is surreal, like a dream. But darn this calendar. It doesn't matter how many smiley faces or silly scribbles I draw on it, the days continue to be marked off with red Xs. As if I needed any more drama in my situation. The red ink marks appear to track only doom, and I do not want to seal my fate with this stoplight color that flashes green to go to the unhoused line. Yet, the pen continues in nonstop motion until mid-month. The day I pitched to myself that I would be in a better circumstance. Not the concept of a plan but rather, gainful employment with benefits, hopefully. I made a promise, not of a majestic scene, more like a simple vision. One in which I would be able to sleep at night. The concept of my bills being paid without prayer, in hopes that one check would hit my bank account before the others did. The "Beat the Bank" game is not fun. I can't remember that ever being a card you drew in Monopoly. "Your check hit the bank before your deposit, move

14

back ten spaces, and pay a hundred dollars in bank fees." With what money I might ask? I sigh.

I think I have added at least ten more gray hairs to my head. I know the exact amount because I counted them. Hair dye is not essential right now, so I have to walk around like a bird pooped on my head. It's like a splatter of gray that has no rhyme or reason. And it only shows where people can see. Why can't the gray be in the parts that don't show? Where I could easily hide it? It's an embarrassment, to say the least.

I sigh. There it is. Circled in bright red. The 17th. This was the number that was determined after I ran all the numbers. The numbers in my bank account, the numbers needed to exist, and I had just enough to make it to the 17th of this month. Not next month. There was not even a cushion put into this date. This destiny. This "choose your own adventure" of choices you wish you hadn't made. This version had no fail-safe. Not like the rumored extra miles in the new cars that tell you how many miles left you have in your tank. I often question this rumor that has been spread around, that somehow the car manufacturers tried to preempt drivers from their tanks going empty. My car is not one of these "new cars" and, thus, I have never had the chance to test this rumor. But given my current predicament, I could probably be the spokesperson for the validity of the existence of this gasoline insurance theory.

I do not have extra resources available to add any type of protection. I have no extra savings. I have no health insurance. I have nothing other than a bucket of hope. Until the new D-Day. Disasterville was upon me, whether I wanted to put my head in the sand or not—the gas was going to run out. These are the facts. There is no sunny filter to brighten my reality of the implosion of my bank account. Or the notification of any of my utility services being cut off. Texas with no air-conditioning is not an experience I care to partake in. Global warming, climate change, or "But I remember it being hot back in my day" are side characters to the reality of the hot Texas sun. I can put my thermometer on seventy-four, keep my blinds and curtains shut, and my cozy place will still be at an average temperature of seventy-eight degrees even with the AC on full blast all day long. Lord knows I do not want to see what would happen with a blackout. No power due to my lack of funds or another failure of our power grid. Things could have been fixed to save some lives in Texas, but there were simply not enough Texas House Representatives who were focused on saving the lives of people freezing in the winter or having heat exhaustion in the summer, yet. One of the many reasons I wanted to run for office. I hoped to add to the minority party and get the necessary votes for the people in all matters.

Each time we have a power outage, it can cause drastic consequences for marginalized communities. Death is the most extreme. But even if no one dies, it can take away from the meals that were purchased. Groceries that were spoiled. Missed work due to no alarm. After the last hurricane, I had to move. It's another one of the reasons I am running. To give a voice to those who were put in the dark. The people whose homes filled with water, no electricity, no answers. No concept of a plan. Can you imagine having no electricity, no water, and no real plan? I can. I was there. But I am able-bodied. I can get to clean water. I can find someone to help me. I have more than minimal technological skills. But you know who doesn't? Our elderly folks. They were stranded. Alone. This is not right. I don't want this to happen again. And it will. We will have another catastrophic weather event. But we can have pro-active legislation. Not reactive.

One of the things that crushes me is that I had started out on the right path. I had been investing and saving for my hopeful retirement. I had over six figures saved in my 401k. This did not include the six months of emergency funds that I had in a high-yield savings account. I had a good credit score. I had a house, that I bought myself. Until all of my funds and house were wiped out as if a tsunami had pounded in and suctioned everything away. My credit score went from a solid seven-eighty to a four-twenty. And no, that's not a fun number to bring about any munchies. My divorce was like an uninsured terroristic attack on all of my money.

I have reached the end of my "savings" to save me. Which, was not much. I was left with very little. Or rather, I was offered little to nothing to finalize things. To make the divorce official, even though it was official in my mind long before we signed the agreement. Ha, if it can even be called an agreement. It was more of a heavy-handed offer that I, unfortunately, could not refuse. It is hard to negotiate when you are not the one in power. Power can come with or without financial resources. Something I realized throughout the numerous legal documents I had to navigate on my own. I had barely any power to fight with, and my family was not from money, nor were they in the picture. I had to accept the hand that I was dealt. Which meant not a great one. I would have appreciated an extra round to sub out some cards, but the game was over, and I did know when to fold them and walk away.

That's right, I folded my cards when I realized that the fantasy house of cards I had been living in was just that. A fantasy. With one tiny tap on the corner of the Queen of Hearts, the entire deck came down. It was brutal. *Brutal* is a rather kind word for the situation. But I would rather not go into all of that right now.

Back to the facts, I am forty and unemployed. This is the first time since high school that I have been unemployed. Over a decade of building up a company as their director of operations only to be kicked to the curb, and no, that is not a metaphor. I am also that horrific

D-word. No, not Devil, but I have met him. Which led me to the word: DIVORCED. But that's not the worst D-word in Texas. We have evolved a bit and come to terms with "broken homes" and "broken families." How nice does that sound? Good grief, how trite for children to hear they are in a broken home. Words matter. Why would anyone want to present to a child that they were from something that was broken? Or that their birth or existence was illegitimate? Why? Why would you say that? To state that a person's birth is illegitimate because they were born outside of marriage is not only discriminatory but also hurtful. I cringe when I hear the words "visiting parent" when the matter of custody is discussed. What in the world is the implication of the idea of a visitor in the child's life? Words matter. Always. Yet, there is one word in Texas, or at least this part of Texas, that is considered by many to be the worst D-word of all. The most horrible, nastiest, dirtiest, lack-of-morals, baby-killing, gun-stealing, D-word to some is … Democrat.

Yikes, the delivery. The ideology that all things associated with a concern for a change in the status quo and transfer of power to the people was wrong or not for the greater good. The idea of corporations not being equal to people? Yup, that's me. Whoosh. It's true. I am a Democrat and, even better, I am one of two people in the Democratic primary to be a State Representative for a double-decade Republican stronghold seat. Praise be, send prayers and all good wishes.

I know it might seem a bit peculiar to be on the ballot to be a State Representative and also unemployed, but I didn't exactly plan it this way. I had planned to be married and after the final straw of the game of "Let's Guess Who He is Cheating with Now" I'd had enough. I had already filed to be on the ballot, and then I filed for divorce. I didn't exactly win with the divorce order, other than my freedom, but maybe the election will have a better outcome. I am hopeful.

But you know what? After the escape from ten-ish years of a miserable marriage and whatever you want to call that hot mess of a relationship that nearly killed me, I have never been better. Better, in that, I do not live in fear. Other than the fear of my bank account and the calendar. Yeah, Venice. I see you.

Regardless, at forty and with minimal options, I am on the ups. I will manifest a happy life and a job.

I can do this. Only ups. Breathe in and out. It's time to kick out all self-doubt. Manifestation and creation. Let's go!

I take in a deep breath and survey my room. It's not exactly the most inspirational. But I did get a Ficus plant. And I think it's doing all right. Maybe even better than me?

I need to focus on good energy. Zero shade, only sunshine in this room. I pull up the blinds and immediately close them. My view, if you want to call it that, leads to the parking lot of my apartment complex, and I am not about to allow anyone to check out my four walls. No one is going to get an "OnlyFans" view of my life. I am not at that point in my bank account yet. Gosh, I don't want to ever go there. I sigh.

Until I have a proper view with some space between myself and the neighbors, or at least a larger parking lot, I will have to use electricity to light up this space. That's right, we will just have to go with the delightful fluorescent lightbulbs one can find at any discount retailer and the most awkwardly placed fixture in the far corner of the room. How is that for setting the mood? It doesn't matter. Zen. Zen. Find my Zen. I want to be on cloud nine, airy and carefree. I want to float into the non-existent reality of bills and bank accounts. I wish it were as easy as these self-help books of mediation and manifestation make it seem. Have these authors ever had to pawn their TVs to keep the lights on? Was there a manifestation of the rich life with a bowl of popcorn as their nightly meal?

But I have a possibility. I have an interview. This could be it. My cheeks warm as reality sinks in. I am not on a boat floating into a fantasy of being in Venice. I am on solid ground, and I need this job.

My phone timer goes off. Yes, I set alerts for everything, and this one is a reminder for the interview of my life. The position is for the Executive Director of Operations at a technology company. *Executive!* Every time I have glanced at the job posting, I have done a little happy dance. I haven't even had the interview yet. Did I mention I need this job? For the past ten years, I have helped to build up my ex-husband's company. Well, technically, his family's company. At least that is how his attorney presented it to the court. That the company wasn't really his and that he didn't have any resources that were his. Yeah, okay. But somehow, he had the resources to bury me in legal fees and give me a "deal" that had me kicked out of the house I purchased and with a custody order to share time with my dog. *My* dog. *Mine*. It's been less than a year since I moved out. The singe is still there.

I swallow hard. *Focus.* It doesn't matter. I can take my experience of what was described as "help" versus the actuality of what I did. I took a Mom-and-Pop shop and turned it into a corporation with multi-state stores. A success that could only bring him to bankrupt me into an escape from the bad, bad life, which I don't want to discuss. No, I am only going to focus on good things. Like this situation. This job is like a dream, the thought of benefits and a good salary will truly save me. Especially since it is not tied to someone with a marital contract. A contract that ended with no actual rights. I digress. *Mia, do not slip into bad memory land.*

22

Focus.

This is different. I can do it, too. I have the experience to prove that I can run multiple companies with proper business plans, and I know all the corporate jargon like "bring it to scale," "table it," and "nuts to bolts," etc.

I am confident in my experience, but three months out of work can weigh on one's self-esteem. Let alone the bomb that glares back at me in a constant reminder that I only have two weeks to get myself gainfully employed. Tick tock. I got this. I let out a sigh. Two weeks before everything implodes.

My phone beeps again, a not-so-subtle reminder.

It's showtime.

"Hello?" I smile as comfortably as I can into my camera.

Zoom interviews are so odd. My smile is as good as one could hope for with a "meet and greet" via the internet. Technology. We've come so far but yet still a step back because there is a difference between a screen versus a human face in front of you. The shake of one's hands can't be replaced with an image of pixelated facial expressions. I want to present as capable and sure of myself. Yet, I see a break in the lines of the image on the screen, and I know that there is no way they can grasp my presence in the same capacity as being in person. The notion of shared air. Not like in my SCUBA deep dive incident where I had to literally share air, but rather oxygen in the same room.

I take a deep breath. This air is all mine.

Two to one. I am alone in my little apartment and they are in the room together. The papers stacked in front of them seem a bit odd. Hopefully, that is not a stack of questions. A blue pen casually lies over the stack. My resume is only one page. I can't help but wonder what the other papers are. Maybe just filler? I glance up as a man's voice begins to speak.

"We appreciate you taking the time to meet with us today. Your resume and pre-interview questions were quite helpful in assessing your character. But what about your character when no one is looking?" Jose pauses in an awkward moment.

I am not sure what facial reaction to display. This is not a question from the "How-to of Job Interviews" books that I found on the 75% off-the-shelf at Katy Budget Books. Is this a morality question? How could anyone get this wrong? This seems simple. I wait to respond as he hasn't released the torch of his question.

"We have moments in our industry where we may or may not be audited. How would you treat your client or account with the foresight to know that you were not going to be audited in that particular case?" His eyes pierce past the 5.5 megapixels, and it is as if we are not in a screen-on-screen interview but face-to-face.

I can't figure out if his gaze is concerned about my true character in a bad choice or hopeful that I make a good one. I take in a tiny breath. I don't want to seem as if I am put off one way or another by the question. Confidence and a sense of calmness is the only way to answer this one.

"I always work as if I'm being audited. Why change the routine if it's a good one?" I let out a light laugh and do my best with an unforced smile.

Oh, yes ... Mia, very natural.

I catch a glance at my reflection in the small rectangle momentarily, then I switch my gaze back to Jose and Mallory. Jose seems like maybe he's in his forties as well, a little bit of gray highlights his dark shiny hair. Mallory resembles one of Ginger's, my best friend, cousins. The dark red hair and almost translucent skin. I glance down at my resume with asterisks in front of me. There are a few highlighted sections. I scan them in case there are any specific questions from my resume that I might need to reference.

Jose smiles back at me and nods. "Good answer, sometimes we do have to make decisions on the fly and—"

Mallory interrupts, "Sometimes lines can be blurred, but we need someone on the team who keeps the rulebook as their guide, always." She licks the bottom of her front teeth and lets out a soft blow. If I were actually in front of her, I would possibly not have caught it. But being zoomed in on her face does add a different level of scrutiny. I will have to look this up later as to what that means, it's always good to learn more about facial expressions. Ginger probably knows. She is good at being able to read people.

"How important would you rate rules, promises, and agreements?" Jose's eyes narrow in on me.

My shoulders pull back. "A promise is a commitment and one would hope that it would be followed through to the end, but I can see where under certain circumstances it might not be possible to follow through." I take a deep breath.

I hate not being part of the world of always following through on commitments and promises … makes me feel like such a failure. I never wanted to be a part of the divorcee crowd, not that there's anything wrong with them. But I feel like a failure. I feel like a fraud for not being able to stick it out after the "I do", when I had to say "No, I can't," and I had to be an "I don't want to be married", and file for divorce. Even though, it wasn't an "I don't want to be married" but rather, "I can't be married to someone like this, that treats me like this, that ignores our actual marital vows."

I let my anxiety simmer inside of me. The back of my throat fills with bubbles of salivia. This question is not about my marriage or the failure of marriage, this is about business. And regardless of what any business person tells you about business being personal, marriage is not supposed to be a business contract. And with that thought, I feel a bolt of reality hit me.

It was business. It was not personal. It was not a marriage or a promise. It was only a business proposal. My ex-husband wanted the contract and I wanted the partnership of marriage. What a fool I was.

I pinch my leg, which is out of sight. I can process this realization later. Now is the time for me to conquer this interview.

I take another breath. "Agreements and rules are easy. The parties agree on the terms and follow through, if anyone doesn't follow through on their agreement or follow their rules, then the entire arrangement is ultimately null and void." I let out a sigh.

Mallory has her eyes on Jose. His eyes are on his paper. And I am left with the possibility that we had a technical mishap. I tap my fingers on the side of my legs. I will count to twenty and then try to refresh the screen if there are no movements from either of them. One, two, three

… my count is interrupted by a different tap. They are still here. No technical issue. *Good*.

Jose taps the paper in front of him. "One final question."

It's like the final round of *Do You Want to Be a Millionaire*? And the answer is yes. Yes, I do. I want to be a millionaire, not that this job is a million-dollar salary, but I do want this job. I want it bad. I need it.

"Yes, so, Mia, can you tell us when was the last time you felt under pressure and how you handled it?" Jose asks me. He has read this from a pre-formulated interview question list. Thankfully, "Where do you see yourself in five years" hasn't come up or my spirit animal. However, I love to answer that one. It's a shark. I love sharks. They are the best. Sharks don't sweat, they don't worry about their next meal or whether or not their children will be okay. Because their pups are sharks, too, and sharks are always okay. Every day they swim and conquer and survive. Not once is there a hesitation in a shark in the process of food. Hunger, survival, every day they live life to the fullest. Chomp. Chomp.

I laugh. "Other than this moment?"

I can't help it. It's true. I am under pressure, and I have to sound confident but also happy. Like, I'm on a third date and coffee is part of the scene. But it's not. Interviews are intense.

This is a constant struggle in the interview process. Be natural but be smart. Be confident but don't act arrogant. Smile but not too much. Share your accomplishments but don't sound braggy. It drains my soul. But it has to happen. The sides of my mouth pull up into an upside-down frown. I'm calm, cool, and collected, like a shark that is on a typical swim along the seal-filled coastline. Lots of opportunities. No big deal. Breathe and let's go. Don't strike too soon. Let the seals enjoy their moment too. Only go in for the attack when you are ready and sure.

I continue, "At my last job, I had a major project that was due and we also had a crisis come up at the same time. It was difficult because I had to manage my time appropriately to make sure that the crisis was being attended to and also that I was going to make my deadline on the project."

"Interesting, what did you do?" Jose and Mallory glance at me with pensive gazes. My response has an answer to a test they will need to use in the future.

Relax.

I force myself not to shrug. Even though naturally that is what I want to do. But I can't. To shrug is to present as if you don't care or don't know. This is not the case. I do know and I do care. But my shoulders would be a way to lighten the situation at any other moment. Like a cool breeze on a warm summer day as your feet hit the sand and it's too hot. The breeze comforts that bit of heat, and you exhale as if things are going to be all right.

"I made a to-do list accompanied by a timeline. I used this to monitor what I'm doing and when I'm doing it to make sure I stay on task and hit my deadlines and stay on top of everything else that is going on. Every item has an executed time expectation. When I get close to the deadline, I have alarms that go off to keep me on track."

Jose and Mallory both nod in unison. "Great, we will be in touch. Thanks for taking the time to chat with us today."

"Yes, thank you." We all nod.

Before I know it, the screen is dark. I lean back and blow the hair from my face. With a slight bounce, I sashay my way into the kitchen and pull my house wine out of the fridge. Yeah, it's a box. I'm being earth-friendly with this wine. It's got like four bottles in it, which means I am part of the bigger picture of reduction as my Tuesday afternoon drink is a major contribution to society. I give myself a high-five and take a long sip. Two more sips later, and I slump back down into my chair.

No, no, Mia, don't sulk.

I click Danza Kuduro on my music app. The *thump, thump* beat pounds through my computer speakers, and I immediately bounce out of my chair. As Don Omar sings "La mano arriba, cintura sola" I follow like a student in class. My hands are up and my hips sway like a palm tree at the beach. It is physically impossible to listen to this song without being musically forced to dance. My chair slides back, and I'm on my feet. My hips move from side to side. Don Omar sings to me, and I agree with him. I am not tired. This is the beginning. I twirl my body around the room. Blood rushes through my veins, and I'm alive. No longer trapped in a funk. The song finishes, and I take another swig from my glass.

The green light on my computer camera is so bright I drop my wine as if I have been blinded. Glass shatters everywhere. I drop down to the floor and move my hand over to the mouse and click close on the Zoom app. I don't even want to know or check to see if anyone was still on the call. My insides cave in, and I can't breathe. No air. It's gone. My ability to breathe and the possibility of this job. Dammit. I choke as if I have come up from being drowned. And I have, I'm in deep. Deeper than I want to be. I had just got on the raft and now all my insecurities rise to the surface, and I am being forced to face them.

No. I pull myself into a mini pretzel. I want to bend myself into a tiny particle and to be swept away with the broom of life and disappear. Pain burns inside of me, and I glance at the red trail of blood that has formed against my skin next to the shard of glass that is stuck in my hand.

Bright red blood trickles out of my hand. Great. Could this moment be any more metaphorical? A merge of pain between my emotions and physically being able to cry from pure agony. Not the sorrow of what has transpired this last year. But pain. It starts to throb. It's too much. I eye the glass. It's really big. And it is deep. I know what has to happen.

A scream roars from my lungs. *Dammit*. It's stuck in deep. I can't pull it out. It hurts so bad. I'm in a crux of glass in my hand that needs to be pulled and not able to find the strength to make it happen. I am weak. The pain oozes from my hand. It's like the blood is a reminder that I am about to die of a small slit because I do nothing. I let it fall. Like I can't be moved to make a choice. To stop the bad situation from the moment of a change into a worse possibility. I swallow hard. Too many times I watched my life slip away. My choices. My voice.

My decision to stand up. No more. I made a promise to myself not to do this anymore. I will reclaim my time. No one knows how long they are here, and while I am, I will not be a background scene. I will be a participant. With this, I can no longer remain on the floor in pure mortification and the only option is to tend to my injury.

Why didn't I close the app? Why would I leave that open? That makes no sense. All the time that went by. A mini-reel of my last actions and movements runs through my mind as I relive everything I did after what I thought was the end of the call. Maybe no one was there. Maybe they had closed their windows and were not able to see mine. I have to talk to Ginger. She will know what to do or at least prevent me from any further moments of stupidity. Besides, this is a major injury, and she is a doctor. My hand is a disaster. Too much blood. I swallow hard. I want to vomit or pass out. This is too much.

I press her name on my phone and wait for the sound of her voice.

"I need you." I slide onto my couch and realize that not only was my little serenade of awkward or improvisation dance moves a piece onto their own but also sans pants. Yes … nothing on but my little pink panties that should not be seen by anyone. Great. I had bought these on a whim after I had trashed all of my undergarments and anything that had ever been touched or seen by *him*. All fresh. These were not my normal look, but I had thought, *FFS, why not?*

I roll my eyes and the throb of fires that blaze in my skin knock me back to the present and reality. It doesn't matter at the moment about the interview. I have to handle this cut.

"Hey there, chica, what's up? What did the douchebag do now? Meld your locks close so you can't exit?" A slight sigh falls from her voice.

I want to laugh, but I'm deep with mortification from what I just partook in and who might have been a witness. *Lord, can I get a witness?* No, scratch that. *Lord, please make it so that no one was a witness to me or my dance or any of that.* What can I do to ensure that? A wish on a star? Eleven on the eleven for the next eleven days? Anything. I will say eighteen Hail Marys and Glory Bes, I will dedicate every Saturday for the next month to the soup kitchen. *Whatever you need, Lord, please send me a sign, and I will sign the line.*

"No, I almost wish it was something as easy as that." I pull at the skin on my thigh. I want to go for a run. I've got to get out of here. Mentally, I need to escape, but I'm impaled by a piece of glass that is no longer clear but a smudge of red goo. *Yuck.*

"What is it?" I can sense the urgency in her voice. She is probably on two feet and ready to pace into a plan. Ginger is all plans and execution. She is a professional at problem resolution. Whereas I seem to be heavy on the problems and not much on anything else. How did I end up so lucky in this friend equation? I'm out on the murky seas of uncertainty, and she is constantly there with a bucket of hope and a life preserver to get me out of the dark and into the light with the possibility of land on the horizon.

"I had the interview this afternoon, remember?" I hesitate for a second. I couldn't feel like a bigger loser. But Ginger is aware of my flaws and downfalls, all too familiar. "Well, I thought I had closed out of the chat after it was over and, anyways, everything went, well … I guess that is the good part."

"What's the bad part?" Ginger is calm and cool as if I'm only about to offer a simple story on how I wash my dishes to avoid spots before I put them in the dishwasher. Yet, that is not the dirty details I have to share. The pain pulses in my hand as if through the fury of blood it is an attempt to speed up my speech.

"I did a bit of a celebratory dance, and then I realized that the green light was on." I swallow hard. There, I said it.

"Okay, that's not a big deal. Just shows you are enthusiastic. Nothing graphic, right? Like, you weren't working a pole or dipping real low?" Ginger laughs.

"No, but um … well, remember how you said pantless was no big deal for a top-shot interview?"

"No." Ginger gasps.

"Yes." My lips press together. It is bad, as I assumed. It was really bad, and her gasp confirmed all my fears and anxiety.

I move from my living room to my bedroom. I hit the speaker button. If she has anything to say, she can do it while I change. I

35

have to get out of here. I have to run. This is the only thing that will fix my mental state at the moment other than a gallon of wine, and that won't be the best thing for when I wake from a wine hug. No, I need to run. I fall to the ground.

Ouch.

Dammit. It's too much. A small scream falls from my mouth.

"Mia, what's wrong?" Ginger sounds far away from my ear. I try again to pull the glass from my hand. I wince at the pain. I take in a deep breath and release. I pull with as much might as I can gather until it's at the very edge of my skin. I tug the one last inch of it, and the glass is free and so is my blood. It is in full-force gush mode, like a waterfall of red has exploded from the Hoover Dam.

"Fuuuuudge it," I screech.

This is too much. I can't take it in. I rush to my kitchen and grab a towel and wrap it around my hand.

"Ginger, I dropped my wine glass and my hand is gushing blood. Bright red blood."

"Oh my god, Mia, go to the doctor. Call 911. They can drive you." Her breath has picked up, and she is obviously in full-pace mode. "It will take me twenty minutes to get there—can you wait?"

"I can wait to overpay for a ride to the emergency room. You know I have no insurance, right?" I am going to be sick. Where is my toilet? I am dizzy. I grasp onto the sides of the counter.

"I'll have Uber pick you up. Stay put—they will be there in two minutes. I'll meet you at the hospital."

The sound of numbers being typed into the phone corresponds with her voice. I don't know if being a multi-tasker is a prime doctor skill, but it is one of her strong points. Ginger is with no doubt in full pursuit of the arrangements with Uber.

"Mia," she calls out from my phone. My vision is blurred. I can hear the sounds of her voice. Loud and intense. *Word. Word. Word.* There is a rhythm, like a chorus. But the sounds are going away. Far away. I can't hear them anymore. It's completely silent.

Chapter Three
"Thicker than blood, but thinner than skin."

Yeah, no big deal. I'm sure lots of people have passed out because of a slight cut to their hand, right? Well, to be perfectly honest, it's not a slight cut. Six stitches to be exact, and I'm glad that I was not awake for the surgery. Because I am not a fan of needles or blood for that matter, hence the reason for a proper faint scene in my kitchen. Almost as if Daniel Day-Lewis had arrived at my apartment and began to talk to me about milkshakes, as in yes, there was blood. Lots of blood. But that is not my scene in a movie or real life, instead, I would opt for the documentary and advise everyone to … exit through the gift shop. Both films are artistic brilliance, unlike my situation at hand, or rather my damaged hand. Now, I will have to cross-hand modeling off my list for possible side hustles. I digress.

I tap both my legs. Both work. This is good. I tingle my left hand, also okay. I try to move my right hand. Not possible. It's wrapped up in a bandage. I glance at it and then up. Ginger is next to my bed. Her green eyes are in full inspection mode. She must think I am an absolute mess, besides the current situation. Bits of pieces of memories flicker in my mind. Her image and some shouts. A car ride. Maybe an ambulance? I am not sure. But I am sure Ginger got me to the hospital.

A decision of mine that worked in my favor. Ginger has a key to my house, as she is my designated life partner. A life partner, kind of like a guide and keeper of all things important. We decided a long time ago to be each other's guide in difficult moments and decisions. It seems as if I have been more of the receiver than the giver. I think about this often and how I can equalize things, yet this moment has not occurred. Ginger has always had it all together. Which is a good thing, I just wish I could even it out a bit.

At one point, I had given her all the passwords and keys to everything I owned. She didn't blink an eye with this level of trust. Her sensible focus has guided my way ever since. This has been my best decision ever, other than Schatzi.

"Hey there—you okay?" Ginger moves my hand out of my hair.

I glance to the side. Any other person and I would've been under the cover of this makeshift blanket and stayed under until they left the room. But Ginger has seen every aspect of my soul and my life.

"I'm such a mess."

"Nah, girl … you are looking fantastic, and I think the ER guy might like you … definitely liked those pink panties, so that was a definite good choice on your part." She nods, and I can't help but groan.

I glance under my covers. Okay, I am finally wearing clothes.

"Ginger, what is this?" I pull the cover down and tug on what was a skirt that used to cover the bottom half of my body. Well, mostly, but still.

Ginger laughs. "I couldn't find anything else, and this was at the top of one of your boxes."

I smooth out the green and white fabric. "Ginger, this is my high school cheerleader skirt … you couldn't find anything else remarkably suitable for a visit to the hospital?" I toss my head back on the pillow. I am in a button-down white blouse with a cheerleader skirt. It resembles a really bad portrayal of a Britney Spears video. And I'm not the one that wants to be hit one more time. I've already been hit enough. I need a break.

"Mia, you realize that your flat is a mess, right? Like, you haven't unpacked yet. What is that about?" She grabs her phone like she is using her calendar to count how long it's been since I moved out of my house. She slides her phone back into her purse and nods. I'm sure she has probably read some articles or books about depression and my situation. Ran through the numbers if my avoidance of unpacking my things was within normal limits or not. I must be okay for now, or at least she is not going to address the situation any further.

Ginger taps her fingers on the side of the bed.

"I planned to finish this weekend. I just had so many boxes to get through." This is a lie. I barely had any boxes. Most of my things were put in a laundry basket or stuffed into trash bags. I remember when "*Satan*" threw a box of hefty black bags at me. "*Here, this makes sense for your things*," he had said and then added, "*Hurry up and get out of my house. Schatzi and I have plans.*" Which was more disinformation from the distorter of all things. He never did anything with her. This made things even more painful. It was not salt or vinegar in the wound but rather a burn of acid. The wound was still open. When would I heal? Probably never.

"You get Schatzi this weekend, right?" Ginger raises an eyebrow at me.

"Yes." The lump in my throat grows into a mountain of pain. I can't talk about her. It's too painful. I merely try to survive when she isn't with me and not focus on the fact that she is absent from my life and I am absent from hers. The most relatable thing I have read is the pain of a parent who grieves not seeing their child because of a narcissistic parent who keeps them from the other parent. Parental alienation. Which I am sure children do not understand. I can't imagine how Schatzi must feel. This is my life. I won't focus on the negativity, but I have to push down the pain of what I cannot bring to the surface at the present. Right now, I am in the depths of the ocean with the only option to continue to swim. And I do. I dig in further into the waves of life, and I pull the water around me

41

and over my skin. I push it past me, all these indifferences and moments of strength where I am supposed to rise.

"Okay, we'll get it sorted before she comes back," Ginger says something to the nurse, and I ignore it. It doesn't matter. I want out of here. I need space. I need air. I need to run. I need to escape and clear my lungs. The lump of despair is swollen and I can't breathe.

"All right, chica, time to say hasta luego to this place." Ginger laughs as the nurse begins going over the checkout procedures. They slide me into a wheelchair because obviously, it's necessary for a minor hand injury. FFS. I force myself not to roll my eyes as we roll along the hallway.

No. No. No. No.

"Stop, stop the chair," I say with as much firmness as I can mutter but also keep my voice low enough not to cause any unwanted attention.

The chair makes an abrupt stop. "What's the matter, Ms. Verita?" The nurse has a bit of concern on her face.

"Can you find a different route? I don't want to go that way. It … um … it doesn't look right."

Great, Mia, that is quite brilliant in terms of creativity. It doesn't feel right. FFS.

I can't come up with anything better than that. Face to palm … if palm was not full of stitches. The chair begins to move again. We are en route to the elevator. And right next to the elevator, I see him. Not him as in "*Satan*," but

42

more like "*Satan*'s" apprentice or right-hand man. I do not want to see him or talk to him or breathe the same air as him. If it were possible, I would take a deep breath and not release it until we had passed. I do not want to have anything to do with this horrible person.

"Oh," Ginger says.

"Yeah, more than *oh*. Please turn us around." I glance up at the nurse. Her focus is away from me and my concerns and my humiliation. She cares for none of this. I am a number. An exit ride. My emotions do not count in her world. But they do in mine.

"Please turn us around. I'm not ready. I think I forgot something in my room." Yes, that's it. The chair pauses for a second.

"What did you forget?" The nurse peeks her head around and eyes me with a level of inspection that would surpass any TSA agent any day of the week.

"Um ..." I bite my tongue as if I don't want to say what I have forgotten, but the reality is I have forgotten all possible reasons and I am at a loss. "Nothing."

I roll my eyes at myself. I can't help it, lies are not my forte. The wheels begin to move forward and the distance between the fiery gates of hell and my eternal salvation are so close that the heat is going to peel up my skin and little flakes will fall off. Bubbles of fear and anger surface, and I want to bolt. To go against the hospital protocol and avoid this intersection of hate and humiliation.

43

"Oh, hey there ... um, Mia ... are you okay?" Maxwell Graham, with all of his fake niceness. The audacity of my ex-husband's attorney to attempt to speak to me outside of a courtroom or while we are not being recorded. Heck, he probably hit a record button before he began to speak. Good ol' fashioned Texas laws allow for anyone to be recorded as long as one of the persons on the recording knows they are ... Yeah, no violation of privacy in that.

"Yeah, I'm great." I look away. Move on now. I responded like an adult without being prodded by the judge. Move along. I don't need nor do I owe anything to this man. He is pure evil.

He slides back and holds the elevator door open for us. The nurse pushes my chair in and turns me around. What the actual fuck is he doing in the elevator with us? I am sure that he had just gotten off before our arrival. Why does he think it's okay to be in the same space as me? He is the prime example of men who refuse to move on a path and will literally run into a woman if she doesn't heed. Or the man spreader with legs gaped open on the subway like we need to realize his manliness is so large that he needs to take up at least three seats. Get out of here, dude. No, thank you. And yet. He stands in the elevator next to my wheelchair. I couldn't be in a more compromised position if I tried. A wheelchair, a sewn-up hand, and a bad Halloween costume circa Britney Spears. I almost want the stitches to open and let me bleed out.

Stop with the negativity, I tell myself. Nope. Not going to go down that path. I take a breath in.

"Why are you here, chasing ambulances or something?" I let fall from my lips. I know Ginger has silenced herself from a nudge in my direction or a reminder of the use of "filter." She always advises me of the need to filter myself. And I agree with her in general, but not with this guy. No, he doesn't deserve a friendly filter. Nope.

A low chuckle hums from the back of his throat. "Not today, unfortunately, there has been an ambulance drought lately."

"Of course, you would see that as an unfortunate." I flitter my eyes and clench my jaw. I can only hope for an immediate exit out of this small space of hate.

"Mia, I'm joking. I'm actually here to visit a relative." He clears his throat.

"Wait … to visit?" I cock my jaw and glance up at him with his steel blue eyes of pain. They don't glimmer or sparkle or radiate happiness. None of the good stuff. But they do pierce.

"Yes, to visit." He nods.

I shake my head. "So, you haven't visited them yet?" I want to clear my throat, but I let my shoulders relax as he delivers the answer.

"That's correct." He nods again.

The elevator rings and the doors open. The nurse moves my wheelchair forward, and I look back at Maxwell.

"Interesting."

This is the part where my nurse moves faster than Maxwell and lets me leave the conversation with the lead and the mic being left on the floor. Except my nurse didn't get a copy of the script. Instead, she decided to ad-lib and to stop my wheelchair abruptly to go and hug another patient. Zero loyalty these days.

I glance at Ginger. She gives me the one-finger salute, as in she will be back. Obviously, going to get the car. And I am left alone with Maxwell Graham. Not anyone I would want to be alone with ever. *Ever.*

I look at my hand. This is my focus. No need to even acknowledge his existence. Whether he is there or not. I have no idea, as I am too busy with this hand inspection. Like maybe I will go ahead and read my palms. What is in my future? What lies underneath all these lines? No big deal. I can do this. I can fixate on my hand. I can draw lines next to the lines of my palm that line my life and every line that has led me to a problem where I thought I was at the end of the line. The idea was that I had no more room on the sketch. The pen was out of ink. I trace my heart line and let my finger drop to the headline. I dig a little deeper. There is a dot in the middle of my headline. I am not sure what it means, but I kind of don't want to know.

"If you don't mind me asking, what happened to your hand?" Maxwell asks as if he is a concerned person with no agenda.

"I mind." I sigh. The gall of this guy. I don't want to be anywhere near him. I would rather have a conversation with a pigeon about whether or not old bread is better than stale crackers. Seriously, why can't he take a hint? But then again, he is not here for hints. If anything, he is here for more reasons to argue for less time for me to have with Schatzi. Like, "Check this out—she hurt her hand and had to go to the hospital. Obviously, she should not have as much time with Schatzi as '*Satan*.'" Yes, that's my ex-husband's name in the legal papers. Okay, maybe not. But who cares, it makes more sense to refer to him as "*Satan*" than the name he was given at birth before he decided to become a horrible person. Except, if you think about it, DaVile as a last name does sound like Devil or Evil … I should have known back then … he was a red flag.

"Understandable," Maxwell states with a purpose. One that I am not going to even think about.

I touch my neck. The little piece of the sawed-off key that hangs around my neck is a constant reminder. I only take it off for the shower. My eyes squeeze tight. This token of so many wrongdoings does not belong anywhere near me. It has been a daily reminder of what I have been through. I told myself the weight of it as it lay against my chest would be a reminder that I could get through hard things. Bad things. But not really. Arg. Just another mistake. How foolish, to wear this piece of gaslighting abuse as a symbol of empowerment. Instead, it was a token of his crimes and immoral acts.

Here I am again, with the fool's path. It isn't powerful to wear a painful reminder of the past. The memory is still so vivid. The young locksmith had seemed a bit confused as he removed the sawed-off key from the door. The key to the garage had been severed inside it so that it could no longer be locked. This was after the outside garage door had been broken so that it could no longer be closed. Anyone could easily walk into our house. The house I had purchased on my own. The house I had refinanced to take out cash to support his family's business and add him onto the title. Because we were married. Because we were going to be together for eternity. Until I could no longer take it. I still feel like a failure. Not that the path was my choice. I was only a fool by my naivety in that scenario. But I did choose to end the official couple part. Even though we did not live as a couple. Instead as a hostage and violent abuser.

"Mia, you have to file and get out. How many more signs do you need?" Ginger's green eyes had pierced back at me full of reason, full of care. I knew she was right. But it was hard to fight. To fight back against him and my upbringing and marriage until death do us part. How could I go against what I was raised on? It was all so hard.

The memory is still so fresh. I had said, *"I know ... but what will I do?"* The metal of the key had been so warm in my hand, almost like it had been in a fire. It hadn't, but at that moment, I was about to jump from one fire into another one. I had tiptoed in every aspect of my life back then. I had done everything I could to keep the peace to a degree but more importantly to keep my distance. The last encounter had left me with a trail of blood on my leg and bed. I didn't want to relive that experience.

"You will do whatever it takes. You will find another job, and you will be safe. You will get Schatzi out, and y'all will be safe. Right now, it's anything but safe. Mia, he asked if your life insurance was up to date. He is setting up your house for a home invasion. You will end up on some Dateline Show about being missing unless you get out now." Her lashes had fluttered. The flutter was not of a flippant moment, but out of concern. She had done her best to be strong in front of me, but she was worried about my impending death. I knew she was right, and her lashes tightened enough to push me to what I needed to do. Ginger was serious. It wasn't a joke or some forced-upon non-reality. It was one of those moments where I had wanted to stick my head in the sand and not react, but Ginger had been right. Too many signs and too many things had been done for me to have been passive and pretend it was okay. It wasn't. Nothing was. I had to get out. I had to file. I had to push past my fear and make a move for freedom. I knew it would be uncomfortable. I knew it wouldn't feel good. I knew I was going to enter the unknown and it would be scary. But the reality was that not filing

49

was also a scary situation. It was a decision to end up on *60 Minutes* or maybe be miserable. I chose to be miserable and alive.

And so, I did. It was my life, and I couldn't exist in it with another Christmas of being chased around the house and called every awful name in the book. Nope. No more.

"Okay. I will file." I had nodded.

I didn't want to go down this path but, sometimes, when you are in a corner, you can either crumble or you can rise and push your way out. I had to do the latter.

I inhale a long, deep breath. That memory was too fresh but also long enough for me to take back the mic. I glance up at Maxwell. He is a large man. Family law is never fun, but there should be special training for abusive relationships.

Maxwell had sat unmoved in mediation. Like everything *"Satan,"* my ex-husband Mike DaVile MD, had said was true. Never any facts. Just nonsensical statements. And when Maxwell questioned me, with each answer, he had been pensive. Unemotive. He had seemed like a robot. It was as if I was not a human in the room. Absolutely awful. Now, I'm next to him in the present. Goosebumps form against my skin.

I tap the sides of my legs. *It's okay, Mia, you are out of that room. You are in a better place. It might not be the best place. You might have to share custody of Schatzi, but you are out. You are free.*

50

Now it was time for me to make a move. Being confined to a wheelchair would not restrain me. A hospital full of people that needed assistance, but I was not one of them. The hospital walls were anything but full of a disinfectant appeal. I unlatch the necklace hook from my neck. Oxygen and intention fill my lungs. Constriction of pain is wrapped inside of me. I have to release it. Steady and slow. *Mia, you can do this*. The sawed-off key was so heavy. It began to warm my hand.

"Maxwell," I state with confidence.

"Yes?" His eyebrows raise as if I might provide some good news or be less abrasive. Neither is the case. It was time. Time to let go. Time to move on.

I let out a tiny breath. One that most would not notice. It was only enough to let me breathe for a second. I only needed a tiny breath to deconstruct my lungs. The sawed-off key is hot against my skin. So heavy. It didn't belong in my hands, let alone around my neck. I glance at it for a second. A hard swallow and I knew what I had to do.

I hand Maxwell the necklace of the sawed-off key that used to hang around my neck. It was so tight. It restricted me. And I didn't even realize it. I didn't understand why it didn't belong. This piece of pain that used to hang around my neck. No longer.

"Goodbye." I let the chain drop into Maxwell's hand.

There's a surge of energy that runs through me as the necklace no longer touches my skin. I grab the wheels of the chair and kick up the brake with my foot. I don't know where the nurse went. But I am free. I am empowered. I can leave the hospital, with their rules but on my accord. I roll my way to the hospital exit with a moment of clarity and freedom that I had not experienced in over a decade. I had thought the necklace had brought me power when in reality it was a lead foot against my neck. It was a reminder of being locked into a moment in time where I ignored all the possibilities and let myself be locked into an abusive life. Today, I freed myself from that lock without a locksmith. I did it on my own. I broke the chain and let the freedom run through me like the surge of a dam. Bad memories began to evaporate and good energy began to heal. The air feels crisp against my skin like fresh laundry from the dryer. Clean, warm, and ready to be worn. New memories are being created as I roll my way to Ginger's car. Had the weight of my sadness been lifted?

Chapter Four
"To all we are, are we to be?"

I rub the ointment over my hand. Not too much of a scar. It's only been six weeks, but I think it will fade away unlike the memory of my dance. This unfortunately lives on in my mind from time to time. A tiny bit of hope circles in a rhythmic motion that maybe the job offer with Jose and Mallory is just delayed. I have heard of job offers that can take over three months. This is not the amount of time that I have. However, I thankfully found some contract work and am going to be able to keep the lights on a little bit longer. Life is finally back to an ebb and flow. I continue to click submit on eighteen million job applications as I adjust my resume for each one. My cover letters begin with even more saccharine-filled confidence. Venice is a constant state of mind that I cross off each day as we get closer to the day I had originally projected not to be able to keep the lights on, even though I moved that date with the contract work income. The date still exists. But I guess that would be the same for anyone who is not financially independent. How nice that must be! Not a worry … well, at least not financial ones.

I have abandoned the sinking into the depths of despair—cue Anne of Green Gables monologue in a makeshift notebook. I have other plans, it is time to bring in a Wonder Woman scripted scene. I am here to conquer this situation. I can do it. These internal pep talks are the only thing I have going for me.

I click through my favorite one-hit submit option on what is one of too many applications. Obviously, the job hunt is a numbers game. But this one-click option makes it seem like a far-fetched endeavor. I want to wave my resume in front of the computer screen and say "Hello? Is anyone out there? Am I only in a submit, repeat, cycle with no end?" It doesn't make sense. How could I send out so many resumes with zero response?

One of the most difficult parts of the hunt is the required cover letter and a statement of intent. Cover letters were the bane of my existence. They took up so much unnecessary time. Each with the requirement of design to speak directly to each and every company differently. How far we have come with technology yet, and how far have we regressed further than decades ago? Cover letters are hard. My anxiety always runs over my skin and clogs my brainflow. I don't want to sound fake. I want to be genuine and "real," but that doesn't exactly drip onto paper with confidence. Like, *Check out how smart and competent I am, but also, don't worry, I am not arrogant.*

I used my best Southern charm to enchant the reader as to why they should want to interview me and not skip on the next. I can imagine the person as they peruse each application and whether or not they want to swipe right and invite me on the interview date. This is so similar to dating apps. Everyone presents their best, most filtered side, and the reader must decide if the filter is too much or if there is substance underneath the grainy photo and text. Needless to say, I went all in on my cover letters.

Your company and my experience seem like the perfect fit. When can we set an interview to try this out for size?

I'm so perfect for this position because of this exact moment and experience that I have that will be the biggest asset to your company.

Yes, definitely. I absolutely can do that.

Oh, for sure, I can do that and that and everything you could possibly imagine. Or so I would hope.

How many over-exaggerations or thoughtful moments of hope do we put forth when applying for a job? How many blurred lines become so changed from our actual resume do we give just for the opportunity to be given a chance? And further, why do we as women always shortchange ourselves? In a research study, women were asked, "Would you consider running for office?" Most said they weren't sure or would have to research the proper qualifications and learn the role first. Same group, different gender, and ninety percent of the men stated, yes, they could see themselves as president. Not president of the PTA, but rather the United States, and given the current scene … this is not hard to imagine.

I sigh. Regardless, I have to find something and fast. Unemployment benefits are not enough to cover the bills, and I need a constant in my life despite not being able to survive without a source of income.

Each day, I wake up with the same routine. Coffee and then put my attention to the plethora of applications and who knows how many submits of my resume. I have gotten to the point where I am able to one-click quick apply on so many job application sites .... almost as bad as one-click buy on Amazon. It drains me. I want to be wanted. I want to be a participant in the workforce. To make a difference in some aspect. I need to be able to have a sense of fulfillment. I remember being able to fill up my grocery cart with no hesitation. Oh, those were the days. A smile forms on my lips with the memory.

The job search was such a drain on my soul and self-esteem as if my self-esteem couldn't be any lower. Try applying for a million jobs and not even a phone call. I was like the kid in gym at school, stinky sweat ran through the room, even with my Teen Spirit. No one wanted to pick me. Not even the last one chosen. Not even an offer or a fake nod. I sat in my fresh clothes and no one cared. They did not want me for their team. I was not the one that got picked last, but rather not at all. It was as if the teams were already even, so I had to sit on the sidelines and watch. I didn't want to be on the sidelines. And neither did my stomach. I was hungry for more than just a job.

A growl rose from my insides. It wasn't like a dramatic, "I'm going to handle life" but rather … "I am hungry, can you please get some food?"

Have you ever had empty food cabinets? Like literally the shelves are barren. Not even a jar of corn seeds ready to be popped? Have you ever experienced that? The idea of no options but only one possibility? That's where I was with my groceries and where I was post-divorce. I did not have any type of pick-and-choose options. It was eat or not. And I wanted to eat, given that if I didn't, I would die. I wasn't so far down in the hole to understand that I had to eat to survive. I was not in the slumps of anorexia, but I had lost some weight through this whole ordeal. I can't account for the process of the divorce, my grief, or lack of income as the number one source. But my business clothes no longer fit. My pants hang on my hips like I am playing dress up in someone else's clothes.

I merge back and forth between what I can present as work attire and then my walk attire. After my daily routine of job application spree, I assign myself a set number of doors to hit for my campaign. Hit with my knuckles. Block walking or canvassing, whichever word choice you prefer, is essential for my kind of campaign. The only way people in Texas are going to vote for a down-ballot candidate like myself is if I actively go to their doors and ask for their support. This became a must after the end of straight ticketing voting in

2018. Courtesy of Texas Republicans who knew Texas Democrats would be drop-off voters. People in politics know that Republicans fall in line with their chosen candidate, but Democrats have to fall in love to vote for theirs. Despite many unsuccessful bids to express to voters that an election is not marriage, you can choose for someone else next time but at least vote this round for this person. Don't skip a race. Finish the ballot. Can we please get in on this idea? You don't have to like every single policy stance a person has, you can be okay with some differences. We are going for the majority concept, and we have to start doing this in Texas, or we will remain in the minority party for the entire state.

Each and every door is an opportunity to change the fate of my state. There is a bit of serotonin hit when a voter is not going to vote in the midterms and you convince them otherwise. The silver lining in not having a job currently while running for office is that I do have a bit more time on my hands than I would if I were employed. In case you didn't know, running for office alone is a full-time job. Not only are you knocking on doors and on the hunt for votes, but you are in a constant meet and greet. Each campaign event is an opportunity to present as the most qualified person for this position. Which, by the way, is in by no means a position to provide a proper salary or life. Texas is old school. Like way old school. Like, kick it back to plantation days and only white men who owned property.

I'm not talking about a house; I'm talking about acres and acres and money upon money. Family money, like decades and generations of financial security. Nothing like your typical Texan. But here we are nonetheless. In this moment of expectation, it is a reality that not much has changed within our Legislature. How far have we come and yet how far have we remained?

Remained more likely, it's where we are a hundred-plus years later. We still expect legislators to be able to "leave" their jobs and home lives for six months every other year and to be paid $7,200 a year. This "salary" is while they are expected to live in Austin, Texas. Which the Austin housing market took off over a decade ago and has not stopped. A lot of folks from California came over with their tech-millionaire success and bought up a ton of property. Houses that used to cost $150k in the early 2000s, now cost over 1.5 million dollars. But the salary of a Texas Legislator has not changed. Let alone the budget for their staff.

Okay. That makes sense ... this is going to create the mold of a legislator that represents the people. No average Texan could do this. How is it that a person who can leave their home/career et al for six months every other year going to be able to understand the needs of their constituents, and on a salary of $7,200 a year?

Which is where I come in. As I am an everyday Texan, once I am gainfully employed again, I will figure out how I will balance a proper work of nine to five while also being a legislator.

I didn't plan this part out, as some things you can't. Sometimes you have to wait until the cards have been dealt to determine how you will play them. This was the stage of the game of life I was in. I was ready to be hit with an ace. However, it might have already been played.

I stand in front of a green door. I always size up the door and house and any descriptive piece. You can tell a lot about a person/family by the exterior and items outside of their house.

Let's get something straight to begin with. It is not soliciting to ask anyone if they are going to vote or to encourage them to do so. That being said, I will also be real with you. If there is a *No Soliciting* sign on the door or anywhere in the yard. I am skipping this house. I know legally I can knock on their door. But why? These residents have already told me they do not want to be disturbed. So, if I am hoping for their vote, why would I go against what they have already stated is their wish? I don't care that "legally I can talk to them"—they said no. *No* means *no*. Even with voting. Let's please be polite and honor the right to say no and acknowledge their preference. That is a much-needed behavior.

I check the next address in my app. The name pops up with their age range and their voter history. I walk in the direction, as it is only two houses away, which is kind of like a gold mine in Texas. More times than we would like, the distance between houses is streets, not only a couple of houses. I check the voter info. I also do not assume that the person/people in the app are going to be the person who answers the door. Further, I don't like the concept of speaking to a stranger by name like "Hey, Mary Gonzales."

No. Don't say their name. Even if their doormat lines up with the name in the app. If you knew my name before we began to speak, I would be on the defensive. I am not going to want to hear you out, as I am going to be concerned with why you know my name. Which means my mind is going on the hunt for how you have my name versus why you are on my doorstep. I don't read from the app. I read the room.

The sound of the doorbell chimes through the house. I only use the doorbell if I think my knock was not loud enough. I am sure people love their ring devices. But I can tell you it creates extra intimidation for canvassing. Too many people have posted videos on NextDoor and Facebook asking why people were at their door with flyers for an election. Good times.

"No soliciting," a person yells through their device.

I nod and head back toward my car. This is the end of my two hundred doors for the day. I try to do at least a hundred doors on the weekdays. It is harder to catch people at home during normal work hours. Or if they are at home via a remote job, they have already fully embraced the reclusive lifestyle and are not interested in a conversation on their doorstep. They are more likely to say "Leave it on the doorstep and get the hell out of here," circa *Home Alone*.

I tap the *Submit* on my app to turn in my door count for the day. The app is great, don't get me wrong, but there is more to being in person than the AI of this device in my hand. I have to use skills that cannot be programmed. People always say to me "You have to have thick skin to run for office."

I smile politely and say yes. I get that. I knew it would not be easy. But I had been focused on the idea of more than thick skin for a while.

In my marriage, I had to focus on my gut instinct and what was real or not. Things were not surface level. They were twisted every which way to the point that I was left spinning, wondering which way was up when all I wanted was out. Gaslighting was a daily form of abuse. The idea of trying to make someone doubt themselves and not being able to determine fact from fiction can destroy your self-esteem, among other things. Yet, I was able to pull myself out of the deception. I survived, barely.

The concept to survive. When we think back to our ancestry, we think of their survival and what they did to exist. The ideology of survival of the fittest was probably not considered with the concept of grocery shopping. How could one think that grocery shopping would be correlated to survival of the fittest? You would have to think about technology and decide if that is going to be considered in this reckoning. Is grocery shopping a modern-day survival of the fittest? Or is it dumbed down to a fun event like an impromptu party, or is it laced with a stressed-filled bubble where you have to count each and every penny to make the balance of the total of the bill for the party or rather grocery bill? Some people don't understand the notion of not being able to make ends meet. The ideology of necessity over desire. How can I make a dinner for less than two bucks? Very simply. A pack of ramen and a bag of frozen vegetables.

I blow the air out through my lips. It's fine. Everything is fine. The budget is okay. Yeah, it's totally fine. I'm not to the ramen part of the chapter. Yet.

I peruse over the picked-over produce at my local supermarket. I am almost to the point of being a member of an ugly produce sign-up service. I don't mind produce that isn't pretty. I prefer to avoid the time waste of the pick-and-choose at the grocery stores for something that looks edible. Anything can be edible with the right spices.

Except time is on my hands. I don't need to crunch numbers to figure out where I can save time to find the perfect crunchable veggies.

I put some veggies in my shopping cart and glance up.

If a record was being played right now, it would scratch. Meaning, at this moment, I must be being played. Hardcore played. What in the world? I shake my head as if I have fallen into a deep sleep of nonsense and need to be woken to reality. Nope. No such luck. I glance at my feet. I need to be grounded. Not again. My eyes narrow in on the tall suit. Crisp and clean as always. Like he walked out of the dry cleaners, and probably even smells like Versace or something. But seriously … why of all grocery stores does this douchebag have to be in mine? There are at least five in a two-mile radius. I'm dumbfounded as to this chain of unfortunate events. Did I subscribe to something I am unaware of? Is this because I didn't forward the nonsense chain mail over the years? Or the "Hey, have a happy day" via Facebook messenger chain reply all? Pass on this "smile to ten others." Nah, I wasn't a part of that scene. It's not who I am. I don't subscribe to those forwards and pass-alongs. I didn't forward it, because I didn't want to.

But is this retribution of a karmic equation or something? I disagree with this thought process. I should not have to be a part of this nonsense. I toss my head back and sigh. Really. Are we doing this again? I am here to grab some salad, maybe a little hummus, and celery, and then bounce. I hightail it to the next display of vegetables and pretend that I don't see him. And no, not "*Satan*," who others might refer to as Mike DaVile or my ex-husband. But instead, it's "*Satan's*" equally douchebag-esque evil lawyer, Maxwell Graham. Don't lawyers add esquire to their names …? This makes sense for his new moniker in my mind. If I could conjure up vomit at a moment's notice I would properly vomit on his shoes. His fake-ass brown leather shoes with ties. Like, *Check out my ties*. Whatever, dude. Tie them around your throat and get out of my way. I bet every morning he ties them with a level of hate for all women. He probably imagines himself with the strand as he wraps each lace around their throat like he wraps up his divorce cases with venom and ignores the pain he creates. His vengeance- and hate-filled representation. Zero remorse. Zero compassion.

I shake. *No. Don't think about him, Mia. That was over two years ago. You don't have to deal with him anymore. It's over. It's long over. You only have to deal with the exchanges of Schatzi.* Which is nonsense too. It's not right or fair at all. But who is here to care or listen? Not the court. No... they have too many other cases to deal with than a custody battle of a "rescue mutt dog" as the judge stated in the final order. I cringe. I know Schatzi probably wouldn't be able to understand the words that were said. But they were hurtful and mean. Just like the Texas Family Court system. *Garbage.*

"What are the odds?" His voice is like a flamed torch against my skin. The sheer presence of him invokes the smell of my skin being burned. Evil.

"I can think of a lot more odds that don't make sense," I let rip from my pursed lips. Like the idea that he would represent "*Satan*" and fight for me to have less time with my dog. The dog that I adopted. The dog that I ran with daily. The dog that comforted me during the most painful moments of my life. The dog that gave me the strength to continue. To put one foot in front of the other. The dog that knew me better than me.

Yeah … this was not the guy I wanted in my same space. Today was not my day either. Nope.

I swallowed. *Be present, Mia. Be in the moment.* I glance back at Maxwell. His sharp suit. Pressed. Fitted. Professional. He pierced me with his blue eyes. I shuddered. *No.*

A laugh tumbles from his mouth like a bunch of overgrown weeds that do not belong. "Well, that leads me to believe you're delighted to see me then?" He effortlessly tosses some lettuce into his basket. I want to grab the basket from his hand and smash it over his head. And shout "Enjoy your chopped salad!"

"Your cue card is as bad as your bar card." I grab my celery do a full about like a soldier and march toward the checkout. I'm thankful for a crowded store because I can blend into the people and avoid another encounter. The air in my lungs is about to combust. I do not need to self-destruct at this moment. It is important to always consider where I am and who is there. In this world of immediate social media fame. I have to be cognizant that anyone can record at any time. Even though the State Representative seat I am after is not a hot target. I have to be careful. If I were to blow up and let myself be as I want, that could be released to the internet and a quick sayonara to my campaign would incur. Our society is too ready to film on the spot, and I'm not ready to go viral for a lapse in judgment. I'm better than that. I can hold my tongue and wait till I'm alone to be who I want to be and let my emotions truly come through. To be true, like my pal Shakespeare wrote: *To Thine Own Self Be True*.

It is so hot. I rush through the parking lot. My car is in sight, and I let out a sigh of relief as I slide into my cloth seats, once again a reminder that leather is not always better. Especially in Texas. I press Ginger's number. As soon as the dial ends into a slow ring, I begin to speak.

"You're not going to believe this." I wait for her to be invested in my news.

"Shock me, I'm all ears." She lets out a small laugh.

"He was at the freaking grocery store with me. Me. *My* grocery store." I groan as I back out of my parking spot. I casually glance in my rear-view mirror. Only a small part of me thinks that I might hesitate and not hit him if he happened to be in my viewpoint. The lane is all clear. I switch gears and veer out of the lot.

"He as in '*Satan*'?" I can hear the dismay in her voice.

"No, '*Satan*'s' assistant. His lap boy. His evil monster helper. His vile, awful, cruel—"

Ginger interrupts my rant. "Wait a minute, I'm not sure who we are talking about."

I let out another groan. "Seriously, you know how awful he is. Why does he have to keep popping up in my life? I just want to vanquish his very image from my mind and never have to see him again."

"I know, but you're better than the days of yore, and I don't think you want to add witchery to your bio." She laughs. "Besides, it's not good for your appeal to the Rs, and you're going to need a few of them to vote for you. If you have dog mom, hurricane survivor, marathon runner, and witchcraft on the side, the percentage of people that that will appeal to is like less than .0000000000000000007 percent."

"Ginger."

She continues, "And those people don't even live in your district."

I can't help but laugh. "Every vote counts though."

"True, but let's whisk away from witchery. Trust me on this one."

"Okay. But why is he popping up everywhere?" I merge onto the freeway with the store in my rearview. My mind is all over the place. I don't need to give him one thought. None. Not a one. I have bigger things to consider.

"Who cares? More importantly, where are you popping up next? We have an election to win. How are the people of the district going to know you are the better representative?" Ginger clicks her tongue. She is right and always pulls me back to the path of success. Even though my path has been jagged and not exactly paved with a ton of wins. But the path I am on gives me something bigger than a lot of things … it starts with an *H*.

Hope.

Chapter Five
"Swipe to the left or slide to the right ... which side do you fall?"

It's another Friday night and Ginger has agreed to leave her man to have a ladies' night with me. She truly is the best. Her man is not bad either, since he has given up a top weekend night so she can console me in one way or another. It's been three months since my last date. I feel like I'm reporting in at an AA meeting ... no joke there, simply a confessional of my last hit of any interaction with the male species. This era of the swipe has become so commercial and non-committal. We live in a society of FOMO ... fear of missing out. People on these apps have formed their version of ADHD, as they can't stop the swipe game regardless of the possibility in front of them. The never-ending chaos of what could possibly be if we continue to swipe. That quickie dopamine hit of serotonin when someone responds with an affirmative of being semi-interested to swipe their finger on a technical application filled with so many hopefuls and hopelessness. I can't imagine this is what we are supposed to do in order to "meet the one." Especially now, no one is interested in anything more than a superficial discussion. Especially the divorcee crowd. Good grief, we should all be in a "meet the right therapist" application instead of

69

the circular maze of endless options for more of nothing much and insecurities.

If it weren't for Ginger's generosity of being my wing lady tonight, I would be sitting in the comfort of my home and swiping. I would grab my bottle of cabernet and pour a nice healthy amount. My friends have told me to go and sit at a bar and let men approach me. This is not anything that appeals to me. I want to be home and be safe. I can scan through hundreds of men in the area. There are so many single men on these sites. I have a little game I play with myself called "Can I swipe to the end of the app?" I have yet to do it. But I can only read so many profiles. And good grief with these profiles.

"I'm a busy professional but can make time for that right person"

"I'm looking for my partner in crime."

"I'm height- and weight-proportionate, and you should be too."

"I'm tired of these other guys that make it difficult for us nice guys."

"No drama. No, I don't want to give you money."

"Quit posting group photos for me to figure out if you are the hot one or not."

And the photos that accompany these profiles. I know I live in Texas, but when did a dead carcass equate to sexy? I don't get it. And the shirtless mirror selfies. That's an automatic swipe left. My guy, if you have to put that in your profile, then the level of substance is not enough to even make it past the appetizer at a semi-okay restaurant. Pass.

Given that I am now on the official general ballot for November, my swipe days have come to an end. I can't continue to be present on those sites. It doesn't seem smart. It seems like the exact opposite. Which brings me to a ladies' night date with Ginger instead.

"Darling, how long have you been waiting?" Ginger slides onto the bar stool next to me as we kiss cheeks. She brings such happiness into the room. It doesn't hurt that her red locks cascade around her face and her eyes are like actual emeralds. This is why she is not single. Well, that and she is a pretty awesome human as well. Luckily, she met her man in her twenties, and he turned out not to be a douchebag, cheating a-hole. What can I say ... somehow, without those pieces of broken vows in the relationship, it worked out for them.

"Forever ... look how old and decrepit I look." I pull at my hair. Despite my best efforts in my most recent box touch-ups, there always seem to be at least a few strands of gray. Like, "Hey, check it ... you're old." Yeah ... thank you, Mother Earth, or whoever thought I needed another visual reminder. I have a mirror, and my eyes, regardless of my age, work quite well. No need for corrected lenses at this point.

"Stop. First of all, you are gorgeous. Second of all, we are not doing any negative talk. Ever." Ginger grabs my hand and squeezes it.

The bartender approaches. "Can I get you ladies a drink? The guy at the end of the bar has asked for your bill to be added to his tab." He nods over at a gentleman who licks his lips. Why? Why can't a nice gesture be accompanied without a nasty move that makes me want to vomit?

"Yuck," I murmur into Ginger's ear.

She squeezes my leg. "Remember, just because people do stupid things doesn't mean they are stupid. Let's let this play out. Hold all the judgments until later." Ginger clears her throat and directs her attention to the bartender. "Well, that is certainly nice of him. We will have two of your best reds. The dryer the better."

The bartender nods and makes his way to the wine cellar. Who knows how much that costs? Definitely not in my budget. Obviously, Ginger, and her gorgeous locks, have brought the big ballers to the table, as always.

In our second round, the "gentleman" had decided to move from his spot across the bar and join us in a discussion of politics no less.

"The party is just going too far left … especially for Texas." The man, who is yet to identify himself, nods as he takes a swig of his bourbon.

"But is Texas the same as it was, say, four years ago, even?" Ginger's eyes sparkle. She loves to engage in political discussions despite my need to downplay amongst unidentified parties. Always need to play it safe. I have had too many run-ins with people from my canvass app who had identified as a Democrat and turned out to be a far-right Republican with a gun in hand to shoot me off their property. Canvassing is not for the weak of hearts or slow-paced runs.

"Oh, you know what they say about Texas—weather and politics, if you don't like it, wait a minute and it will change," Unidentified Man states with a chuckle.

"Isn't that the truth … By the way, what's your name?" I raise my eyebrows. It's a bit odd that he hasn't already introduced himself.

"I'm Brian Stevenson." He offers his hand.

Ginger shakes it first. "Hold on, are you with the family law center?"

"Indeed, are you a lawyer?" He inspects her face as if he is able to review the facial profiles of professionals in his mind, like a computer in search of a match.

"No, I only play one on TV." Ginger laughs. Brian's eyes squint. "I'm kidding. My husband is a lawyer. Not family law, but he has mentioned the family law center before. Your name rang a bell in this rolodex in my head." She taps the side of her head.

"Ginger has a bit of a photographic memory … might have been what got her the never-ending scholarships to every top medical school in the nation." I smile with pride.

"Well, there were a few in Europe too." Ginger shrugs. She can make a slight brag sound like downright humility.

"All right then, another round in celebration of the brilliant doctor's mind." Brian raises his glass and nods at the bartender. Red splashes into our glasses as warm amber slightly fills his tumbler. Friday night suddenly is all right.

"Now that we have our professions out of the way. Don't be shy. Your turn." Brian winks at me.

My chest tightens and my fingers begin to tingle. *Breathe, no big deal*. My cheeks begin to heat. It's okay. I *almost* have a job, at least one … surely I will be offered something soon. There are three jobs that I am in the second if not third round of interviews … there must be a statistic for over/under on a job offer for at least one of them. And further, if I am to win in November, I will have two jobs then. Because, obviously, I will have a job by November, even if I'm working multiple server jobs. I will get it done.

I run my tongue along my bottom teeth. *Breathe*.

"Well, Brian, here's the thing, we are actually in fortunate company tonight, as Mia is the Democratic nominee for Texas HD 193. The district we are sitting in right now!" She gives his arm a minute shove.

Brian's eyes widen, and he clears his throat. "Is that right?"

My lips are pressed together, even though I want to scream with thankfulness once again to Ginger for always being the person to toss on her superhero cape and save the day. Or me rather.

"Yes, that's correct." I nod. "Just won my primary. Now onto the general, I go." I laugh as if I'm pretending to move my arms in a jog motion.

"Who's your opponent?" Brian taps on the side of his glass.

"J—" I stop myself from saying the not-nice addition I normally add to his name and focus on being proper. "Dick Mikelson." If it were me, I would only ever go by Richard, but, honestly, it makes sense that Dick goes by Dick, especially given his voting record in the House. Who votes for rape insurance?

"Oh, Dick … that's a character for sure. That district is pretty red though, yes?" His fingertips are tapping over his phone like he is pulling up the district makeup.

"Yes, it's been held by Republicans for several decades. But I don't tout party lines when I'm knocking on the door. I talk about things that matter to all of us, regardless if we prefer a D or R next to the name of the president." I know how to remain party neutral, especially among unknown lineation.

Brian nods as he places his phone on the counter and motions for the check. "I like your way of thinking … We'll see how far it gets you in November." He signs his name on the line and passes business cards to each of us. "Let me know if I can help."

"Thank you." I slide his card in my purse and sigh. The level of doubt was there. It echoed through the small bar. It was a small hum; you might miss it if you weren't keen on the noise. But I was. I had been aware of this chatter for a while now.

The *"Who does she think she is?"*

"She doesn't have any experience."

"That's a red seat—it's not going to flip."

"What a waste. Why would she even think it's possible?

And empty *Oh*s of non-interest. The immediate write-off. I take the final sip of my wine and glance at Ginger. Her eyes are on me. I know what she is doing. Probably in a plan of some sort. It will have to wait till tomorrow. "My Lyft is here." I nod at Ginger.

"Are you serious?" Ginger squeezes my arm. "Tell me it's because you didn't feel like driving?"

I laugh. "It's because I didn't feel like driving ... and my car not being capable of it tonight might have been part of my decision." I press my lips together. I can't lie to Ginger, but this is not the place to discuss yet another nail in my tire.

Ginger closes her eyes. "Okay, we can circle back to this later."

I nod and make my way to the exit. It's a quick *two-step, two-step* to the car. I verify the license plate to the letters in my app. I always check to make sure the car I hop in is the car that is supposed to pick me up. The ride is swift, and I rush into my empty house. Schatzi is nowhere in sight. The emptiness is so loud. I lock my door before I lay my head and let the dread of the unknowns disappear into the vast cloud of what-ifs.

Chapter Six
"All knights wear armor, but not all are shining."

Due to my current custody schedule, I only get to see Schatzi on Thursdays from 6 to 8 p.m., whereas the rest of the time begins at 6 p.m. on Fridays and ends at 8 a.m. on Mondays, depending on what the first Friday of the month is. As if that is equal. Whoever came up with that number, I have many words for them. Who knows, if I do become duly elected, I can put my mark on the Texas Family Code which hasn't been updated since 1995. Time for a change. And I get it. I know that most do not compare a dog to a child. I totally understand this. However, I have to follow the same custody schedule as humans, and yes, I'm venting from a dog mother's perspective, but I'm still bothered about it from a human perspective. The Texas Legislature decided that if you make eye contact with your child (or dog in my case) that counts as a day. A day. Eye contact in exchange for twenty-four freaking hours.

Ahem, let me clear my throat. No, eye contact does not equate to a day. Not in anyone's eyes, and that is bad for the children (or dog) and bad for the parent who is considered the "visitor." The visitor in their child's life. What kind of cruel label is that? A parent is not a visitor. The "visiting parent?" What? Who came up with this terminology? Not anyone with an ounce of empathy or compassion. And I can guess who came up with it. A man. A man with most likely no kids or grown kids. A man who does not think about the effects of the soul-destroying pain a parent suffers from not seeing their child every day to then only a couple of hours during the week. To further label them as a non-consequential actor in the child's life. It's just wrong, on so many levels.

I lock the door behind me and unfasten the leash from Schatzi. I had taken her out for a quickie walk, but she knows our routine. Rush in the door, grab her leash, and walk her around the property until she relieves herself. Usually, this is quick, but sometimes it seems to take an eternity. But this was what we did.

After our quickie walk, I pour myself a glass of wine. I can usually make it to about three to four sips before the tears start to fall. They are like a slow leak at first. My tears are as if a Ziploc bag had been filled with ice and melted in the summer sun. The bag is stuffed beyond capacity, and it is only a matter of time before the water bursts through the seams of the glued-together sides. Ziploc is great and all, but it doesn't matter the amount of ultra-non-penetrative adhesive they have on the plastic if you have a mother (whether it's a human mom or a dog mom) who is in utter agony about missed time with her children. Nothing will keep the dam of emotion from breaking through and soaking an entire continent. And thus, I take my fourth sip of wine.

A warm drop slides over my lower lash and onto my face. I know what is about to happen. I prepare for this every day. Part of the wine is to let it happen without being able to have the entire amount of pain hit me so hard. The wine eases it. Kind of like K-Y before a situation you don't want. Imagine your legs are propped up on the stirrups. You are naked from the waist down. The doctor is in front of you, with the nurse in the background. Now she puts the K-Y on the probe prior to the entrance. This was my appointment with reality. Complete exposure. The absence of pain with the K-Y wouldn't make the experience any better than what it was: a stark, cold, awful moment. I wanted to evacuate as soon as possible.

I place my glass of wine down on the end table. The only end table I took. I left the other and the matching coffee table. I took the longer couch. I chose the steel gray one because I liked the color. I left the greenish one for him and the L-shaped sofa upstairs. I took less than half of everything. I would have taken less if it hadn't been for my friends Kevin and Cheri. They had helped me move and insisted I take more than what I had planned, even though at the end of the day, it was still less than half. It was only things. The rest of the furniture was left in the house. The one I purchased and was kicked out of. I even had to leave Schatzi that day. It wasn't my day. He wasn't even with her, and it didn't matter. I had to leave her. Alone.

Back in the painful moment of my reality. I hate this. I hate to be sad in front of

Schatzi, especially given we only had two hours. I'm trying to get past this moment. We are doing better. I used to spend an hour in my closet as the tears fell from my eyes and moans from my lips. Some days are tougher than others.

I make it to my room. Schatzi follows behind me. Even though she knows this is the place where we will separate for about an hour. She still does not leave my side. She is the best dog and companion. Dogs do love you despite all of your flaws and weaknesses. They look past your imperfections and still wag their tails and are generally happy to see you every single time you return.

Every time I say "Schatzi," she will rush over with anticipation as if I'm about to deliver a truckload of Christmas presents, but I'm not. It's only a pat on the head, scratch behind the ears or back, and even a hug. She is a good hugger. I love her. She is a mix between a German Shepherd and a Border Collie. The prettiest eyes are surrounded by caramel circles. And now I have to leave her. I step inside my closet. The latch snaps as I let my body fall to the floor. The tears are in full-on mode. They push past my lashes and pour onto my skin. My body vibrates, a hard rattle of a wounded animal that is about to die after being hit by a car. I shake and shake as the tears fall over and over against my face. I can't stop them. I don't even want to try. I know this is part of my day. Normally, I give myself till 6 p.m. to cry, but given today is our day, my start and end times will alter. Today will not be like every other day. I am going to do better in my closet time. I gave myself a rule. I have an hour to cry on days that I don't have Schatzi. When I have her for our two hours on Thursday, I force myself to cry for less than an hour. Otherwise, I would indulge myself. I would allow myself to cry.

I know it's impossible to run out of liquid. This is an overflow of emotions that will never end. And it won't. I could sit in my closet all night and cry, maybe even until I was reported on a "last seen" flyer. I try not to focus on the sadness when I am not in my closet. I compartmentalize outside of this space. I don't think about not having Schatzi full-time, losing my house, and the reality that sometimes life can be downright cruel outside of my closet. Outside I focus on everything else. I hold all of my sadness in. I compress my emotions into tiny sealed bricks of storage. I am the compartmentalized warrior outside of this one spot.

In reality, I let the tears run down my skin. Let the hurt out. Acknowledge that I am in pain. I am in physical pain. Emotional pain. I want to die. I would rather die than not be with Schatzi and get rid of this pain. But that's not an option. I can't die. I can't let myself go. I have to keep going. I have to let myself have this moment, this self-indulgence, and then I have to stand up.

I rise, open the door, and exit the darkness of the closet. I am back in the light. The sadness is still there, but I leave it in the box that I have compartmentalized grief. I have to be able to get through the day. The night, the next moment, and I have to rise for more than myself. I need to fix things so that others don't feel this unbearable pain.

This is another reason why I chose to run. There were too many things about the laws and the way certain policies didn't help out those who needed the help the most. It was time for someone to be a voice for the voiceless. For the ones that can't leave the sorrow of the closet. I get it. I live it. And I am going to stand up for us all.

More specifically, for the survivors of human trafficking, who need a real path to rehabilitation that doesn't involve a gala for the elite while they are brought out on stage to share their trauma, only to be forced back into the life because a fancy dinner with an auction is not going to provide a young mother with a skill to provide for her family. These women need real solutions. Like assistance obtaining their birth certificates and identification so they can find work outside of the life they escaped. They need programs for affordable housing that doesn't include a two-year waitlist. Where are they supposed to live in the meantime? Affordable childcare and healthcare that doesn't require a thirty-page form with no assistance in filling out each page. The current process is too confusing for the average person let alone someone who is struggling with the emotional trauma and perhaps lack of education due to being in the human trafficking world. The world where they are frightened of the door knob because they were beaten if they touched it. But we are to assume they can get through a government documentation program without any guidance? We can do better than this. The over 300,000 known victim-survivors of human trafficking in Texas deserve better. I intend to make this one of my focuses among many others.

I slide my shoes on. Schatzi wags her tail in utter happiness. She knows this isn't about a quickie walk in the apartment complex but rather a proper run where we can both be free and enjoy the trails.

The idea of being able to run makes my veins pucker up with happiness. Run. Yes, let's do this. I know Schatzi loves it, too. Being able to run is therapeutic, both physically and emotionally. Physically it gets your serotonin levels to flow and is healthy beyond being able to keep you in shape. Emotionally, it takes me to a place where I am able to clear my mind and find clarity on issues or situations that I might not have been able to reach in a stationary problem. Since I was in middle school, there has not been one run that I have taken where a problem has not been solved or tempered after a good run. My thoughts have been able to properly digest, and I can gather more about a situation. I ran a marathon. Yes, I did. I never thought I would run a marathon. I always thought a: that's too long, and b: I couldn't do it. I love to run. I like to run 10ks. Then I ran a half marathon. I was proud of myself. Being able to train for a half marathon was a big deal. Except a little cloud to my sunshine of self-esteem was being told by him that a half marathon wasn't that big of a deal if you compare it to a full marathon. Like I was only half successful in my race. Even though the race was literally for the half, and I finished it. But no. He had to diminish me and my race.

Even with this information, I did not once think about the fact that he had never run any race, not even a 5k. But I was challenged. I trained to run a marathon—26.2 miles. Ran them. All of them. Finished before the gates closed. Got my medal. Timed my music properly and crossed the finish line as "Welcome to the Jungle" by Guns n Roses played a private but loud serenade in my ears. Yes, I had joined the jungle of marathon finishers. Boom. And wow. It was incredible. That is something I can tap on and say "Hey, Mia, you got through that. You can do this."

A quickie four-mile loop, and I have to get Schatzi back to "*Satan*." This is such BS. There is no reason she shouldn't be with me or at least spend the night. But no, I have to bring her back to him. Like, why? I shake my head as we hop into my car. Let's do this. I rub her head. She is such a pretty dog, and I tell her as much. Her eyes look up at me with pride and a bit of sadness; she knows what's about to happen. The part that kills me the most about this drop-off is the idea that she thinks I want her only for the two hours. Not in my life. But she is a dog. I can tell her how I feel, but that doesn't change the actions of the two-hour turnaround. I know she is a dog and not to be in comparison to kids. But I can imagine how painful this must be for the drop-off parent to have to say goodbye after less than two hours, especially if you count the commute time within that timeframe. *Garbage.*

I walk Schatzi up to the door. She has the exchange leash on her. The door opens. He has obviously been waiting at the door. I swear if I were not to arrive exactly at 8 p.m., he would call the police.

"Hey, Schatzi girl. You miss me? I bet. Come on back home. I'm so glad you're back." His voice oozes of infidelity and betrayal. *Miss him, as if.* And home is where her heart is, which is with me.

I hand the leash to him. I make no eye contact. I learned a long time ago not to look at him. Regardless of the number of horrible things he has done to me and continues to do. If I make eye contact, I will feel bad for him in some capacity and momentarily forget about the pain he puts upon me. So, no eye contact is essential. It is imperative to go *gray rock*.

I shudder once I get back into my car. I pull up to the next light and swipe through my apps. I click on my Meet-Up App. What a lifesaver it has been. Whoever created this needs to be thanked. It is so perfect to scroll through different possibilities of get-togethers in your local area. I am pretty sure there is a chess meet-up on Thursday nights. Maybe it's still going on. Not that I want to show up in my workout gear. But, honestly, I just want some social interaction and a distraction. Chess would be perfect and no suitor is even better. I scroll through the daily calendar. There it is. Yes, it started at seven. Well … maybe they started late or are on a second round. Either way, I decided to give it a go and head toward the hotel destination. Which seems odd for a chess meet-up. I could see how maybe singles meet-ups might meet at a hotel, but this is for chess. Seems out of the ordinary. Regardless, I pull into the lot and check my face. It's decent, and I head into the hotel. I scroll over the meet-up notes again. "*Meet us in the dining room.*" Well, okay then. Here we go.

I make my way toward the room and see a gathering of only men. Obviously, I need to clue my single lady friends into this. The odds are definitely in our favor in this spot. I peruse through any signs of availability. A middle-aged man approaches me.

"Can I help you?"

"Yes, I'm here to play chess—this is the Knights Meet-Up, right?" I scan the room once more to ensure that I did indeed see the chess boards.

"Yes … oh, okay." His eyes are widened as if he has seen a ghost. Maybe my outfit is off-putting or maybe my pheromones are too much for this testosterone-filled room. I don't know.

There is an open seat in front of a board, and I sit down. "You ready to play?" I ask.

A young Persian guy jumps back and flitters his eyelashes.

"I'm sorry, I didn't mean to startle you." I scoot in the chair.

"Ah, no worries. Yes, I'm ready." He pulls on his collar and hits the timer button. He moves his knight out onto the board.

I smile. Nice move. I move one of my pawns forward two spots to clear the board for some moves for multiple options.

We continue on for about five moves before I hear "Checkmate." I swallow hard. This was not something I expected.

"Okay, well then. Well done." I offer my hand to shake.

He nods and scoots his chair out. Apparently, he does not want a rematch. He moves through the room with all efforts to avoid a possible exposure to the plague. Like, dude, you beat me fair and square, not sure what that was about. I know the game was quick, but that was a bit rude.

I look over my shoulder and see the waiter approach. I nod. Yes, I definitely want a drink. I'm sure this low-key hotel has only the best of house wines. Ha! But what the hell, the night can't get any less significant than it already has been.

"A cabernet, please."

"Make that two." A heavy voice echoes over mine. Much louder or maybe it wasn't. Maybe it's just the sound of that voice that sounds louder than any other voice in the room.

Especially in the courtroom. But not here. Not now. I glance down at my feet. Yes, sneakers. Maybe I should make a run for it. I know I am in my workout gear. The shorts are still stuck to my thighs and the nape of my neck is still damp from my run. Despite this, I had an ounce of hope that I was not actually in my workout gear. Not another misfortunate appearance encounter. A mere fantasy could be that I was not actually here. That this was not real. Not again. First, it was the Britney Spears look-alike outfit, then my blockwalk canvasser clothes, and now I am dressed down again. While he, of course, is in a suit. When is Maxwell Graham not in a suit? I wonder if he came out of his mother's womb with a tweed blazer and some beige slacks.

No wonder I lost that first round so quickly. My luck is off, my game is off. I need to have my chakras balanced or something.

I tap my feet and blow the hair from my face. I want to pretend and not acknowledge the person in front of me. He is so carefree in this casual atmosphere. His long fingers grasp onto his knight as he places it back in position.

"Hmmm," I let out. That's all I could come up with. Why was he here? And, of course, in that suit. All crisp even at the end of the day. While I sit across from him in a tank top drenched in sweat—*Thank you, Texas*. No. This is not right. Surely this is a dream/nightmare. It doesn't make sense. Why would he be here? Why?

"What are you doing here?" I press my eyelashes together in an attempt to wake myself up. I need to wake up.

"Oh …" He nods and runs his finger along the collar of his shirt. "Well, this is a chess meet-up, a place where people who enjoy chess meet up to play." His blue eyes flash at me like they are in an effort to twinkle, but I will not accept that. No, they are not. They are blue, moody, gross, hurtful, yucky eyes and so is his outfit. Yes. I am the one with the power in this position. I have obviously been working out my body, and now I am working out my mind.

Mind over matter, Mia.

"Why are you *here* though?" I bite my lower lip internally.

Self-control. Be cool, Mia. This is no big deal.

"I'm one of the people in this room who likes to play chess." He pushes one of his pawns forward one space. "Your move."

And so, it is.

I pick up my rook and swipe one of his pawns. It's a small win, but, hey, a win is a win. I know that I will most likely lose my rook after this, but I wanted to take at least one of his pieces. My lungs tighten. I need to gather some composure. I take a sip of my wine.

"Nice." Maxwell nods at my capture. He runs his index finger over his lips as if he can't decide his next move. It's clear as day he should take my rook. Any novice would know this.

"How is your hand?" Maxwell ignores the obvious choice and moves his bishop a couple of spaces.

I rub my palm. "It's okay. I am not sure if I will have a scar or not, but that would be the least of my worries." I let out a laugh. My shoulders slump for a second, and I lift them back up. He probably didn't notice.

"Houston Medical is really good. How is your race going? Is that what you are worried about?" His eyes are clear, like they could be trusted and this is real empathy. Unlike the faux-empathy that my ex-husband had displayed in our marriage. His initials always made me laugh. MD for Mike DaVile. You would think he was a doctor the way he presents himself. Always had an answer about everything. Like he had been to medical school and law school, and had his MBA from Harvard or some other prestigious school. He had achieved none of the above. Rather, Mike had barely graduated high school.

Yet, Maxwell has this different level of empathy, like a school administrator who wants to help someone out and make a sixty turn into a seventy on one too many grades. But that's impossible. This is the same guy who chose to believe "*Satan.*"

I glance back at the board. I am not sure why he didn't take my rook. I run the various options of where my pieces could go in contrast to how that would play out from his perspective. He could end this game in a handful of moves. Maxwell has lined up all of his pieces to be protected but also to attack each one of mine. How did he do this so well and without me being able to predict it?

I let the bit of pride I had earlier slip from my lungs. I move another one of my pawns up two spaces. It can easily be taken, but it is only a pawn. Maybe he will let me die a slow death rather than the one-two move and claim my queen.

"Um ... well not really worried about the race. I can put in the effort and hope that voters will believe in me and do their part," I finally give in and respond to his question. I scan the room. It is emptier than when I arrived. I tap *the Home* button on my phone; it's nine o'clock.

"They will," he says with a level of confidence I wish I could bottle and keep for myself. He avoids my pawn and moves another of his pawns into a position for me to take it. *What is he doing?*

"I guess we will know soon enough. So, do you do these meet-ups often?" I take a sip of my wine. It's dry but not too heavy.

The sides of Maxwell's mouth pull up. "I've been to a few. I had plans earlier, but they were canceled, and I didn't feel like going home." His shoulders shrug. There is a level of uncertainty about the way his arms move. Like the confidence has softened.

I press my lips together. "No one to go home to?" I zone in on his face for a reaction.

"Ha, no, just me. Not even a pet." He *tsks* and takes one of my bishops. There it is. I knew he had a plan to take a more powerful piece.

"Some people wouldn't consider a pet an *even* … some people consider pets to be family." My insides burn. I wish I had Schatzi to go home to tonight. But it's not my day. And I have to share because of the guy in front of me. Who apparently thinks she doesn't matter or is an *even*. I move my queen out into the open. I'd decided it was time to sacrifice her and call it a night.

Maxwell nods. "Yeah, I had no idea how important some people feel about pets until your case." He rubs his chin with his dexterous fingers. "Well, I mean, from my client's point of view. He felt so strongly about the dog. I almost thought it was a little out of the ordinary." He waves a hand in the air. "Actually, forgive me, I shouldn't be speaking about this."

My eyelashes are doing a dance of destruction against the pupils of my eyes. I try to focus on what he has said and simultaneously attempt to maintain my sense of composure. Unfortunately, I am capable of neither.

"No, he did not feel strongly about the DOG. Her name is Schatzi, and she is my dog, my family, not his. He only did this to hurt me," I blurt out before the tears stream down my face. "I have to go. Goodbye." I grab my purse and wipe my eyes as I rush out of the hotel. My only bit of grace is that I am in fact in my running shoes and can make it to my car without any hesitation, something I wouldn't be able to do had

I worn heels. Hell might hath no fury like a woman scorned, but I would think hell on earth is the reality of a woman who has mourned the loss of her baby. Schatzi will always be my baby, pet or not.

Chapter Seven

"Let the games begin, and we will see who is here to win."

The air is not crisp. It's sweltering hot. It's "I think my skin is going to melt off my body" hot. It's "Am I in a volcano?" hot. I wipe my brow with the back of my hand.

"Whoo baby ... I don't know if I can take this heat." Beverly uses some of my lit to fan her face.

"Same." I glance at my app. "We only have a few more houses to go—do you think we can pull through?"

"For you, yes ... Anybody else?" Beverly laughs. "No way in hell, and I feel like we are already there!"

We both laugh as we make our way up the sidewalk to the next house on our list. I knock once and then ring the doorbell. A little extra effort on the door doesn't hurt.

A large man in a Buc-ee's white T-shirt and red shorts opens the door. "Yes?"

"Hi, I'm Mia Verita, and this is Beverly. We wanted to see if you had plans to vote this year?"

"Hump, nah, I don't vote." He shakes his head with disgust at us.

"Oh, why not?" I cock my head to listen for whatever reason or reasons have discouraged him.

"Because I know the system is rigged and my vote doesn't matter. These Republicans have been in charge forever and nothing changes."

"Well, that's all the more reason to vote. Mia is a Democrat and she really needs your support."

"I appreciate that, but I just can't get with the government."

I pull my head back. "What do you mean?" I am not sure that I even want to know his answer, but I am a bit curious.

"Ever since Harvey, it's just not right."

"Oh, did you have some flood damage?" I glance at his house to see if I can notice any watermarks on the bricks.

"Nah, I ain't worried about that. I am mad 'cause they caused it."

My eyes squint. "Do you mean the government could have prevented the mass destruction if there had been proactive legislation in place to prevent the damage that was done to homes and buildings? If so, that's one of my action items if I am elected to represent you."

The man shakes his head. "No, I mean they made the rain happen. Opening up the sky with that damn weather machine."

Beverly and I make eye contact. It might be time to close out on this house.

I can't help myself, but I have to clarify to be sure what this man is trying to convey. "You think the government had weather machines that caused Hurricane Harvey?"

"That's right. And do you know why?"

"No idea," is all I can muster.

"So they could round up all the kids in Fifth Ward and vaccinate them. I saw them driving them up in buses and doing it at the mall."

In my best effort, I did not laugh. I realize though, in theory, this is nuts. However, this man truly believes the government has a rain machine that caused millions of dollars of destruction and lives lost. I would be speechless, but I need to quickly end this conversation. "Oh, okay. Well, I hope you consider changing your mind about voting. Have a good day."

Beverly and I nod at the man as we move with speed off his sidewalk and further down the road. I wait until we are far out of earshot to speak.

"That was a first." I flitter my eyelashes as if I can blink out the wacko situation we just encountered.

"Yep, that was nuts." Beverly laughs.

We make our way to the next door and I knock and ring the doorbell. I almost hope no one answers, as I am not sure if I can handle another wacky conversation. We stand in silence for a minute and I click *No answer* on the app. I guess I shouldn't wish for things that I don't want. I really do need to be able to speak with as many voters as possible. As we make our way back toward our cars, there's a young woman with her dog.

I wave.

"Hi there, have you made plans to vote this year?" I hustle toward her to offer some of my lit.

She shakes her head. "Oh no, I'm not the voter in the house."

"What's that?" Beverly asks.

"I'm not the voter. My husband votes for us."

"Are you registered to vote?" I shuffle through my lit for a voter registration card.

"No, and I'm not going to. *He* is the voter."

I press my lips together as she passes us. No need to cause any further agitation, but what world are we in where a young woman is not using her voice to vote? Women died for the opportunity. I am crushed.

"And that is why, I am out here with you. People like that ignore all the hard work the women before us had to do for these youngsters to just ignore it." Beverly shakes her head.

"It's a bit horrifying actually. To think if all women felt this way, we would be in a full reenactment of The Handmaid's Tale."

"Again." Beverly wipes her brow. "Don't even get me started on the real Handmaid's Tale."

I shudder. "Absolutely, terrifying." We hug goodbye, despite the heat.

I have to hurry and get home. I have plans tonight. Part of the campaign trail is events. Money to raise at fundraisers, time spent en route to events, being present for events, regardless of what has been offered about the event. It's always a gamble. You never know if your time and/or money will pay off. So, you put on a fancy dress, buy the ticket or table in reference to your budget, and you attend. Always. It is important to be everywhere, always. If you are not at an event, the host(s) will think you don't care about their cause, and thus not support you financially or in other "in-kind" offers. An in-kind offer means sending out some campaign fliers for you or something else where they foot the bill but do it as a donation to your campaign indirectly.

People who vote expect you to be at their event, whether they will indeed vote for you or not. One of my friends told me about a certain congresswoman that would show up everywhere. Someone would have a thirteenth birthday party for their niece and, all of a sudden, this congresswoman would be there, find a big cooler, and announce to everyone that "There is no place I'd, rather be than right here celebrating the sweet thirteenth birthday of Lisa Montrose." And not one person in the crowd would think there was a slight doubt in this. Because this congresswoman did appear everywhere. She was a woman of the people, and this is why she had the tenure she did. She was there, she cared, and people knew it.

Which is why I had to show up. Even if it's only for the grip, grin, and click from the camera lens. Get the photo, always. Nothing says, "I'm here for this district", then a splurge of photos of you being everywhere. This is my new normal. Thankfully, I am single and don't have to worry about my significant other and can attend everything and anything. Although, it would be nice to have a plus-one for at least a few of these events. Especially in dead-ass, kill-me, boring conversations with racists or misogynists. I would love to have a partner, cue me out of the scene before I go off. I'm fortunate to have Ginger; she is there for the majority of my events. The lady loves to mingle, and she is perfect at being the best hyper. Obviously, her career is much more distinguished than a hype girl, but if she ever had a brain injury and could no longer be a doctor but still had the hype skills ... clearly that is what she should run to as a profession. I would endorse her any day of the week. I could hear her in the background: *"Okaaaaaay, peopppppppppppppppppple, did you hear that? Mia Verita endorsed me as the number one HYPE Lady ... Yes, Houston, let's do this ... Can you feel me?"* The crowd obviously would go wild.

"Are you sure about tonight?" I glance at myself in the mirror. The age-old battle of *Should I wear this or that* has ensued.

"Mia, are you seriously doing this again? Are you in front of the mirror? What is wrong with that mirror in your place? You should call the super and have it replaced. I think it might be one of those carnival ones or something. You never seem to appreciate the way you look. Like you seem put off by your appearance and, honey, that doesn't make sense."

"I don't know ... I know it's a casino night, but I feel like maybe this dress is too much." I stare in the mirror. It's a red sequin dress with a deep V. Jessica Rabbit from *Who Killed Roger Rabbit* would be thrilled. But I'm not a cartoon character. I want to be taken seriously, and I think this might be too much of a *no* for that idea.

"Too much what?" Ginger sighs. "Hotness, what? What is going on in that brain of yours?"

I let her question dangle in the air. I don't know what's going on in my brain. Sometimes it's too much. Too much everything. Like I want to be elected, but the constant in the back of my mind "Is this okay?"; "Is this too much?"; "What could be said about this?"; "Am I being electable?" which is my favorite. I remember when a certain lady candidate was running for president of the United States, not the PTA, and people kept the conversation going, "Is she electable?" Seriously, the level of misogyny and internal misogyny is almost too much to stomach. Thankfully, there were some smart people … marketing people with an edge for reality who began a T-shirt and bumper sticker business to address this electable notion. Their slogan: "Yes, she is electable if you vote for her."

What?! Mind blown. Hold on a second. She is electable if you vote for her. What? I am still in the midst of being able to wrap my head around that deep concept. Electable. Yes, she is electable. Stop with this nonsense. Can she do the job? Yes, then vote for her. The end.

However, I can rant any day of the week, but when it comes to me and my campaign, I shrink into one of those wall flowers of uncertainty, not aware of where I should go or how I should act. I'm forty effin' years old. I know how to act. I know where to go. Why do I doubt myself? Is it from years of trauma and constant gaslighting? Being told that I should shrink because I was taking up too much air in the room by my mere existence?

Or is it because of my internal misogyny? I don't know. But I need to shake myself of this doubt and dissonance. It's time for a new move, a new groove, and I don't mean like the emperor in a quasi-Disney movie. No. It's time to move forward without any more doubt. I need to have the faith in me. If I could afford it, I would go to therapy. I have read through a million psychology online articles, papers, and books. I get it. I was in an abusive marriage. Emotional, verbal, physical, and financial. All of it was abuse. I have to accept this. It is hard to say. Especially out loud. When I had told my attorney about what I thought might have been abuse—the blood, handprints left on my skin, broken nails, all of the destruction he had caused in what had been my home, to then be a shared home, to then be a home that was taken from me, along with everything else—my attorney said, none of that mattered. She said I would have to have a bloodied face and broken bones and, get this, even with that it would be an uphill battle to prove. Can you imagine? I felt like an imposter to even use the word *abuse*, given that I had no broken bones. Broken nails, yes. Broken dishes, yes. Torn-up woven baskets I had made as a child, yes. Broken stereo speakers, yes. Shattered glass, yes. Blood down my leg from the horrible violence of non-consent, also yes. But even with all of those broken things and pieces of me, I didn't qualify for a temporary restraining order. These horrible things didn't matter enough to be put in a court document to prove that I was a victim of abuse. I was an imposter, as I had no broken bones. Where was I to turn if the courtroom couldn't even help me? This was when I realized the laws were not written for people like me.

How can I have a level of confidence in myself when I constantly sink back into the lack of confidence in our legal system? The system of justice is the backbone of our country. If it crumbles for the most vulnerable, how am I to stand tall and act like Lady Liberty is not a farce? These levels of doubt make me return to those moments of insecurity. I constantly question if I can do it. I don't know. Every time I give myself the millisecond of a pep talk, I fall back to, "But can I?"

It's a battle. Internal. And I realize this. I am trying. I am trying to be stronger than I was the day before and not sink into those moments from my past.

"Mia, snap out of it. Take some vitamin B. The dress is good. You are fantastic. This event will be fun. I will be there, so you will laugh at least once. Which is more than you can count on by being at home," she laughs.

Ginger is right. The event will be worth it. I need to stop being so ho-hum and drum. I need to shake off the sadness and embrace the possibilities. One never knows when an ace will show up, especially in the game of blackjack.

"You're right, see you in a minute." I hit the *End* button. Time to sink my feet into the sparkly red heels. I might need to tap my ankles by the end of the night. I am ten toes into my shoes and ready to play. The moment of the story in which the heroine reflects on her shoes. This is my time to shine. As if I might pull out a red heart in a game of blackjack when I have already doubled down.

Does that even mean anything? I don't even know at this point. I look at my Lyft app. Two minutes. I had to call for a Lyft. Besides the expense of new tires, the car rides in exchange for the use of my car definitely add up. I have yet to be able to prove if anyone is actually puncturing my tires, but they continue to find themselves with nails.

I grab my lip gloss, ID, and a few credit cards. I can't be at some sort of unfortunate moment and have a decline. Always have a backup. Always. This is my mantra. I know cash would be good. But that's just not my scene.

I bend down give Schatzi a big kiss on her head and snuggle her for a hot minute. My phone buzzes. The Lyft has arrived, hopefully, free of any nails in its tires. Time to go. Let's do this. Maybe tonight will be a winner.

"Hold down the fort, Schatzi." I blow a kiss to her and lock the door.

I verify the license plate and make and model of the car. Yup. Nissan XYX – 337, Juan as the driver. "Hey, Juan, how are you?"

"Good, Mia, yes?"

Man, it feels so good when the drivers verify that I am the rider. It makes me feel safer. Too much has happened to too many people, and this little bit of security helps to restore my faith in humanity a bit.

"Yes, that's correct." I check out the distance. Only five miles. No big deal. I'm ready to have a good time. I take a deep breath. Every ride goes like this. I try not to say it. I know we all try not to ask it. But I can't help myself. "How long have you been driving for Lyft?" There, I did it. I can't take it back. I know it's not right. I know they are asked it every day who knows how many times. But I can't help myself. Whatever. It is what it is.

A small laugh echoes in the Nissan. "This is my two thousandth ride. Exactly." He glances at me from the rear-view window. "You tell me, how long that is?"

I flitter my eyelashes. Is that a sexual question? I'm not sure. Obviously, I am not going to answer if it is. But where is he going with that?

"Come on, take a guess," Juan semi-pleads. His voice has a sense of subtle anticipation, but like he is not fully committed to the conversation. And I get that, as I definitely am not.

I check my map: less than two miles. "I don't know, Juan … What would an average ride look like, mile-wise?" I try and swing the conversation back to a semi-professional tone.

"It depends on the rider." Juan lets out a low chuckle.

Of course. This conversation can only be fueled by sexual innuendo. I am not here for it. Not with the Lyft driver. Let's swing back to professional land, please.

"I'm not sure what you mean. Maybe you could explain?" There, I really threw it back on him without going sexual and giving him an opportunity to be polite.

Juan stifles and drops the ball. With nowhere to turn in a polite matter, his silence is the force that guides me to my destination. I hop out and click my heels on the concrete sidewalk as I make my way to the entrance. The music is loud and I haven't made my way inside yet. However, I hear Demi Lovato in full-on mode to let women express themselves, not like Madonna. But rather by being confident. Be you. Walk into the room with shoulders high, chest raised, eyes locked in, and boom, let's do this. Yes, I'm ready to feel confident tonight.

I check in at the table. Tag myself with a nameplate of "Mia Verita for TXHD 193." It's actually a good thing to wear a name tag, that way, if people don't know who you are and they want to, this is a helpful hint without anyone being awkward. I'm here for this. I scan the crowd in pursuit of a familiar face. Nothing. I glide through the room of sequined gowns and seer-suckered suits. The wine is good. There is a small bar top in the back with a tip jar. Crap. I don't have any cash. This is not good. I don't want to be that person. I saunter a little slower as I make my plan. Maybe they have one of those QR codes or something. I hate to be so unprepared to participate in a society of tipping, even though the origins are not good. We really need to get rid of the whole concept of tipping in general … Maybe when I'm elected. I internally smile. I glance up at a man with intense eyes that move from my face down to my chest.

"Hey there …" The man looks at my tag. "Mia, can I get you a drink?"

And in one small moment, I'm thankful that I let the Jessica Rabbit fear that hovered over my brain dissipate and instead opted to go with it, and now my tipless fears are gone.

"Thank you—that would be fantastic …" I hold my hand out and wait for a name in return.

"I'm Brent Moss with the Realtors Association, nice to make your acquaintance." Our hands shake. His is much older but not rough. He must be part of the group of men who get routine pedicures or he has good genes. His hair is like a white fluffy cloud, and his eyes reflect that of a happy moment. He is sure of himself, which is nice. That's the thing about older men, they have a level of security and assurance that younger and middle age men don't always carry.

Otherwise, they have this level of doubt and insecurity. But once men pass the age of about fifty or so, they don't care. They have zero shits to give. You either want to be in their presence or you don't. They are assured that they have something to offer, and if you don't want it, they know someone else will be around in a hot minute to recognize this.

Women are at a disadvantage past the age of thirty. Not that they can't find their happily-ever-after or hold their own. But if we are to look at the numbers, men have held the cards of fate for quite a while. It's on us to make the change. Not to spread and bend over, but to change the course and demand equality in all aspects of our life. However, that change has to come within, and I mean internal misogyny. We can't make changes if ladies don't stand together. It's impossible. Unification is the only way. And it is possible.

"I'll take another bourbon on the rocks, and the lady will have …?" He glances at me, and I have to break my internal rant about misogyny and choices to go with, "I'm low on cash." Might as well accept a free drink. I owe nothing in return, regardless. It is what it is. Chivalry doesn't have to be dead or unaccepted to also have equality in the same room. Both are possible. That's the thing that a lot of people don't get, and I mean both genders. They think it's an "all or nothing." Like if I want equal pay for equal work, then I can't also accept a drink with zero expectation. Hey, y'all, we can do both.

It's totally cool. And, also, when women are making the same pay as men, then let's have a revisit on the convo, but until then … accept the drink, no big deal. Really.

"Oh, I would fancy a cabernet." I let my lips purse together out of habit, and I anticipate the taste of a nice sip. I know I shouldn't have a crutch of a sip of wine, and maybe it's a placebo, but it does help to settle my nerves, and when I am alone, I am uncomfortable. I need a little help.

"The lady fancies a cabernet, top shelf if you've got that for wine?" Brett asks the bartender, who nods and gets a key to unlock the wine refrigerator. Well, okay then. I can appreciate a locked-up wine. Bring on the fun.

Brett slides some cash to the bartender and hands me the properly poured glass of wine. There is only an inch or so from the top of clear glass. I can't help but take a long whiff of it before my taste. I'm not in the least pretentious; I shop at Goodwill and other second-hand stores predominately. However, I can appreciate a good glass of wine, and this one was unlocked, so I want to have a good sniff before I take the first mouthful. The aroma is delicious and deep. Like a walk through a thick forest after a heavy rain. The ground is damp, but the soil is solid and not soft enough to even begin to sink your feet. Barely able to make a footprint. And then a small amount of a blossom. My lungs fill with this essence, and I let the liquid travel over my tongue to avoid the delay. Brett has his eyes on me.

The sip is full, like the wine. The notes open even more on my tongue, and I can see why it was locked up. This is a wine I would want to lock up in my home. Not because I wouldn't be able to control myself but rather to save it for special moments. This is a "special moment" wine, and I'm touched to be in it. I clink my glass against Brett's bourbon. "Thank you, this is quite delicious."

Brett's eyes light up with a small reflection of the lights against the windows in the ballroom. He seems satisfied but not anything out of the ordinary. This man is obviously used to this level of enjoyment of a simple glass of wine. And in that moment, I get it. I'm not in my league. This is outside of where I am right now in life. Despite our age difference, and some might measure us on appearance, I'm still the underdog. I am not in the right corral. This reminds me of the first 10k I ran out of high school. I didn't think about the difference in line-ups. I only remembered back in my cross-country days the necessity of being in the front of the pack. So, with all my naivety, I put myself in Coral A. With the fastest runners. Of course, with the sound of the gun, I kicked off my run with a speed that mirrored everyone else's. I had the surge of adrenaline and the inexperience of being in a race past high school to fool myself into the notion that I could keep pace with Coral A. I made it to about the halfway point, and then my pace began to drop drastically. I couldn't keep up. Several races later, I realized that not only did I not need

110

to be in Corral A, but I also needed some chill music to start the race and tame my adrenaline before the kickoff. I needed a proper pace to make it. I learned, and several 10ks later, I did much better.

Here I am at a fancy event. I paid to be here. To exchange campaign cards with business cards, to mingle, and even when paired with a well-to-do man and an incredible glass of wine, I was out of my comfort zone.

"Well, hello, Brett, I didn't know you were well-acquainted with the Mia Verita." Almost as if my guardian angel dropped Ginger exactly into this moment. She squeezes my shoulder and lightly kisses my cheek.

Brett laughs. "Oh, Ginger, you know I'm always keen on the next who's who of Texas. Now, fill me in on how you know this lovely young lady?"

It was my turn to laugh. Young ... okay ... granted, I was way younger than Brett, but I don't think anyone would describe me as young. Not even a person aged to the point where they have one foot in the coffin.

"Mia is my dearest friend. And I am so proud to see someone with integrity and commitment willing to represent TXHD 193, don't you agree?" Ginger points at his chest.

Brett grinned. "Yes, it's always a good thing to have people with integrity run for office."

"I knew you would agree." She nods and her eyes flicker, as if she has an incredible idea cross through her mind. "Which makes only sense if you and the Texas Realtors Association were to host Mia a fundraiser!" Her lips spread into the widest of smiles, like one of a beauty contestant as they wave to the audience.

Brett shakes his head. "Now, you know we don't go against incumbent representatives." His eyes run over my face in an attempt to read my electability and if he should go against his rules in a gamble.

"Well, see, that's why we keep ending up with people that vote against our interests. Even when we get someone for the people, they don't have the financial support to even be a contender." Ginger shakes her head. "I thought you had more character than rules for the rich who already have financial support?" Ginger sighs.

This is the most awkward silence. I take a deep breath. "Why don't I send you our win numbers, and maybe we can discuss the possibility again after you have had a chance to review the idea of a different outcome?" I offer.

Brett nods. "I can't make any commitments for TRA on my own. But I am not against checking out the numbers. Here is my card." He hands me over a card that is clearly a premium stock. I can only imagine the type of fundraiser he could design.

"Thank you, I will, and thank you for the wine." I link arms with Ginger. "I want to introduce you to the major donor I mentioned earlier, I need to thank them in person." It was my turn to be confident.

"Good to see you, Brett." Ginger taps him on the bicep, and we turn toward the far left corner of the room.

"Oh my goodness, what miracles have you got up your sleeve? Who is this big donor?" Ginger squeezes my side.

I jump and let out a slight giggle. "Uh, hopefully Brett. I don't have anyone lined up. But we need to work this room and see who is willing to support a non-incumbent in this race."

"Gotcha. All right, I see some other people from the Medical Association we can chat with. They might be willing to go against an incumbent, depending on how he voted for the Nurse Practitioner Bill. Do you know?"

"Oh man, I don't remember, let me check." I pull out my phone and scan for the Nurse Practitioner Bill; it's a bill that nurse practitioners have been trying to get passed for several years. It would allow them to practice on their own without the supervision of a doctor. As you might guess, doctors are completely against it. I find the bill and scan through the yays and nays.

There it is. "He voted for it!"

"Perfect." Ginger guides me toward a group of two men and a woman, all dressed impeccably and deep in conversation.

"Hello, team! Don't y'all look fantastic!" She taps on the man's shoulders and hugs the woman.

"Ginger, how good to see you out of scrubs," one of the guys says with a smile.

"Oh, come on, you know my doggie scrubs are the cat's meow!"

They all laugh. Apparently, she actually has dog scrubs. I rarely see Ginger at work or in scrubs.

"Let me introduce you to Mia Verita, the candidate that totally opposes the Nurse Practitioner Bill and is running against the tool bag that voted for it last session."

Ginger pulls me into the circle. We go through the introductions and policy speeches.

One of the men grabs my hand. "Mia, how can we trust that you will vote against this bill?" His grip is intense, like his stare. I try to pull back, but the grip is locked. The only way I can release it is with my answer.

I rub my lips together and nod. "Yes, you can trust that I will review any bill before I vote on it and that I will always have an open door and ear to hear your thoughts. I will listen as to why I should or shouldn't vote for something." I try to pull back again. His grip tightens.

"We want a real answer, though." The man's eyes are dark, like a coldness I wouldn't want to experience in an alley at night. And then the grip is released.

"Dan, that's not how you encourage someone of your concerns." A voice I have come to know all too well is at the end of the statement and his hand is around Dan's wrist. I take a step back.

Ginger lets out an uncomfortable laugh. "Oh my, how, er, nice to see you again." She nods at Maxwell.

"Yes, good to see you too." Maxwell's chin acknowledges Ginger, and his eyes focus on me. The contrast between his eyes and Dan's is surreal. This is beyond awkward. I don't know which way to go from here.

Dan nods at Maxwell. "Right, remind me again how it is that you win your cases? Is it with a smile and a light handshake?" He laughs as if his statement is not something he pulled out of the sky. There is a history between these two, obviously.

"Dan, why don't I buy you another round? Looks like your glass is also empty." Maxwell lifts his glass.

"Ha, you buy me a drink ... more like me buying myself a drink. Yeah, sure why not. Ladies, how about another round? It's on me ... or me via Maxwell. Right?" Dan's eyes have lightened up but the tension around the corners of his mouth does not amplify a real smile.

"That sounds lovely, two more cabernets, thank you both." Ginger flashes a pearly grin and grips my wrist like she thinks I am either going to faint or run away.

I am going to do neither. This night has taken an odd turn, and I don't know what to think.

Maxwell eyes me as if he has some sort of concern about me. Which I do not understand at all. When has Maxwell ever been concerned about my feelings or safety for that matter? And

115

no, it didn't feel safe. It was odd. Dan's grip was too much. Yes, I am in a crowded room, but this man felt comfortable with a level of restraint on my arm that I did not want. I am doing my best to stay in the present and not return to a memory of pain with similar hands that gripped my wrists and refused to let me leave. *No. Not here. Mia, compartmentalize.* I take in a deep breath.

"Are you okay?" Ginger rubs my back.

I nod. Like an automatic response that has no care as to what emotions lie beneath my skin and what visions run through my mind.

"Mia, I'm sorry. I am not a fan of Dan's, but I didn't know he would be so aggressive." She bites her lip. "Do you want to leave?"

"No, I have to get through these types of things. It's part of the job or hopeful job, right?" I roll my shoulders back as if I can roll away bad moments that I wish never existed.

"Here you go." Maxwell offers each of us a glass of cabernet. Dan is nowhere in sight.

"Where's Dan?" Ginger scans toward the back of the room.

"Oh, he had some call or something." Maxwell raises his glass and takes a large swallow.

"Well, thank you for the drink, or him, whoever it is we should thank." Ginger laughs.

My cheeks warm. It is not from the wine. This is only my second glass, and after that first round of uncomfortableness, I am like a dried-out sponge on a windowsill. The suds of truth have washed away and the sink is empty.

116

"Right, well, he did confirm he will be hosting a fundraiser for you. So that will be with his money." Maxwell clinks my glass. His eyes flicker at me. I take a step back. I am in a level of uncertainty that I am not sure I want to remain.

"Really?" Ginger squeezes my arm. "That's great, he has a fantastic network."

"Indeed." Maxwell nods.

I rock in place. "Oh good," is all I can push out. My strength in compartmentalization is not at a high at this moment. Memories from my past cut through my brain. Slivers of pain roll through my mind. The lies. The shoves. The destruction of property. All the times I tried to leave and was blocked. The key. I take a sip of my wine. It is earthy with notes of leather, like a horseback ride through the mountains in a country south of the border. I wish I could escape into this vision and feel the wind run through my hair. I am not okay and feel uncomfortable. Next-level anxiety is upon my skin. I need to leave.

My throat is dry. I take another sip of my wine and cue up my Lyft. Thankfully, there are several nearby.

"Um, thank you. I have to go—my Lyft is here." I wave my phone at Ginger and Maxwell as if I need to prove this to them.

Ginger's green eyes are wide underneath her wrinkled brow. I lean in and give her a hug. It's the best I can do at this time. My gaze lands on Maxwell, whose shoulders drop as a smile is forced on his face. If I hadn't been so keen on the identification of facial expressions I wouldn't

117

have noticed it. He reaches out his hand to shake mine. I let my hand meet his as if there are no hard feelings between us and everything is cordial. If only.

I make no waste as I hustle to my Lyft. The ride is somber and quiet. I am thankful for that. The intensity of the evening has become a level I do not want to repeat, and I am happy to be back at home.

I greet Schatzi with a big hug and dump out my purse on the counter. I shuffle through the cards and write my notes of each person that I spoke with and managed to grab one of their cards. This will be my circle-back list for donors or endorsements. Anything that can help move me a few steps closer to the finish line and the end of this campaign, which is quickly approaching. I glance at my reflection in the mirror. I had just touched up the bird poop spots, but they are beginning to show. Arg. Maybe that's why Brett had called me young. Maybe his age had dimmed his capabilities, or maybe he did see my bird poop at my roots and wanted to be generous.

Or maybe he sees me as young and not yet at the point of being described as anything different. Like once a woman is no longer described as young, she has hit a particular age in her life. The one that announces to the world she has hit her limit. Term limits. It's the end of her term as a woman of visibility.

Tonight, I was definitely visible. I am not sure what to make of all of the different interactions. The interaction with Dan was like a warning that lit off from deep in my gut. Something was off. I always get the light ring of danger whenever Maxwell appears, but I have to question if that is more like Pavlov's dog reaction in that everything I associate with him has to do with "*Satan*?"

Is it possible for him not to be dangerous and I am hypervigilant from the history of abuse in my marriage? Or are all of my worries real? All of these questions run through my head. The level of self-doubt is so difficult to muddle through when it grasps hold of my body. Is it possible that I am not able to think straight, because I haven't truly worked through all of my past?

Chapter Eight
"Some secrets don't exist."

Silence is sometimes louder than Grand Central Station in the midst of rush hour. The echo of darkness is almost like being in a cave with not even a flicker of light. I let the phone drop from my hand. The call has ended and there is a surge of blood that has rushed through my fingers. My heartbeat is a pitter-patter, it is intense, almost painful, and I am left feeling numb. Like I can't hit the red button. I don't have to. The call has disconnected. I glance around the room. There are no videos on me. I nod. Yes, it's real. It's real. I click the phone app button and scan the call log. There it is. Jose with Foundershare company. The company that I was sure had shredded my resume.

How long did we talk? Ten minutes. Yes, it's impossible that he would have called to talk to me about anything for over two minutes, other than what actually happened. I am in such disbelief. I run over the conversation through my mind again. No one would call to give bad news and stay on the phone. Normally, people don't call to give personal rejections. But if they do, it is a quick missile of bad news delivered with some sort of message, like, "It's just not a good

120

fit, but we wish you the best of luck in your search."

I glance at the call time again. The conversation was simple, nothing out of the ordinary. Jose began with the regular, how are yous and a highlight reel of the interview. Which led him, as he had phrased it, to the point, where they wanted to extend the job offer to me. I bit my tongue so as not to gasp. Jose offered me the job. He did!

My breath is still not at a normal pace, and though I have run through the whole exchange several times over, I can't help but be in disbelief. Maybe they didn't see my dance show after the most horrific interview experience of my life. Maybe I am not as unlucky as I thought, or at least not at that moment. I let my lungs fill with oxygen again. In and out. Okay, what did I accept? How much money? When do I start? *Mia, it's totally fine.* Jose said he would send me an official offer letter. Perfect, this is perfect. I'm still shocked. But that's okay. I go ahead and do the next, most important thing: dial Ginger.

"You are not going to believe this!"

"Go for it. I'm ready to be shocked—it's a Sunday afternoon and my day has been spent poolside, I'm in the mood for excitement." I hear a splash of water, probably from her toe against the pool. She has an infinity pool and those fancy lounge chairs that sit in the water in a shallow end. You can dip your toes in the water while being totally relaxed in a stationary float.

The wave of acceptance runs through me. "I got the job!" I shriek so loud I am sure she either dropped the phone and I owe her a new one or it barely missed the water.

"Whoa, Mia that's incredible, and finally. But more importantly, which one?" There is another splash. Either she is in motion or did, in fact, drop the phone.

I get this. As, Lord only knows how many resumes, applications, and interviews I have gone on and Ginger has had to quasi-live through. Each interview, whether in person or remote, has had a prep meeting, a fashion show, and finally a recap. Then we have the weekly run-through of any status updates from the multitude of job applications. Possible interviews that have not been offered or declined for whatever reason. This job search is a job in and of itself. I can only imagine how difficult it would be to find a new job while simultaneously being employed. The worry of being discovered for the idea of a better opportunity for oneself could leave you jobless.

"The one where after it ended, I was in stitches, not laughter but tears, and a hospital visit. You remember that one?" I obviously said this facetiously because who could forget this one, let alone Ginger?

"Yes, little lamb, I of course remember that and your medical bill … Texas really needs to expand Medicaid because your bill was out of this world. I don't put a price on our friendship, but that one was more than an all-inclusive weekend in Tahiti." Ginger sighs.

My stomach clenches. I hate this. I know Ginger is "doing well," but I don't want my friends or anyone to be put out by paying for my bills or anything for me. I feel sick. I swallow the nastiness and inhale. *Just breathe*. "I know … that was awful, and you are truly a wonderful friend—thank you."

Ginger laughs. "You already said thank you, silly … I am just pointing out why we need to get you elected!"

"Agreed. Can you get together to discuss the details? Do you want to meet up for a drink? We could celebrate?" I glance at my Fitbit and tap it. It's only 4 p.m.

"Yes, girl, let's meet between six and seven at Local Bar." Ginger laughs because she knows that this timeframe is so subjective, but it's fine. I'm fine with it.

I need to go for a run. I hate running without Schatzi. I have thought about reaching out to shelters to see if I could run the dogs there … but I'm a bit nervous to do so … the uncomfortableness and not knowing exactly how things would go. I know I should just go and try it out, but I just haven't. And even though Schatzi wouldn't technically know, I would feel bad if she "found out." Like she would feel betrayed that I was on a run with another dog instead of her, which, of course, would not be my choice.

I nod. "Sounds fantastic, see you soon." I click the red button and head to my bathroom to switch to my running gear.

The thought of Schatzi and a betrayal run without her flows through my spine. I am fueled with a red wave of anger by this very concept. It seems so wrong. If she were here, she would be in circles around my feet like a shark in chummed water. It is crazy wild how she can know before I even get my gear ready that we are about to go for a run. I wonder if my pheromones have changed or something. As soon as I get the ice for my water bottle, she is right there with that look of, "Oh, are we doing this?" She is so smart. And, of course, I'm like, "Yeah, let's do this." But she isn't here. She is over there with him. He doesn't even walk her. From what I have ascertained, he keeps her locked up in the backyard, not running the neighborhood or trail, no dog parks or runs to the store. She is excluded from life but kept as a prisoner for him. To continue to imprison me. It's horrible.

I make my way down the trail and let the warm Texas sun heat my skin. I don't worry about the sweat or the thickness of the air. I let my feet lead the way through the trail that connects my apartment complex to the old neighborhood. So many memories of Schatzi and me, and our runs. I make my way through the mini hills and quasi-bridges until I am on the street that I had discovered several years ago. I found the house. I narrowed down the numbers to less than ten. This house, this one, this is the one that I chose. I knew it was the perfect spot to buy. The neighborhood was built in the '70s with big trees and nice lawns. A good school district. Neighbors that smiled. This is where I put my down payment and signed my name on the mortgage paperwork. Purchased the house with my credit. Me. All mine.

In my fury of memories, I somehow veer my way to my old house. There it was. The lawn could use some work. Trees need to be trimmed. The outside faucet had a slight drip. The hose had yet to be replaced. And there in the backyard was my dog. Tied to the pole that was attached to the porch of the house I chose, bought, and later on lost in the divorce along with everything else.

Schatzi lets out a soft cry as I approach. Not a roar of affirmation that she exists but a painful sound that she needs help. I peer in through the fence slats. There was no bowl of water. Only Schatzi with her hard tug on the chain and an attempt to be free. I am on the outside of the fence as I squint my eye through the fence slots. There she is. Her sweet puppy dog eyes are in full view. I stand on the outside of this faded cedar fence in a place of freedom and she is tied to a chain link rope. Like an inhumane prison. I can't walk away. I open the gate and crumble to the ground to hold her. She licks my hands with the only possible amount of water left in her body. I let a small tear fall from my eyes as I begin to unchain her from this horrific prison. Schatzi didn't deserve this. This fake "war" of a custody battle in the divorce wasn't about her. It was about me and my decision to leave him. And yet, he kept the noose tight around my neck by his latch on Schatzi. Being able to obtain joint custody of my dog was the final way for him to control me. To be a permanent marker in my life. A no-exit strategy. Despite my presence no longer being existent in his life, he demands it through the exchange of Schatzi.

I couldn't believe it when he obtained primary custody of my dog. The dog that I adopted from BARC. Not him, he wasn't even listed on the paperwork, and yet, he was able to finagle primary custody of her via his horrific accessory to the crime of abduction of rights of my dog because of his cruel lawyer. Obscene. I pulled Schatzi in closer to me. The idea of us being at home and safe was so surreal that a loud noise of a man's voice startles us both. Schatzi growls. Her white teeth are in full sight.

"Mam, I need you to step away from the animal."

The animal? What? Who said that? I glance around the backyard. No one is there. An ice-cold chill races against the back of my neck. My skin is colder than an icebox in a North Dakota winter. A dark shadow blocks out the Texas sun that covers my skin. Near the entrance by the gate stands a man in a dark uniform, his hand on his holster. Like what in the world is going on? I take a deep breath and let go of Schatzi. I slowly stand up and wipe my damp fingers on the sides of my shorts.

"Put your hands in the air, slowly," the officer commands.

Schatzi is no longer in growl mode but full-on bark. It is louder and louder; she can probably sense my bewilderment and fear. I am almost frozen in time with his direction. What on earth? I ignore my dismay and slowly lift my arms into the air. I have never had a police interaction before. *Ever.* I've never been arrested, nor have I ever called the police on someone else. I did think about it with him. But I never followed through. I glance toward the bay window of the house and see a figure I know all too well. His arms are crossed over his chest, and I can see the gleam of his smile through the dirty window pane. Sick.

"All right, miss, I'm going to come behind you. I want you to lower your hands behind your back, and do not resist me," he directs again with the same misogynistic tone. His voice echoes that of someone who is in the midst of armed robbery, where several lives are at stake vs. a woman who is worried about her dog that is chained up outside in the hot Texas sun without any water.

I am in complete and utter disbelief. I stand still and in silence. I have lost my voice, again. The officer firmly fastens the cuffs around my wrists and I let out a wince when my skin pinches in between the clasp.

"Stop resisting," the officer shouts as if he has an audience of fifty people instead of me and my dog, who is all teeth and barks for the whole neighborhood to hear.

Schatzi is beyond concerned for me. The chain is stretched as far as it will allow. The pole waves from side to side as Schatzi jumps at the officer. I am for once thankful that she is chained so that she can't sink her teeth in. I can only imagine what her fate would be if she attacked a police officer. I would probably also end up with an assault charge to go along with whatever the current cause of action is.

"Now, I'm going to walk you to my patrol car, do you understand what I'm saying, or do you need an interpreter?" The man pushes my shoulder as he shoves me toward his parked car.

I laugh. What the hell? An interpreter. "Um, what kind of interpreter would I need?" I try to glance over my shoulder at him, but it hurts too much.

"Don't get sassy with me. We have a special place in the pin for mouths like yours. You comprende that, don't you?" He shoves my head and it barely grazes the ridge of the car door roof.

Just like that, I am in the back of a police car. A police car. My lord ... where am I?

Wake up, Mia, this is a horrible nightmare, time to end it.

I blink several times. I want to shake myself awake. I shake my head. Still in the back of the police car. I close my eyes and take a deep breath. In and out. I open my eyes again. Still in the car. No. I shake my head and breathe faster.

"You okay back there? You going through withdrawals or something?" The officer eyes me from his rear-view window. He starts the car.

"Yeah, of my dog," I mutter. Tears gather in my eyes. I need to remain strong in this situation.

Focus, Mia. It's okay. This is a huge mistake, obviously.

I let hope seep in for a mere second. Denial is not just a river in Egypt. I know this is not a mistake. This is by design. If I imagine, hope, or give way to the possibility of anything other than what it is, then I have not made any progress at all since the divorce.

I bite my lip. Metallic. Yuck. That was obviously too hard. But it is blood. Blood or death. Let it drain out, sink, fall, or swallow it, and plan for my next moment to change this course.

"Never heard of that, must be some new trailer park shit. Y'all are always coming up with something new to smoke." He grunts.

I shake my head and glance down. I am not going to engage any further with this guy. I lean forward, my stomach is like a bucket of darkness. What have I gotten myself into? A place I had never envisioned for myself would be in the back of a cop car. My lungs fill with air as if I can weather balloon myself out of this mess. My only option now is to think clearly and confidently, which I try to do for the remainder of the ride.

The car pulls in front of the booking lot. I am not familiar with anything about this station or process. Yes, the police station. I am still in shock, yet able to move my legs instead of standstill in fear. The rough, tough officer leads me in for my booking. I still can't believe I am in this predicament. But I have not let my disbelief muddy my focus. I follow through with all of the directions and grab the phone for the mandatory phone call. There was only one person that I would call for this.

"Hey there. Please tell me that was a joke. I am three margaritas deep." Ginger laughs into the phone.

"I wish. No, this is my one call. I can't go into details, as I only have one call with a short time to get it out. I went by the house, saw Schatzi chained up outside, and so I went in the backyard." I glance at the clock. Time is almost up.

"You broke into your old house?" Ginger gasped.

"Yes, I mean, not really ... my name is still on the house. And it's my dog." I squint my eyes. I know these are details that do not matter to the state of Texas or anyone in this police station, but they should.

131

"Mia, you know he doesn't care about that and will do anything and everything he can to find ways to torture you. Why give him such an easy pitch?" Her glass makes a loud clink on the counter.

I sigh. "I wasn't trying to give him an easy pitch or anything, I was worried about Schatzi. It's hotter than the flames of hell out there today, and she was chained up, with no water in sight." My voice cracks, and I don't want the people around me to see this display of weakness. Everything I have ever seen or read about prisons has made it very clear to not look like a victim or prey.

"Okay, so what are the charges?" Ginger lets out her sigh. I can imagine the three margaritas have evaporated into my reality of nonsense and now she is focused on solutions, as always.

"I'm not sure. They said something about trespassing, and I think possible attempted kidnapping or something?" I try to scan my memory for what the officers had said as I was being booked. It's all a blur of non-reality. I am still in disbelief.

"Mia, I can't come get you, I've been drinking and you need a lawyer, not a doctor. I am going to call my legal aid that I have through my work and send someone over to get you. We need to make sure you are properly represented from the beginning. Sometimes when a lawyer shows up to nonsense like this, they can quickly have the charges dropped." The clicking of her nails against her phone is in full effect, and I know she is already in pursuit of this as the solution we need.

"I hope you're right." I bite my lip. "Ginger …"

"Yes, love?"

There are so many things I want to say but only two words make sense in this moment.

"Thank you."

Chapter Nine
"Acts of service cannot repair a wound that is too bare."

The inside of a county jail cell is stark and full of depression. If the actions that caused you to end up inside this box of bleakness weren't already filled with confusion and uncertainty, there would be none to be found here. Most offenders of the law end up in county jail until they can afford bail or get moved on to a detainment center. I gulp at the concept of being taken from this barren spot. Being caged is unreal, but being in the county jail versus being taken further away from society makes the fervent blood in my veins run cold. This is almost too much to take. But I am focused on my pursuit of freedom. From this cell and whatever erroneous charges have been filed against me.

I lay my head back against the wall. The tile is probably from the '70s, asbestos most certainly laid behind the porous walls full of various scribbles of obscenities. No idea how many markers or pencils got into this room. After the thorough strip search, I received courtesy of the only female officer, I can't wait to get home to my shower. I want to have a silkwood scrub down and forget that this day ever happened. No amount of bleach can splash down on my eyes to wipe away the existence of this penitentiary impropriety.

134

"Mia Verita?" The warden taps on the gray bars and laser light focuses on the room of only one person: me. She nods at me, which I hope means I'm being released. The magical key from her ring unlocks the cage of hollowed-out moments hung together by steel bars of frustration. I follow behind her to what I believe is the exit, despite no exit sign in sight. She swings the door open and a man is at a small table. The kind you see in interrogation scenes in the movies. But this face is not one from the movies or a cop drama. This is the face of my nightmares. His eyes are not the typical inspection. A crease lines his forehead. His suit is pressed and fitted. His lips are cruel and unnecessary. He does not deserve to have a mouth or a voice. My eyes rest on the face that plays the role of "*Satan*'s" assistant. I take a step back and grab onto the door.

"Easy does it. You coming down off some drugs, honey?" The warden scans me up and down. She reaches for her radio. "Are you going to be all right, or do I need to get the medic?"

I didn't realize there was such a drug issue here. Good grief. I take in a long deep breath and shake my head at the warden. One could only picture what a visit from a prison medic would resemble. I flinch, still in trauma from the pokes and prods before my booking.

"*Satan*'s" assistant stands up. "Mia, it's okay I promise." He opens his hand and motions for me to take a seat.

135

"You promise? I'm sorry, why would your promise mean anything to me?" My nostrils flare and pricks of needles dart in my eyes. I don't want to seem out of control. I let the anger sink deeper into my skin and try to regain control of the room and my life. I glance at a square tile on the floor, part of the corner is chipped. I trace the empty space with my eyes, then circle it once more. As my breath steadies, I turn my head toward "*Satan*'s" assistant again.

"Well, with all fairness, I have never broken any promises to you." He nods, and his blue eyes flash like he is full of honesty.

I examine his demeanor and remember how it was in court. All the times he objected to simple requests. Like an actual day with Schatzi and not the bogus two hours. The idea of an equal split of time and his mile-high objections, motions, upon motions that he filed. All to keep me from my dog. Let alone his inconceivable notion that the house that I bought should belong to "*Satan*" himself. While I was kicked out and lost more than half the access to love and care for my dog. My dog. No. Thank you. I shake my head. Some hair falls over my shoulders. I lift my handcuffed hands to wipe it away. Handcuffed.

"Mia, I know you might not care for me, but I'm all you've got right now, and you need a lawyer, given the situation." His gaze leaves my face and touches the stack of papers on the table.

I do not want his help, but I do need to find out what this nonsense is all about. I slide into the chair and pick up the papers. A list of charges longer than I care to read runs down the pages in black in white. Much like my attire. I sink further into the chair.

"I'll be back in a few. Knock on the door if she starts to go into major withdrawal," the warden says before she closes the door behind her.

Maxwell nods at the warden as if there is any truthfulness to her statement.

"Tell me what happened," Maxwell says as he sits down in front of me.

I glare at him and look under the table.

"Are you recording me? I know, technically, you can, given the ridiculous laws of Texas but, still, I think it would be dishonest if I ask you point blank and you lied." I press my lips together. Too many times have I had this conversation. There are studies about recording a person and how it erodes their perception. We are not meant to be under a microscope. Everyone acts differently when recorded. And when someone else is the recorder, there is a huge change in their voice and display of how they react to their victim. They become eerily calm and controlled because it is about control. They corner their victim and say "Go ahead, flip out … show everyone how crazy you are." When in reality, it's often the recorder that has caused such trauma to make the victim react. It's disgusting.

Regardless, as a rule, I try to never say anything that I would go back on, but there is a level of trust that two people should be able to have without the concept of playback. It's not healthy. But then again, nothing really was about that scene. The marriage was more of a contract than a fairytale dream that he had presented to me. I was such a fool. I had believed in a happily-ever-after. I had believed in the concept of love being able to conquer all things. But the reality was that love cannot conquer all things if love only exists on one side of the table. Unrequited love is not something that can overcome anything. Ask Juliet.

If I wasn't here in this cold room because of "*Satan*," my mind would not keep this pattern of the pain of our marriage revisitation.

I shudder.

"Are you cold?" Maxwell begins to take off his jacket. As if I would even consider being clothed in anything that has touched his skin. Hells to the no.

"No, I just happened to think about your client, which makes this a rather odd situation, for how could you represent me, when you also represent him?" My insides are in flames.

"Mia, to answer your first question—no, I'm not recording you, and yes, I agree, it is not okay to record someone if a person asks point blank if you are recording. I think honesty is key. Despite what happened in your previous case." His lower lip motions in as he pretends not to bite his lip.

Is he in some weird attempt to be seductive to me? Gross.

"Further, I am not representing your ex-husband in this case. This is completely separate from your divorce." His large hand clamps down on the papers. "These are criminal charges, whereas the divorce was a civil case."

"Civil. Ha. Yeah. Okay." I roll my eyes.

Maxwell laughs. "Agreed, but laughter aside, these are serious charges." His eyes stare into mine, and I break away first.

"I want to help. I was hired to help by Ginger—that's your best friend, right?"

I nod. I want to clarify that she is my LP, my life partner. Not in a sexual way (not that anything would be wrong with that if she was single and we were both lesbians, but she is not single, and we are not lesbians). Anyway, I digress. Life partner, as in after the horrific divorce and horrifying experiences that happened, Ginger said she would no longer be only a best friend but rather a life partner—she'd be there for all major life decisions and ensure that I didn't end up with another *"Satan"*-like person or get into any types of bad contracts of any sort.

Yet, here I am, with *"Satan's"* assistant that Ginger has hired and, yeah, I'm in a bit of disarray, to say the least. Why would she hire him? She has never done anything to me with an ulterior or bad motive. She is not a vindictive person. But this, him, Maxwell Graham being here. It does not make sense. I don't care that he helped get a fundraiser for me. This is the last person, or rather lawyer, that I would want to be with me in a jail cell. The last lawyer. The last lawyer standing. Why would she do this?

139

I don't know what to do, and I have already used my one phone call to call Ginger. I sigh. If I weren't locked up, I would not even consider a conversation with this guy. But, I am. I have no choice. I don't want to be here. I need help. Sometimes in life, help is offered in a package that you don't want. Not that I am begging but I do not want to be choosey in this situation. I want out.

"Okay, well, Mr. Legal Aid, what is your suggestion?" I blink again in an effort to one last time wake up and this not be real. I let my eyes stay closed a bit longer than normal. The insides of my lids are dark and dismal. I had hoped for something else. Something. But nope. Despite my eternal hopeful demeanor, I was out of luck. I open my eyes. My jaw is clenched. Still here.

"First, my name is Maxwell, you can go by Mr. Tibor if you prefer. Your choice. Given that I do know the person making the charge of this case, I don't see these charges being dropped."

I laugh. "You think?" I shake my head. "Of course, he wouldn't drop nonsense charges. But who calls the police on someone for wanting to take care of their dog with no water?" Tears form in my eyes, but I blink them away. *Be strong*, I tell myself. There is no way I will let him see me in any moment of sadness. Never.

"Yes, it's quite unfortunate. But we have to figure out the game plan. I am going to get you released on a personal recognizance bond—you have no priors … right?" His eyes scan over me

140

as if he is able to see my life history written over the lines of my body. Not the horizontal black-and-white polyester blend that is slung over my skin. It is so itchy.

"Nope, no priors. Your crazy client is probably at home gloating about this right now." My mouth is dry. I want to get out of here. How much longer before I can breathe fresh air? I know it's only been a few hours, but I'm parched. I am on edge. These walls are so dismal. It is scary and awful and I want out.

"Well, my crazy client is here right now, not at home. But I'm going to do everything I can to get her safe to her home. Give me a minute, and I'll be back for you." He stands up and pauses near my shoulder as if he wants to pat it but doesn't. That would be weird. This entire thing is too weird.

What seems like a grain of rice unable to push through the hourglass of time finally comes to a pause when Maxwell and the female officer return.

"All right, you can follow me." She cocks her head to the door. The exit of this cold room I had feared would be my peril. I make my way past the other steel-rung cages, most with people with their heads down as they lean over on a plastic bench that has been soldered to the floor. Only one person makes eye contact with me. A young woman might only be eighteen. Her makeup is smudged under her eyes. Lipstick barely lines the outside of her lips. Her clothes are wrinkled and unfitted. On her feet are heels that appear to belong to a different owner. I know this look all too well. I press my lips together. I want to say to the guard "Wait—let her out, and let's get her the resources she needs," but I am in no position to do so. Not yet.

The reminder of being unbooked and unhandcuffed is a sensation I hope to never want to experience again. My heart is in full-on race mode as we exit the jail. I don't even want to reflect on this. Later, maybe. Later maybe I can think about how being locked up can cause such permanent harm. But not today. Not right now. I bury the experience as quickly as I run through it. I glance up at Maxwell. We are outside the ancient building. Freedom. The breath of fresh air is powerful as I suck it into my lungs. I can only imagine what it must feel like to be released after an actual sentence of, like, a decade or something. This is too much for me, and I know I am being low-key dramatic; I have only experienced something that was the tip of the iceberg of being incarcerated. I put a pin in this moment. I am not going to forget about it. But I can't focus on this right now.

Maxwell taps my shoulder like a business partner.

"Come on, I can drop you off at your house." He clicks the remote of his car and a Lincoln Navigator's lights flash back at us. Oh, really, a Lincoln Lawyer? Good grief. This guy is too much.

I hesitate for longer than what would seem natural.

"Mia, I won't charge the account for the ride." He stands still, tall and firm.

I get it. He wants to present as if this is no big deal. But being around him is a big deal. Furthermore, I don't want to be indebted to anyone, and he has already gotten me out of jail. I am good to walk home at this point. I don't want to owe anything else. I guess, technically, I don't. This was Ginger's doing. And I'll owe her forever … that's just a reality. It doesn't matter how successful I become. I will always owe her what she has done for me, and I don't mean things that have been covered by dollar signs. I mean an actual true rescue from a life of pain and misery. *Thank you, Ginger* plays on repeat in my mind. I can't say that enough. She wouldn't even allow it if I did say it every day.

"Okay, can you bring me to Ginger's house?" I need to see her ASAP. Too much to divest in any type of phone conversation, and given my most recent legal matter, I do not want to go directly home. I need to chat in person, and fast.

"I'll take you wherever you need to go, within the city limits that is." He lets out a soft laugh.

Seriously, who has time for laughs right now?

I glance back at the jail as we pull out of the parking lot. I don't want to ever revisit that scene. I will have to do better in the future and follow my father's favorite quote: "Think beyond the moment." Obviously, I didn't do that, and now I'm going to have to pay the price in more ways than one, I'm sure.

"Oh, wow." Maxwell tosses his phone into the console.

"What?" I click my phone open and see a million notifications. Apparently, someone has given the press an inside scoop of my jail visit. Across the local paper is my mug shot. Unbelievable. How would they know about this? I eye Maxwell. The lines across his forehead are creased. Is this his work? Is he the leaker? "Did you know about this?" I show him my phone screen.

"As of two seconds ago, yes—prior, no." He clicks on the turn signal and pulls into Ginger's driveway. "You need to have a response to this before it gets out of hand. They are already calling you Fatal Attraction Mia. Do you have a media team?"

I let out a slight laugh. "A media team? Really, yeah. I have a media team, a publicist, a finance consultant, a campaign manager, I've got it all. Yeah, oh, and you're looking at them … rather, than me. It's me. I am my team." I bite my lip and get out of the car.

I have no one on my campaign team. I have no team, and now I'm a Hashtag trend. For *Fatal Attraction*. They don't even know what the movie is about apparently, because that doesn't even make sense.

I walk up the steps to Ginger's house and hit the doorbell. I need something to wash over my skin, brain, eyes, and altered state of reality, bad.

Ginger swings open her door. She has her phone in one hand a drink in the other and a face filled with worry.

"You saw, didn't you?" I nod at her phone.

"Mia, it's all over the net. *Fatal Attraction*, like these little babies, don't even know what that movie was about. At least pick something that would make sense, like *Lolita Bobbitt* or something else I don't know." She hands me the glass of wine. "Then again, he did cheat on you."

I focus on my death stare towards her. We aren't supposed to talk about that, ever. It's too painful.

"I'm sorry, I know. But he did." She drops her jaw for a quick second. "What is he doing here?" She points at Maxwell, who has joined us on the step.

Maxwell is steady and calm. Zero flinch of insult from the scorn across Ginger's face.

"Oh, you didn't know you hired him?" I push past her and go to the living room. I need to sit down and let the frenzy of this reality simmer inside of me. I sip or guzzle whatever version of the truth comes to mind with this wine.

"I'm sorry ... What? My legal membership hired you?" Ginger laughs loudly. She grabs onto the side of the door to steady her balance. "Oh my gosh, Mia ... if you didn't have bad luck … Well, I won't rub salt in the already horrified wound."

"Indeed," Maxwell states.

"Okay, I'm going to need something stronger. You come in … I need to get all of this information before I think I've got my money's worth from you." She cocks her head to nod him in.

Few can ignore a direct command from Ginger. He follows behind her as she leads him into the kitchen. I sit in the living room and sink into the couch. I don't want to fall into a catatonic state. At best, it's a misdemeanor. I can figure this out. It will be okay. It's imperative to search for the silver lining in every moment to ensure that one doesn't sink into despair and get pulled in by the undertow of a deep depression. I've done a fairly decent job of not being taken under. There have been moments where I've had to cock my head back to breathe in the oxygen instead of being submerged in my sadness. Today, that was not going to happen. I was going to have to figure out a plan. With my "team" or not.

"First things first, since you are hired as her legal team, you can't share anything that we talk about here, correct?" Ginger's eyes are laser-focused on Maxwell.

"Yes, attorney-client privilege exists." Maxwell nods and takes a sip of his wine.

"Wait … but what about with Sa—I mean, Mike-MD? How are you able to represent me in this case?" I rub my lips together. "Isn't this a conflict of interest?"

Maxwell shakes his head. "The way the rules are written, as long as it isn't the same transaction or occurrence, it's possible." His index finger and thumb rub his jaw. "It's possible for him to file a motion for me not to represent you in this case. But anything you say or I hear about is still under attorney-client privilege while I represent you."

I shake my head and begin to pace. "No, that doesn't sound good."

Ginger stands up and puts her arms on me. "We can find someone else if need be … It will be okay."

I let my shoulders relax for a moment, too quick for anyone to notice. Sure, Maxwell appeared like the raft of safety to get me out of jail, but do I really want to forgo all of the past and accept that he would have my best interest at heart?

Chapter Ten
"Label or libel, follow the suit that holds the most weight."

Another day another dollar, literally. Today is the day that I begin to make money. I arrived at my office—that's right, my office—at exactly 8 a.m. sharp. I have said maybe 18,000 prayers that my boss and new company have no idea that I'm the Democratic candidate to represent TXHD 193, and that on top of that, they are media novices and do not read or peruse or even know of the existence of social media platforms. I said a bonus round of prayers that they also do not speak to anyone else who uses any social media and that they pretend to be in a bunker of non-information regarding anything that exists outside of the corporate walls. Hope springs eternal on both. But either way, I'm here.

I have a list of instructions on my desk about how to set up my email and things of that nature. I begin to run through each item and sip on my coffee as I take in the protocol.

"Knock, knock." Jose is at the door. It's odd to see him in the flesh. Still seems surreal that we haven't met before, but it is what it is.

I pop up from my desk and offer my hand. "Jose, so nice to meet you in person." Our hands exchange a firm grip.

"Yes, indeed. I see you found the email and office set-up instructions?" Jose eyes the papers on my desk.

"Thank you, these are quite thorough. My email is already set up, so I'm ready to begin reviewing anything of high importance that you want me to work on." I take a small breath. I need to dial down my enthusiasm. My blood is on a race course around the Indy 500, and I have only had a sip of coffee, so this is not the caffeine.

"Good, just work on getting settled in. Here are some company reports, protocols, and office culture. Make sure to see how our culture reflects yours, and let me know if you have any questions." He taps the desk, nods, then exits my office.

Office culture. I am doing my best not to be paranoid, but does Jose mean the whole *Fatal Attraction* bit? I am not a *Fatal Attraction* person. I would never do anything to my ex-husband. I was only worried about Schatzi being without water. No *Fatal Attraction* in my blood. Even with the thing we aren't ever supposed to mention. The part where it was a list of names that he finally confirmed were not unjustified suspicions but real affairs. Even with that, I didn't do any weird *Fatal Attraction* stuff. I simply asked him to verify each one, as I had my hunches, which he always said was my insecurity and my jealousy. Because it was totally normal in his eyes to leave at 10 p.m. and not return until 4 a.m. because he needed to "think." Or the multiple previous girlfriends that he needed to have constant contact with. Or being on Tinder to see if anyone would swipe back on him. Yeah, he literally said that to me … while we were married.

Anyway, I'm out of that situation now. I glance at my phone. "Free Schatzi's Mom" is trending. What in the world? And my mug shot again. Good grief, if I never have to see that photo again. It has to be one of the worst photos I have ever taken. My hair is a hot mess. I look worn out. Underneath it is a GoFundMe account. What? Who set this up? I click on the link. It's being sponsored by PETA. It reads "*Mia Verita did what any dog mom would do. She tried to rescue her baby and get her some water after being chained up in her ex-husband's backyard with no water. No water in Texas? That's a crime right there! Mia did what any of us would do. But her ex-husband called the cops and had Mia arrested for trying to save Schatzi. Kick in today, so we can protect Schatzi's mom and get her a better arrangement for Schatzi.*"

My chest is tight. I want to crawl underneath my desk, but I think that would be frowned upon, especially given this is my first day. I have to figure something out.

I text Ginger a link to the tweet with the GoFundMe link.

She must not be with a patient. A text immediately flashes on my screen.

Babe, you know I've got you covered, and I would rather pay your legal fees directly.

I laugh and type back: *Ginger, I didn't set this up. PETA did, and now it's trending on the socials.*

Ginger responds: *Oh, good. We could use their help. This is good. Let's do lunch. Noon at Escalantes.*

I send back a thumbs-up emoji.

I need coffee. More coffee. I have to be present here in the office, and I need to get to know everyone. I make my way into the break room. A dark-haired woman in a navy suit and white blouse is filling the coffee pitcher. I nod at her.

"Hi, I'm Mia, I'm new."

"Yeah, so I heard. Where did you work before?" She is doing the size-up routine. I've been there before. I get it. Like, *"Who is this new person?"* Some people don't want to make time investments; they have to have data before they can commit to further conversation besides a simple greeting. It's a bit funny to watch.

Being from a military background, I remember how the "locals" would respond to my family's arrival. Based on previous interactions with other BRATS, they decided if they wanted to invest in anything to do with us because they knew it was possible that we would not be there forever. We could move at the drop of the hat and change their entire environment. Everyone could be consumed with so and so, and then their dad or mom would get another assignment and have to move. Then the whole scene would change. I accepted this possibility of a change of life

151

always. I have only ever counted on death and taxes; those are the only things we can be assured, per Benjamin Franklin, that will happen. Everything else is debatable and changeable and, thus, I have gone with the flow.

"I, well … gosh … I was working with my ex-husband … We had a company, but, well, he got the company in the divorce." I lift my coffee cup as if I'm in an attempt to clink mugs with this woman. Because, really, what kind of nonsense is that?

I swallow. It's so difficult to breathe when I have to contemplate what happened in my previous marriage. And the pain of it all is horrible. But what is worse is the constant conversation about what transpired. *What did you do?* "*Did you do something bad?*" There is this false ideology that in an abusive situation somehow both people are at fault. And the reality is that this is not the case. Collateral damage happens, but it is not because the victim is part of the fault. We have got to stop looking at the abusive scene as it's "two people that can't get along." That is not accurate, and it is unjust and wrong. We have to change the narrative and help the victims and give them the strength to move forward. No more backdoor deals.

"That sounds awful—what was the company?" She sprinkles some powdered creamer into her cup. A mug with some writing on it. I scan it a bit closer: *If all else fails, tell me I'm pretty.* Well then.

"It was a valve company. I was the sales, marketing, and finance department but, in the divorce, he was awarded it, along with everything else." I swallow. The burn is deep and the lump in my throat is too much to ignore. My eyes are filled with tears.

Mia, check yourself. You don't know this woman and no one believes or understands this story. No need to share anything further.

"Oh, honey, that sounds like my friend Rhonda … a tragedy in the making. Anyways, how are you doing now?" She stares back at me with blue eyes that are filled with questions but also thoughts and feelings of someone who does care. This woman isn't asking for her benefit, she is asking because she actually gives a damn about me. How refreshing.

"I'm okay. Anyways, how long have you worked here?" Yes, time to move the conversation. I have already shared too much, and it's not good or helpful information. I need to focus.

"Oh, baby, I've worked here for like five years and been with the ups and downs." She nods as she sips her coffee.

"What do you mean ups and downs?"

The environment of this industry has had lots of ups and downs that are related to oil and gas but also lots of other things as well. I need to be aware of this and focus on how I can overcome it to be successful.

"Well, baby, here's the deal—there are highs and lows with the oil industry regardless, but if you are going to sue someone, then you should know exactly what you are looking for, and if you don't, then you are at a disadvantage. These are the realities that most don't want to see. They want to enjoy the life but not think about the tiny transgressions. How many can they do before we don't have a silent treatment? So many highs and lows, and then you have to take a deep breath and take it all in because the time is only about to begin. It's now over, but, really, it's something that life expects you to achieve, to rise up. Maybe you do and maybe you don't. Only time will tell."

"Understood. Good chatting with you. I better get back to those manuals." I let out a slight laugh. The "Oh, you know what I mean; I'm about to go take care of 'work stuff' that is not exactly fun" laugh. But we've all been there. This level of familiarity is what ties people together.

"You and me both. I'm happy to have you on board." She nods in my direction, and I head back to my office.

I scan my phone and "Free Schatzi's Mom" is still in the top spot. I'm stunned. I shake my head and hit the manuals hard. I want to be on top of my work scene from day one. I have a campaign event later tonight. It's not mine, but it will hopefully get me introduced to people in the know and maybe some campaign contributions. The attempt to fill my campaign bucket is a nonstop train. We only have a few months left until the election. It is go time.

I struggle on the last chapter of the manual and my head begins to nod. It's almost noon. I need to head to Escalantes to meet up with Ginger. Guidance for this hashtag social media scene and GoFundMe is essential.

Ginger picked a proper spot directly in between both of our work locations. Wow, that has a nice ring to it. I am so happy to be employed. My cheeks warm at the thought of being on my own. I will have a paycheck within two weeks. No more unemployment. How gross is it to go on unemployment because your ex-husband gets the business and you get fired? Seriously, the atrocity. I shudder.

Mexican food is on the docket, even though it's not Tuesday. But I'm okay with that. I lean into the booth and kiss Ginger's cheek. "So good to see you. But the bigger question is, do you want to be with Fatal Attraction Mia in public?"

"Fatal Attraction, I thought we moved on to 'Free Schatzi's Mom'? Those PETA people are relentless. Surely the whole thing is over now?" Ginger slides a menu in my direction.

"Over, I doubt it. You know who we are dealing with, right?" I glance at the menu. Despite the many options, I have my go-to. I'm going to have some chalupas.

Ginger groans. "I wish I didn't know … but, good grief, how long is this mofo going to keep going?"

I wince. This is the kind of situation that makes my heart hurt. I know I made the mistake of being with "*Satan*," but my friends and family didn't sign up for this nonsense. And this never-ending battle and battle of BS. I get it. I understand that at any point any of them might say, "No more. I can't." They might say, "Mia, I love you, but I can't anymore," and I get that. I wouldn't fault them. Ever. Because it's not on them. This is some nonsense that I took on by myself. I made this mistake. Unfortunately. I take in a breath.

"You know he isn't going to stop. That's not how this works. Remember all the research we did on psychopaths, sociopaths, narcissists, et al?"

And we did. My mom and I took the FBI profile test on psychopaths, and even without all the information, "*Satan*" scored high. The reality is that most people are not aware of how many sociopaths/narcissists there are in the world. Most people only think of sociopaths as in Ted Bundy, but one in twenty-five people are sociopaths, and we just write off their bad behavior for one reason or another. People assume that there must be a reason for the actions that they wouldn't do. Because people don't think that actual evil and no conscience is a real thing. It's imperative that we heighten the awareness of sociopaths and narcissists, but not in the current way. We need to bring light in and let people see them for what they are, but not in a celebratory way either. Unfortunately, in America, we too often celebrate the culture of disdain for common decency in order to succeed. We worship the success of others despite the immoralities of how they got to their moment of power. We glorify in music, movies, politics, and social media.

"Mia, I'm not going anywhere. I'm a human, and yes, '*Satan*' does wear me out, but he doesn't break me or ever make me want to break away from you. I'm here till the end." She grabs my hand and squeezes it.

And no, the water in my eyes is not from tears, it's really hot outside and the air is difficult to breathe because of the Sahara dust that has flowed over our city. That's all. It has nothing to do with this pure human in front of me that never lets me fade to black. She is always there for me, through the libel that he shouted and now for all the labels. Ginger is one of a kind, and for that, I'm grateful.

"Thank you ... I can't ever repay you for all that you have given me."

"Okay, well, I'm not one for the big thanks, but you're welcome. Now, let's focus on your success." Ginger lets go of my hand and takes a sip of her sweet tea, which is something that resembles Ginger. Sweet and constant. You can't go wrong with Texas sweet tea. If you travel to other Southern states, this is not the case. Like Georgia ... that's a joke. You need a liver transplant or a diabetic counselor on the spot upon delivery. But Texas tea is different. We have the perfect blend of tart and sweet. Maybe even a bit of medicinal property. Yeah, Texas tea—don't mess with it.

Chapter Eleven

"Changing lanes moves machines in motion, but who is behind the wheel?"

Time flies when you're having fun or not. Regardless, the time keeps going despite the mood. Tonight is a fundraiser for another State House candidate Michelle Brown. She seems genuinely nice. A bit overly eager to "help." I say help with quotes because there is a vibe about her that I haven't quite nailed down yet. She messaged me on Facebook when I announced in our local Democratic club that I was going to run for TXHD 193. Michelle was nice, yet assertive. She presents as if she has been a member of the Texas House of Representatives for years. The reality is that this is her first race too. However, despite her lack of candidacy, she has invited the guy with his eyes on the lieutenant governor's spot to be a speaker at her fundraiser. The concept of being in the room before the person becomes the next whatever major title is an intriguing concept, however, I'm here to meet possible donors and volunteers for my race.

I walk into the room with zero confidence and unfamiliarity that runs through my veins like an anxiety attack ready to break through the walls of my surface of solitude. Deep breaths. The room is filled with a mixture of people. You can see proper donors of two hundred bucks on, up to the activists with their khaki shorts and message

T-shirts: "*15 or die*." Not sure that I would require a minimum wage of fifteen bucks an hour or die. I mean, there are other options. Always.

The activist community is a difficult group to deal with. Yes, you need these people to push hard against societal norms and breakthrough with honest truths. They bring a voice to the voiceless and represent the unrepresented majority. They help bring real-life stories that it is not possible to exist in this era on minimum wage. They bring the history of why minimum wage was created. They debunk the capitalistic lore that minimum wage was for teenagers who live with their parents. FDR would be turned over and over in his grave if he saw the Texas business ideology. The havoc that capitalism has wrecked on our public education system has only served to create a general society of ignorance and acceptance of rules that do not make sense or benefit the masses but rather the elite one percent. Yet, even if you agree with the activists in their message and their voices, if you do not agree to everything, they will cancel you. The hypocrisy is a bit much for me.

The crowd is filled with T-shirts of every message possible. Both young and old folks are on display. Only a few people are dressed in suits or dresses. This is not a typical fundraiser. The mixture of activists and old money has merged. Regardless of party affiliation, there is a difference between old money, new money, legacy politicos, and newbies like myself. This group screams Democrats, with a level of inclusivity. These are my people. My happiness goes to the next level.

In the back of the room, I see a familiar face from social media. I cannot attest to all political communities, but in mine, once you start to show up at events, you begin to "friend" people who are connected with other politicos that you know. The idea is to build your group, and show you have the support of the political community. This brings you clout and with clout comes volunteers and donors. Ben Norris is one of those politicos. We haven't ever met in real life, however, we are also Facebook friends like Michelle Brown. The difference is that Ben seems to have a different realness to him that exudes beyond the social media presence that he presents.

I make my way through the crowd and ignore the request to put on a name tag. I have my campaign name tag on. I don't need to wear Michelle's name on my chest. I appreciate the offer to the event, but I am not going to be a walking advertisement for her.

I tap Ben on the shoulder. "Hi, nice to 'meet' you in real life." I air quote *meet* like a complete dork to fulfill the duties of my age and somewhat out-of-touch accuracy with the young crowd. I am sure I have at least ten years on this guy.

"Hi." His voice is soulful. And not because of anything else than the depth of his baritone. "Have we met somewhere else?" He lets out a gentle laugh. Like he doesn't want me to

160

feel bad if I have confused him with someone else. I'm not sure what his thought process would be for this. I know I am older than him, but I am not senile. Or anywhere near that.

"Well, no, we haven't technically met anywhere, but we are Facebook friends." Immediately after I say this, I realize how too into Facebook I present as. I am aware of who my friends are and what they say, and what is going on with their lives. But I might be in a small group that is actually doing due diligence with my scroll. Yeah, I scroll through my timeline. I like every post that I read that is good—now with the heart and care feature, I switch it up a bit. I know this is an insignificant thing to do. However, I also know about how I felt when I would post something in the midst of my divorce and one "Like" could make the difference for me. It's like a serotonin or dopamine hit that happens when we get the notification. Which is necessary, and also sad. But when we are so isolated and the thumbs-up can provide a bit of assurance to someone who is alone, why not click that little white graphic? No harm in a tap on the *Like*. I would rather hit it and give that person a bit of hope than scroll and think that person might be in pain.

During my divorce, I would post pics of my dishwasher and talk about how I was in the midst of the success of a clean dish scene. I tried so hard to find happiness and a spin, pun intended, on every bad moment of my life. I made taco people stories on Instagram. People probably thought I had lost my mind and, in reality, I was

161

doing the best I could not to fall off the edge of sadness. Everything I did was an attempt not to fall into the depths of my despair. And yes, all of those posts were deleted before I announced that I was going to run for office. But they still exist in my mind and serve as a reminder of what had been. The sadness of the suds will never truly fade away, but I have moved on past my dishwasher photography days.

"Oh, okay, well, nice to meet you in person." Ben offers his hand and some kindness to me. He has no idea who I am. I am probably one of his auto friend requests accepted, as I'm pretty sure I friend-requested him. Though I am not a hundred percent on it.

I shake hands with him and both our attention sways to the loud bang on the mic from Michelle.

"Attention, everyone, we are about to begin." She motions for the crowd to find a seat. "Thank you, yes, please find a seat and don't forget the envelopes with pens are on the table. Please don't worry about filling them out while we are speaking. No one is going to be bothered by the noise of a pen on check, am I right?" Michelle laughs.

The crowd semi-mimics her. I glance at Ben. Our eyes meet, and there is a shared moment of cringe. Does she not realize how she sounds?

Probably not.

"People ask me, why did you get involved, what made you run?" Michelle glances at the audience and nods at various people as if

162

she is personally acknowledging them. "Well, I tell them, it wasn't an easy path. It wasn't a path I wanted. It wasn't a path I chose." She looks down for a second. "No, friends, this path chose *me*. And today I'm going to tell you why I am going to choose *you*. Each and every one of you to help lead the way for Texas." She raises her arm and clenches her fist into the air with an affirmation of an oath she has made to us.

Wow, okay. I have to give it to her, she is a good speaker. The crowd is fully engaged. I scan the area, some people have taken her advice and have grabbed the pens on the table to write out a check. Yeah, that is worthy of an applause. The sound of claps begins to fill the room. But Michelle, like a true professional, waves them down. She is slick. I am impressed, but I still am not completely sold.

"Friends, please save your applause. What I'm about to tell you is not applause-worthy. It's not good. Unless you think of the reality of what happened." She makes eye contact with a few people in the crowd again and then back to the ground. Her eyes glance at the ceiling as if she is in an internal struggle. With bated breath, we wait for this secret of some sort she is about to share.

I scan the table. Iced tea and water. Not exactly the type of drink I want to sip on while I'm about to hear about the reality of what happened. But, okay. I grab the iced tea. Ben has his too. We cheer. Obviously, there is this shared moment of, "Yeah, we should be drinking something other than tea. But let's make do." That's the thing about Ben. Even though we hadn't met in person until tonight, I felt there was this similarity and a mutual thought process that not everyone gets. Ginger often tells me that my level is a little deeper than the norm and that the jokes and observations/connections that I come up with are not comparable to the everyday person. I get that. And that's why I appreciate it even more when someone gets me despite the normalness of what it is that they are able to see.

"Friends, I was a stay-at-home mom, with a few babies living on food stamps. I wasn't able to pay the rent." She eyes the floor as if she is doing her best to find the words. Yet, this script is obvious, at least to me, that it's a show. I should have asked if we were going to be given popcorn. She has moved on from inspirational speaker to sad sack case. The range. Quite impressive.

"I had nothing. It was a struggle. An absolute struggle. Until I found work for a legal service company. I was able to do this in my home, while my kids were there." She nods as if people are in doubt. "Yes, and I became their best seller. I sold more than anyone, and I eventually became the vice president of the company." The sides of her mouth are stretched up and flashy pearls are on display.

Ah, the top salesperson, now this does make sense. I focus on Ben. He cocks his head to the right and takes a sip of his tea.

"Next thing I know, I'm paying off my mortgage, and my husband and I are able to take fancy vacations. Until …" She stops and scans the room. Michelle offers a nod to let everyone know that they too are in on this experience and this moment when things changed for her. Everyone is suddenly invested in her life and what happened. She takes in a deep breath and sighs into the microphone so we can truly feel her despair. "Friends, I was driving home from a work event and I was pulled over. Now, hold on a second—I back the blue … make no notions about that—but this police officer pulls me over and treats me like a criminal." She pumps her chest and pokes at it with the mic. A *brr* rumbles over the sound system. "This police offer says to me, *me*." She sighs. "That, I have a warrant for my arrest. My arrest? Me? Have you seen me? How could I get a warrant?" She shakes her head and lets her blonde locks fall over her shoulder. "I digress." Michelle meets the audience with a full-on glare and takes in a deep breath. "And then I get booked. Yes, booked. Apparently, someone had used my name, my identity, and took out a mortgage, and a second mortgage, and a truck payment all with my information." She flitters her eyes. "I was gobsmacked. I didn't know what to do. Who would?" She eyes the audience. "Oh, you would go to your congressperson or representative for help?" Her nods are over-empathetic. She smiles. "Yeah, if only it were that easy. Except it's not. And yes, I did that. I went to all my representatives. All of them. Even my kids' PTA president—oh, wait, that's me." She laughs. "But yes, I consulted with her. What did I come up with? Nothing. No answers. No solutions. Not even an empathy, like *sorry*." Michelle shakes her head and looks down. Her eyes look filled with tears. If it weren't for my doubts, I would be pulled into this moment. But there is something off here. Way off. Too familiar. Like I've heard this story before. Where did I hear it?

I glance at Ben once more. He raises an eyebrow at me. Michelle wraps up. I was only half alert to the rest of her stump speech if you can even call it that. It was more like a Lifetime movie. I cock my head to the side. Wait a minute. Wasn't this a Lifetime movie? I swear I saw something similar in, like, the last five years or something. I pull at my phone and google "*Lifetime movie stolen identity*."

I shake my head. There you go. A movie starring a very prominent actress about her identity stolen via a truck and mortgage. I scan. I can't help but notice the similarities between the stories. Time to clock out of this event. I nod at Ben. He seems nice, but I need to go.

I bow my head and pretend that I can't hear the voice being exuded over the speakers. I need to get out of here. I slide forward and swallow. But I'm not fast enough. A man steps in front of me.

"Hello, Mia, I'm Daniel. I wanted to introduce myself. I know your race is considered a no-go, but I think it's a go. I think you can win. Not easy. But a win. Yes." He nods and lets his eyes run over me. He knows what he is doing. He

166

doesn't care. He is focused. I want to be focused, too, but he is on another level. He doesn't care about what I'm dealing with. He has his only goals and is not interested in anything else. So I take a deep breath and suck in the moment. You have to breathe. Always.

"Nice to meet you—what's your name?" I offer my hand.

"I'm Daniel Lee with Texas Lawyers Group." He shakes my hand, and I smile. I've heard of this group. They were on my call list of people I needed to meet.

"Mia Verita?" I turn around and face a man with a box and a baseball cap that reads *No Worries*. With a smile emoticon.

"Yes?"

Mr. Smiley Emoticon's No Worries Hat hands me a stack of papers. "You just got served." He walks away faster than I can even reply. Daniel is still in front of me, and all of my dreams are in the dumpster fire of my complete and utter embarrassment. I glance at the papers. They are from "*Satan*." What does he want now? I scan through the document as quickly as possible. Every word of his affidavit burns into my skin. "Irrational," "Not capable of making decisions," "Supervised visits," "Unstable," each accusation is like another assault. It rips into my chest deeper as I read. My lungs are on fire. My heart is off the rails. Beads of sweat have formed along my hairline.

"Everything okay?" Ben asks, having joined our small group at some point while I was scanning the documents. His hand is on my shoulder, and I am about to crumble in front of two complete strangers.

Breathe, Mia. Breathe.

I glance at the last page. "*Satan*" has asked the court for full custody of Schatzi. The papers fall from my hand and scatter all over the floor. I drop to my knees to pick up each sheet. Something inside of me has created a level of urgency to grab the pieces of hurtful lies before either Daniel or Ben can see them for themselves. I know that the words are nonsense, but it still hurts, and the reality is that people assume that if someone has enough gall to file an actual affidavit with the court, then there must be some actual truth and merit to their statement. I am not sure if this goes back to the gaslighting part of the history of abuse, but narcissists know how to sprinkle in a little bit of truth to the rest of their lies to make you doubt yourself or think that somehow some or all of what they are saying is true. Especially when they do it with a level of confidence that would make any rational person believe they must be speaking the truth. Yet, "*Satan*'s" entire affidavit is filled with lies and unqualified personal attacks against me based on his opinion and not facts. The paper has my name and that's accurate, but the rest is nonsense. I am reminded of memories of constantly being put down and arguments that turned into word salad where I ended up apologizing for what *he* did wrong to *me*.

The whole concept of "if there's smoke, there's fire" is a falsity and should be seen as such. Sometimes the smoke and fire are started by the same versus the concept of "there are two sides to every story." Maybe. But there is also the truth. Not sides. Just pure facts.

The last page says the law firm of Maxwell and X. Wow. Okay then. I guess Mr. Rescue From Jail was a farce. I swallow hard.

Do not cry here. It could just be business.

I stand up and straighten out my dress. Both Ben and Daniel have crinkled foreheads of concern. I smile at them.

"Wow, so that was awkward. I'm sorry about that. What were we talking about?" I rummage through my purse and grab my campaign card. Might not mean anything at this point, but I don't want to toss this opportunity to meet with Daniel's group. I hand one card to each of them.

"Yes, here's my card, Mia. Let's do lunch this week." Daniel hands me his card and waves goodbye.

Ben nods. "I don't have a campaign card, but here's my business card. Let me know if you need some help with that situation." He nods at the papers in my hand.

I let out a small laugh. "Oh, this is no big deal. Ha. Yeah, it's cool." I force a smile. I guess the benefit of this is being able to handle a horrible situation without having a full-force breakdown in front of strangers. I'll save that for my closet. Time to get home.

169

"Well, have a good night." I nod and turn to leave. I need to get into the privacy of my walls, actual brick and mortar that can provide me a place to hide and let go of my utter embarrassment and sadness of this battle that I have been dragged back into. I can't believe my ex-husband would have me served at a political event, but, wait, yes I can. Any place where he could embarrass me and cause me harm would serve as the perfect place. And this was the most ideal spot. He was always good at this type of planning.

I plan my exit the best way I can and avoid any further conversations. Which is another tick of unfortunate misfortunes on my part. I needed to stay and mingle to get people to come to my fundraiser, to put a face to my name. I'll have to make it up somehow. Right now, all I know is that I need to be in the comfort of my home, so that's where I head.

A few minutes later, I barely put my purse on the kitchen counter when a knock comes from my front door. I am not in the mood for company at this moment. Especially not unexpected ones. I peer through the peephole. I cannot believe the man that is on my doorstep.

"What are you doing here?" I stare at Maxwell, the man who provided me with my deepest level of embarrassment to date only an hour earlier.

"I came to explain." He lifts a bottle of wine from his hand.

I'm aghast. Wine, from a guy that just had me served at a campaign event. Like, are you serious?

"No explanations necessary. Have a good night." I push his wine away from my air space and pull the door shut.

I head back to the kitchen and my doorbell rings. Unbelievable. I swing the door open and find the doorstep empty. Except the bottle of wine with a note. I lean down and pick it up. It is a good wine. And I will not turn away a nice bottle despite the deliverer. The note reads *Please let me explain*, with his phone number.

I pour myself a glass and check the note again. I don't want to be a fool, but I also don't want to jump to conclusions. When Maxwell came to the jail, he seemed like a decent human being who finally understood what kind of human "*Satan*" was. I almost thought I could trust Maxwell. Against my better judgment, I let my guard down, and now I'm angry. But I am not going to beat myself up about this. I need to see what he has to say for himself.

My phone is within hand reach. I text: *Explain in less than five words*.

The little word bubble is in motion. I wait and take a sip of my wine.

Not on the case anymore. He follows it up with a second text: *I apologize for improper grammar, but I was limited in my response. If you give me a minute, I can explain, but I'll need some leniency on the word cap. I'm not one to maintain my brevity.*

171

Not, the response I had ever thought. And it leaves a lot to consider, but tonight is not the night for that. Regardless of what the text actually means, I still have a case to contend with. I need to focus on the scars that have been reopened. Stitches have to be pulled tighter, and that is not going to happen overnight. It's going to take a huge pile of strength, which means a good night of sleep. I'll tackle this next mountain of emotions over coffee. This wine is going to deliver me to a place of zero thoughts. No need to drive. I'm parked in a place of solitude. Alone. No Schatzi. All by myself. Cue Celine Dion, pajamas, and a bottle of wine. If Schatzi were with me, we would be snuggled up together. I hope she is inside for the night.

I place the glass of wine on the table and close my eyes.

Chapter Twelve
"Another battle, another fight—how can one keep up and not lose sight?"

The papers are in front of me. Each word is like a razor blade that cuts against my skin. My tears run over the open wounds and the burn increases. I can't read them again. The fact that other adults participated in this nonsensical filing is what really makes me even more infuriated. I get that my ex-husband is a modern-day *Satan*, and he is going to do evil, cruel things. That is his MO. But other adults with brains who must function enough to process the paperwork? The lawyer— I still have to figure out that situation—or the judge who was willing to sign the order for me to be served? Served at a political event no doubt. I haven't even been elected, and I am on round two of controversies. What's next?

I rub my arms. The chill is like a mix of frostbite in a cabin that can't be warmed by the fire. The level of depression runs rampant inside my mind, it cannot be quieted. This is the part where I want to bury my head in the sand and pretend I am alone until everyone leaves the room or I run out of air. Whichever comes first. I don't care at this point. If there was an oasis of quicksand, I would dive in. The branches of pain and too much struggle would wrap around my limbs and air would be compressed in my body until my heart made the last pump.

173

Ginger is fully on solve mode. "Hey, no ostrich time today, okay, babe?" She taps my hand with her pen. "No tapouts. We are full-on going to end this dude. This is ludicrous." Ginger stands up and pops her knuckles like she is going to handle this old-school style. "Listen, I contacted my legal aid through my work. I have some more time available, and I vetted the lawyer. It's not Maxwell. Though he did a good job getting you out of the pen." She lifts her glass of wine as if she is virtually toasting him.

I will not participate in that. I know he said he could explain, but I saw the law firm's name on the papers when I was served in front of two strangers and left to feel like a complete mess of a person. It is the ultimate level of humiliation to be served. But to be served with a lawsuit in front of strangers, especially ones you are in the moment of negotiating a business deal is a whole new level of horribleness. Despite this, I obviously can't let Ginger down or ignore all of her efforts, both financial and emotional, to right the course of this next-level effery of my life. I have to do my part, which, at this moment, is to be present and let go of my imagination of no longer being able to breathe.

"Okay, so what's the scoop? Who is the lawyer?" I lift my head and stare at Ginger. On cue, the doorbell rings.

"Well then, didn't know you could summon legal services. I was sitting over here logging into my app, scrolling through all the options to find someone, and you just summon

one to my house. Okay then. Nice, Mia … nice."
Ginger sashays to the door and opens it.

A tall man in a semi-fitted suit stands at
the step. His eyes are dark, and I am curious if
that is his disposition, or if he can actually solve
this situation. A small amount of hair tops his
head in what might be a buzzcut or an attempt to
hide the balding of age. The suit is pressed, and a
thin blue line runs through the navy material. I
still want to tap out, but I made a promise to
myself and all things decent that I won't. I let go
of a bit of air in my lungs.

"Hello there, you must be …" Ginger
pauses. She obviously can't remember the name
of the lawyer who was sent over. For all we know,
this could be a serial killer and we are his next
two victims. Well, maybe not, but it is possible.

"Yes, hello, I'm Alex Dominguez. Are
you Mia?" His hand reaches out toward Ginger.

"No, thankfully I'm Ginger, her friend.
Only participating in this battle from the
sidelines. Have you had a chance to review the
file?" She motions for him to join us at the table.

I stand up. "Hi, I'm Mia, the one on the
field." I laugh at my lame joke.

Alex smiles with a level of
professionalism that does not go unnoticed. "Nice
to meet you, Mia. Yes, Ginger, I have reviewed
the case. I must say, I've heard of these dog
custody cases … but this is another level." He
pulls at his tie and sits at the table. "Good news is
that we have PETA involved, and they are on our

side. I'm going to get an affidavit from them to help support our claim."

"Are you sure we want to continue to include them?" I glance at Alex and Ginger.

"Yes, Mia, you are fighting against evil forces. You need the righteousness of PETA to pull up with you. Thankfully, you have them." She *tsks*. "I wish there had been a group of righteous doctors to go against all those BS bad online reviews he spammed the internet about my work as a doctor." Ginger presses a hand against her head. "I still get questions about it, even after paying for that company to push them down or have the fake reviews removed." Ginger shakes her head.

My heart sinks. This is the part where I am reminded that not only do my friends and family have to deal with the emotional trauma of this situation, but "*Satan*" has gone after them as well. He wrote horrible reviews about Ginger's bedside manner on multiple sites trying to kill her career as a doctor and, for the record, her bedside manner is second to none. He is simply horrible.

I shake my head as well. I need to focus. PETA on my side is a good thing. I need to regain my attention on the silver linings at present. This is how I can stabilize and not lose sight of the goal. The goalposts might be in a constant motion of change, but this game still has to be played. Schatzi is supposed to be with me. I adopted her, and this whole thing with "*Satan*" is a farce. Maybe Alex can help. At least Maxwell isn't on the case.

"Have you checked out opposing counsel?" I raise my eyebrows at Alex.

"Yes, that lady … Well, excuse me here, but that might be a bit too generous, as she doesn't exactly have the qualities of a lady." His face forms a grimace.

"Hold on … the opposing counsel whom you are dealing with is a woman?" I squint my eyes. This doesn't make sense. I saw the law firm print on the service stamp. Could this be what Maxwell meant? Maybe I do really need to talk to him.

"Yes, we've had a few conversations. Her voice is very squeaky. She sounds like she is going to cry, but every statement out of her mouth is nonsense. I'm not sure if she was able to pull that kind of BS with her parents and it transferred over to her professional performance, but it's bad." Alex scrunches up his nose.

I immediately like him. He has had to deal with Maxwell's co-counsel, Holly Coursey. She is full-on trash. But to see a man not buy into her nonsense makes my heart soar. I am disgusted by the sight of a woman who has zero restraint and is no holds bar ready to destroy another woman over money. That is trash. She is trash. She was horrible in the courtroom with Maxwell. She presented as if she took pleasure in trying to find anything in her stacks of files that would make me look bad. Or try to find a place where I had lied. I remember how her face lit up when she misunderstood where I said the vet was located. Like she had found the clue to prove why I should not have any custody of Schatzi. I was stating the street, not the town. Her puffed-up feathers deflated in the courtroom, but I took no pleasure. And yet, she continued to flap through her multiple binders, her eyelashes fluttered as she searched. Holly presented as if she were a toned-down version of Annalise Keating, and was so sure she could find some piece of testimony that differed from anything they had recovered from their interrogatory questions from me. She had beamed with pride, with what she thought had been uncovered. But she was wrong, again. How can someone be so thrilled and do everything in their control to try and limit a person's ability to be able to see their dog, their lifeline, their more than a best friend, I will never understand this.

"Agreed, she is a pathetic excuse for a human being, let alone a lawyer, but is she handling the case alone?" I will admit my breath might be absent for a second while I wait to find out the answer to this question.

"She has a law firm that she works with, but she is the sole lawyer on the case." He flips through his papers. "I wish there were someone else to work with. She is unscrupulous. I have heard about her from other lawyers, and she edits orders to benefit her clients. Enters things that are not what was agreed to at trial. Only lawyers that are paying attention catch her on it. Most assume she is honest, but the reality is that she is one of the biggest liars we have ever seen in our Texas family court system. We have a name for her … Hole Full of Lies."

178

I nod. "Yeah, that makes sense. You don't want to know how many transcripts I have had to order and pay for to prove that she was lying. It's just awful. She needs to be disbarred." I shake my head.

"Maybe we can make that happen." He pats the papers. "She hasn't exactly made a lot of friends."

"That's not surprising. But how do we handle this case, excluding the bar reports?" I appreciate all the behind-the-scenes, but I need action now, not later. I know we are on a tick-tick time bomb, and I want to make sure that I am on the right side of the release of the bomb when that happens.

"Well, I will work on things legally. But outside of that, you have to follow all of the orders as they were written in regard to Schatzi. I don't care what you think is significant or not. They will make it seem more important than not. If you are two minutes late to pick up or deliver Schatzi, they will say you are disrespecting the court and their orders. You can't have that. I know life happens et al, but we are not playing in the world of 'life happens.' We are in the world of a 'how can they bury you.' And they will find the way." He rubs his chin. "I know it's ridiculous and not fair, but you aren't dealing with justice right now. You are dealing with the very ends of society and how much they can flex before the case is settled or appealed." Alex bites his finger. "I think you have a case. I wouldn't be here if I didn't think so. But it is what it is." He stands and

179

flexes his fingers. "It's imperative that we know what they are coming with but also not to second guess them." He pats the paper on the counter. "They think that you are irrational and incapable of making decisions by yourself." Alex shakes his head and motions for me to stop.

I am ready to rant, but he wants me to stand down.

"I know you are not incapable of decisions. Let's get a video of you and him at police headquarters doing an exchange of Schatzi. They will crumble." He bites his knuckle. "I want for the court to realize it's all a farce."

I appreciate his willpower, but it doesn't matter. You can show this group the smoking gun, and they will blow it out. Sometimes the level of gaslight is so difficult to temper. Studies have shown that the first people to report the crime are the ones who are believed even if they were the actual perpetrator. The whole concept of what was she wearing. Had she been drinking? All the ownership of the crime is placed on the victim. The questions are rarely focused on the alleged criminal. Why would he do this? Why did he feel it was acceptable to harm another individual? Regardless of what happened. The history of the court is still too fresh to be hopeful. Too many injustices to get over.

I swallow. I wanted to be hopeful, but it was not a hopeful place in the courtroom. I am not sure that I will ever get over that.

"Okay, Alex, besides being on time for my pick-up and drop-offs, is there anything else?" I slide onto one of Ginger's bar stools.

"Yeah, I know this sucks, but litigation sucks, so imagine that every moment you are being monitored and watched. And, technically, you are—I checked out the file. This guy ... your ex ... wow. He really likes to record stuff. I wouldn't be surprised if he didn't have a car out front of your house." He makes his way to the windows and peers through the blinds. "Yeah, totally possible. Anyway. I know it sucks. Totally, I get it. I don't like being monitored/watched, etc., but that is what is happening right now. You have to know that and expect that." He takes a sip of the wine Ginger poured. "Listen, every moment that you are outside of your house, you need to pretend like you are competing in the contest of 'Who can be the best person of Texas' award."

I scrunch up my face. "That's not a real thing."

"You're right, it's not, but it is your life until this case is over. You are in a contest of who can be a better person and, thus, a better owner of Schatzi." He glances at his shoes. "You do want her, right?"

I jerk my head as my heart subsequently sinks to the floor. "What? Of course. She is mine. I'm the one who adopted her. He doesn't even take her for a walk. He chains her up outside." My eyes fill with tears.

Ginger pours some wine for all of us and puts her arm around me. "Mia, of course you do. Alex is trying to make that happen. Let's see what he has to say. Our plans haven't worked out thus far. Now we have a professional on the case. Take a deep breath, and let's trust him …" She runs her hands through my hair, and our eyes meet. "For this moment."

I nod.

"All right, good. The first thing we are going to do is lean into PETA and its social media campaign. I have a few connections there. I will drop a few leaks of your exchanges of Schatzi. We can see how he treats her in real-time. How Schatzi responds to you as well. Maybe even have some bacon or something in your pocket." Alex laughs.

I shake my head. "No, Schatzi likes these jerky strips that are good for her tendons."

"Sure, yeah. You know best. Anyways, we get some video and pics of that and we can get a social media campaign going. I will drop his family's company in the comments and we will see if this brings out the commenter trolls to do their thing, and I think that might draw up enough distraction from his focus on you. His family will not want a public issue with PETA or any other large group, I imagine."

Ginger blows out through her mouth. "Yeah, that's good, he would hate to have anything to cause a problem with his reputation or his family's reputation."

"I don't want to cause financial harm to the business." I rub my lips together.

Alex and Ginger's heads swing a sharp turn like I said I enjoy eating dragons for breakfast.

"Mia, that is all he has done to you. That is all he has tried to do to me." Ginger's red locks shake along the sides of her face.

"I know. I'm sorry. I just don't want to cause others harm." I roll my shoulders back.

"You are being caused harm. You are going to lose Schatzi. You are not going to sit in a puddle and wait for the next hit. We are not doing that this time." Ginger waves her finger at me.

"I need to know one thing. Are we in this to win it or not?" Alex stares his brown eyes down at me.

"Yes, of course." I nod in further affirmation.

"That's all I needed to hear. The campaign starts in the morning." Alex nods at both of us and gathers his paperwork. "Good night."

We both say good night to him. And a few minutes after Ginger gives me a pep talk to lift my spirits, I leave her house.

On the drive home, I think about how much I want to win, I really do. Yes, I want to be okay. I have a plan. Scratch that, we have a plan. I am okay. Schatzi will be okay. I just need to keep this message in the forefront of my mind.

183

I make my way back home. Despite the bit of wine. It's still early, and I need to finish my run. I gather myself together, take a swig of water, and run through the parking lot of my complex. Thankfully it connects to the trail. As my feet contact the gravel, I'm blinded by the light. Literally. I can't see. There are eighty million photographers with flashes and loud commands in my face. I duck and try to run farther away from them all. I am a nobody. What is this about? This crowd is lined over a bridge that leads onto the path. They have signs and bullhorns.

"Free Schatzi's mom" is being shouted through the crowd.

I glance up and make eye contact with several people in the crowd. All eyes are on me. Are they really this concerned? I'm in shock. I blink to check myself. Yep. Everyone is still here. I stop for a second and tap someone. "What are y'all protesting?"

"You, silly. We are not going to stand down and allow some D-bag to take his misogynistic control over a mom who just wants to be with her baby." She stares me straight in the eye and raises a fist in the air. "Save Schatzi's mom" bursts from her lungs. This protester is next-level ready to fight for me. Not just for me. But for Schatzi.

Strangers. So many strangers who know nothing of me or Schatzi, and here they are. Full force in arms, linked side by side. They don't hold back. They are ready for any type of attack. And what are they in this for? Me and Schatzi. I can't help but have my breath swept away. This is almost too much. Yet, my momma taught me right. When a grandiose moment happens, you don't walk away, you thank the giver and accept their grandiosity. This is what is happening right now. I am the receiver at this moment. A moment of disarray. A moment of people not being able to accept things as they are. They are not going to read the words and take them as facts. These are the truth seekers, the keepers of the faith. The ones that are going to rise above everything that we have been involved in. I nod. I get it. We are in this together. Though they might not actually feel the personal outcome of my battle. They see me in it and they are not going to let me battle alone. They have risen to the challenge and will not go silently into the night. These are the people that keep the world in motion and make me want to wake up each day and work harder. Not for me … but for them.

Chapter Thirteen
"Money moves mountains, mouths, and monopolies."

It's interesting the difference between people with money and those without. Those with money can throw together an almost last-minute fundraiser at the drop of a hat. They can book a private room in a restaurant filled with white tablecloths and soft candlelight. The perfect level of dimness from accent lights, almost as if they were the founders of the "no overhead lights ever" theme.

Dan from the Medical Group kept his promise and booked a room at La Griglia for my final fundraiser before the election. We didn't really speak at all about it. I called him and left a voicemail. Then I followed up with a text message, and he sent me the contact of his assistant, Shelby. The text read, s*he can handle it for you.*

I was a bit concerned with the hand-off, but I had no other options and, thus, pulled up my insecurity britches and pushed the call button on my phone. Shelby accommodated everything and asked for my Act Blue links for donations and said she would send out the invite to all of Dan's contacts, which is a literal gold mine of dollars. Despite his aggression at the previous event, he would be helpful in this last round of hope to raise enough money to get one more mailer out to the voters and maybe even hire a few pole workers for early voting and election day. One can only wish for the best.

I check myself in my compact mirror once more before I exit the car. No lipstick on my teeth, a good sign. The night is going to go well. The energy feels right. Even though I lean left always.

It's 4:59 p.m., a good time to arrive. Ginger will be here any minute, and though I do not have an official campaign manager, I was able to get a member of our Democratic club to volunteer as the sign-in person. The key is to have someone who has a little bit of assertion as to not allow people into the room without prior registration. Meaning they paid in advance. Or have them pay on the spot. There are plenty of people who will get an invite, show up, drink, and enjoy light bites on the house and offer nothing in return.

The whole point of the evening is to raise money. Not just be seen. Other than me. I need to be seen, and the one thing I dread … being heard. I have to give a speech. I am doing better, but there is definitely room for improvement. I practiced tonight's speech at least five times in front of my phone in advance. Watched it back for glitches and weird and/or awkward moments. Which, unfortunately, had more than a few.

I nod at Sarah. "Hey, Sarah, thank you so much for doing this!" The sides of my mouth are raised to a level that the Joker might even be put off by. I can't help myself. I get a bit overjoyed when people show up and volunteer. It warms my heart and the side effect is a dopey smile. I guess there are worse things. Ha.

"Of course, this is really nice." Sarah motions to the room. "I haven't been here before."

"I agree, I haven't either." I let out a little laugh.

"Well, get used to it. This is the life of a legislator." I feel a heavy hand on the back of my lower back.

I step to the side with candor and a slight smile. My chest tightens. I take in a small breath and remind myself to be calm, cool, and collected. "That's funny." I internally grimace. What kind of a response was that?

"No, no jokes here. This is the life. You'll see." Dan raises his glass and motions to the wall of "only top shelf, would normally be locked-up" wine.

"Well, I guess we'll see. Thank you so much for hosting for us tonight. I really appreciate it." I let my lips press together and force them not to rub back and forth.

Steady. Steady.

"Of course, then again, if your lawyer Maxwell—"

"Dan, good to see you." Ginger opens her arms for a hug and a light kiss on the cheeks. She never fails to enter the room without major grandeur. She is in a black snug cocktail dress with feathers on the bottom of her sleeves. The shoes have got to be the new Louis she got for

Christmas. If *Vogue* magazine cover were a person, it would be Ginger.

"Ginger, so glad you could make it. I am really counting on you to make sure our voice is heard in Austin this session." Dan's eyes peer down onto Ginger's face and then to mine. No words come from his mouth, but his face suggests an agreement or offer that cannot be refused in the future has been made. The mood is giving Francis Ford Coppola, and I am beginning to sense there could be a horse's head placed in my bed if an offer is refused.

"Now, Dan, you know I have the best interest of the medical community, as does Mia. She is going to be fantastic. Who did you invite tonight with big pockets to help get her across the finish line?" Ginger's green eyes scan the rooms as if she can see into the bank accounts of the attendees.

"I invited Tammy Smith."

Ginger shakes her head. "Dan, how can you talk out of both hands? You can't talk about big money donors and then not include their actual title." Ginger purses her lips. "It's Dr. Smith."

Dan laughs. "Of course, but I knew her before she added those credentials."

Ginger sighs. "And yet, the misogyny remains." Her voice is almost a whisper, but we all hear her.

"Hey, I'm proud of her. I just …" Dan drops his jaw. "Well, I'll be damned, if it isn't our biggest donor of the night." Dan raises his glass as Ginger and I turn to see who his focus is on.

"Maxwell?" I let fall from my mouth before I can use some form of self-control.

"Good evening. Good turnout. Yes?" Maxwell eyes the room.

It's filled with members of the legal and medical community. Most of who I don't know personally. These are individuals who owe something to someone else here. They are giving money for them, not that they don't necessarily believe in me. It doesn't matter what level of life you are, most people in Texas tune out politics. This is by design. But the group of people here know that they need to listen to others that do pay attention and they have put their trust and money into what they have advised. Like Dan and, apparently, Maxwell.

"Hey, don't you have a speech to give?" Dan taps my arm.

My veins tense, but I can hold myself steady. I really need to work on my reactions to normalcy. At least I am somewhat aware of how certain physical touches affect me, even if they are not intended to upset or threaten me. This probably goes back to the trauma of my past, but I cannot let it affect my future.

"Yes, we should get to it before people are ready to leave." I let out a slight laugh, as I would prefer a smaller amount of people here, but that is not what one should actually hope for.

Dan grabs a mic from a makeshift podium made of a metal paper holder most likely

190

used for bands. I wrote out a speech, but I have given enough of them to know not to read from it. I can glance if need be.

"Hey, everyone, if I can grab your attention." Dan claps his hands over the mic. The murmurs of the crowd dissipate. "Thank you. Now, I appreciate each and every one of you who came tonight. But coming here tonight is not enough. That was not the big ask. I know I can fill a room—just look at my 'end of the year' holiday party." He laughs and people from the room join. "That's right, you know Dan will make sure you have a good time and that you are taken care of." He eyes the room and nods at a few select individuals. "Now, I need you to help take care of the state of Texas." He does the classic thumb-up fist gesture, almost as if he is making an impression of President Clinton. "This is a pivotal time for us. I need each of you to reach deep into your pockets and kick into Mia Verita's campaign." He claps his hands together and hands me the mic.

My nerves are like a whack-a-mole in my head. I tap the sides of my leg with my left hand.

"Oh, well, thank you so much, Dan, I really appreciate your kind words." The narrator in my head is in an argument over the words I am speaking versus the reality of his introduction. I nod and eye the room myself. Faces I have barely met or not at all are all focused on me. We are in a cocktail setting. These possible donors do not want me to get to the nitty gritty of your Seventh Amendment right. Or the complex legislation that needs to have multiple lawyers review it before you file your bill. No, tonight I need to bring up relatable easy bills that everyone will have had some sort of experience with.

I have a long list of issues I want to tackle once I'm sworn in. Some are personal things that I experienced and want to fix so that others do not have to go through the same thing. Others are issues that I have followed like rape insurance or pro-active legislation to prepare for the next weather disaster. There are kitchen table issues like Public School funding and whether or not we can open another DMV in their area, time and money always motivate voters. Then there are little issues that might seem small or unimportant until you find yourself having to hire an attorney to help you. These little issues are the kind to bring up in this type of group.

"Words matter, and this is why it is so important for us to elect representatives who will keep the promises that they make but also not ignore words that will change the course of history for you." I rub my lips together. "How many people here have ever had a speeding ticket?" I let the sides of my mouth pull up. "Don't worry, we won't judge you. Ha! Okay, anyone in this room who may have had to step foot in the courtroom or was bothered by an HOA notification of something on their property that was out of place?" The crowd groans. "Right? Oh no, you have a piece of grass growing out of your driveway, that will be $50 and another $25 for them to send you the letter." I nod as the crowd begins to talk. There are grimaces and angry faces.

"I know, these are things that are upsetting to us. But these are things we can work on together to make it better. Some laws are helpful and that will protect you and your property." The group begins to nod in agreement with the possibility of good legislation. "That's right, with your help and investment in my campaign, I can promise you that I will work tirelessly for you and your best interest." Everyone begins to clap. "Thank you—let's go win this!"

I join in the clap with them. As my hands touch in the repetitive motion, the blood flows through my fingertips and somehow at the very top of the final piece of skin that forms my individualized print, I actually believe it's possible to win.

Chapter Fourteen
"Nothing left on the field ... tally the votes."

And so it begins, right back to where I
began this race. So much uncertainty. So many
unknowns. I put my name on the ballot with the
full knowledge that this seat had been a
Republican stronghold for over two decades.
Two decades. Yes, I knew this, but I also knew
that I could talk to people like a regular person. I
know that I could and would represent them.
Even if their thoughts differed or were based on
oppositional ideologies. For the most part, we
would and could agree. I ran on this. Many battles
were had at the door. I engaged in all the debates.
Friendly and maybe some that were antagonistic.
Then Election Day came upon us. What were we
to do? Where was I to go? I took the day off from
my job, so I could work the polls, and yes, I did
make many jokes about this. Even though I am
extremely against strip clubs, that is another
argument. Jose and Mallory were supportive of
my election. They even volunteered to work a few
polls themselves. We were able to be at fifteen of
the thirty-eight key voting locations in the
district. We ended at the last one before the
deadline with an encounter with an extreme far-
right Republican who was literally lying at the
polls about my opponent. And she was so
aggressive. This small woman with her

pamphlets and false promises from a man who probably wouldn't be able to pick her out from a crowd. But she was grandstanding for him. I don't understand that level of loyalty when you have no idea how wrong you are. It's horrible. Our entire system needs to be overhauled, but also, we also need to engage our youth in the reality that is before them. They need to be empowered to make proper decisions for themselves and to know who and what they are voting for. Our school systems are silent on this. Texas is horrible about the education of civics in our public schools. It's almost as if the Texas Board of Education does not want the youth to vote or run for office. Oh, that's just what one would refer to as saying the silent part out loud.

It's a travesty. If elected, I will make it my mission to engage the youth, to understand what is at stake and how much their vote matters.

I take a deep breath. I've been at this location for over two hours. It's early and most people are at work, but I am here regardless.

A man in a wheelchair approaches me. His nails are longer than one would expect. "Hey there, I got your mailers." He points at me.

I smile naturally. It doesn't get old to hear that people have heard about you before you have literally introduced yourself. "Is that right?" I let out a small laugh.

"Yeah, they were good. I could see you at my kitchen table. Ha. The mailer with the calendar of community events. That reminded me of my mom. It really meant something. And I'm a lifelong Republican. I liked them. But seeing you here. You have my vote." He nods.

I offer my hand. "Thank you, sir. I appreciate that, and I promise that we probably see more eye to eye than you realize."

"It's possible. But the way politics have been going, it's hard to see the person and relate." He taps his knee. "But you being single and fighting for your dog. That takes a lot of grit and heart. We need that." He rubs his beard.

"Yes, sir, I agree, we need everyday Texans to represent us, especially right here in TXHD 193. After everything we have gone through with Hurricane Harvey, we need someone who understands what it's like to have your house wrecked in a natural disaster. What it was like to have no water or electricity for thirty days."

"Your house was wrecked?" His eyebrow raises.

"Yes, sir, I guess you didn't get that flyer. House was wrecked. I had a huge four-by-four-foot hole in my ceiling. Lost electricity and water. I know that was bad, but not as bad as some of our other neighbors. We need pro-active legislation to address the issues that happened during the last natural disaster and ensure that we protect homeowners and business owners, not if, but when the next catastrophic event happens." I swipe some hair out of my face. It's November in Texas, but it is not cool weather. It's warm. Hot almost. I need a water break. I smile at him.

"You're a good egg, Mia. I'll let my friends know." He tips his hat and turns his wheelchair to roll away.

I want to say thank you once more, but sometimes less is more. I let him roll with the perfect exit. Let them have some say in how the conversation ends. It's important to read the room and to let the audience participate in the discussion. No one likes being only talked to. Engage them. That is how you win, by bringing everyone to the table. Inclusion is the best resolution.

Some might say the only solution. Those people are not wrong.

My phone brings me back to the present. "Hey, where are you?" It's Ginger. She said she would work some of the polls with me. I didn't want to bug her about it. I figured she could get here when she could. It's not like she doesn't have her practice to worry about.

"I'm over at the MUD Office. It's pretty dead. But I did just flip an R vote in our direction." I can't help but let the pride emote through my phone.

"All right, all right, all right ... I like the way you move those Rs to the other side of the ballot. Good stuff, good stuff. I can meet you in a couple of hours. But lunch first, please?"

I tap my Fitbit, it's a quarter to noon. "Lunch would be good ... I think I can talk to the boss about letting me have a quickie bite."

"Your boss is so cool ... I bet she would be okay with a bit longer than a quickie. But I will be respectful. Greg is going to join. He wanted to cheer you on." She breaks her joyful chatter. Like I would have a problem with Greg being present.

"Wow, Ginger, I am actually quite flattered that he wants to join and, obviously, am thrilled. That's great." It is at this moment that I can take solace in the fact of the matter that I have the best friends. So supportive, and even their partners care about me. That's huge. I truly am blessed.

"Oh, that makes me so happy to hear. Great. Let's go to Ephesus on Mason at twelve-thirty. I'll be the one with the big smile." She laughs.

Of course, she will be there with a big smile. "Ooh, awkward … I was going to also wear a big smile. Okay, don't worry, I'll figure something out. I will be there regardless. Chomp-chomp." I hit the red button and watch as a group of definite Rs march past me with disgust. I see the paper in their hands. The Bought List. It's a Republican endorsement list that this guy sends out to solid Republicans about who to vote for. The reality is that the Republicans who make lists are not vetted for their party values. It is entirely about who pays the bigger amount, that is who gets the endorsement and makes it on the list. Is that who these people want to vote for? Whoever has the most cash? Maybe? The whole thing seems so disingenuous.

I shake a few more hands with people who recognize me. More mailers that they have received with my face on it and, of course, lots of pictures of Schatzi. Such a different race, as my opponent had no idea that there was a chance of being able to flip this seat, so everyone who has approached me has been positive. We came out of nowhere with our mail, and the decades of Republican control did not make them sweat at all about the possibility that I could win.

I can't help but wonder what would happen if the opposite was true. What if they had sent out a bunch of bad mail with my picture with lies? That makes me nervous. I was nervous about this idea before I put my name on the ballot. I thought about the repercussions that could happen with being in the targeted seat. I left an event where this was discussed, and as I was in the midst of downtown Houston, I encountered several unhoused people. I was able to make eye contact with them, and I knew that I couldn't look them in the eye and understand their struggles and not want to get in the fight for them and the rest of Texas. I was not going to let the bankrolled bullies back me down. Nope. If anything, it made me want to fight harder. Even though my "fight harder" has really been about the doors. Foot soldier and knuckle smasher. Ten thousand doors. Ten thousand freaking doors was my count this morning when our app updated.

My phone buzzes. I glance at the caller ID. It's Alex.

"Hello?" My chest is tight. The never-ending doom that flows through the phone or any situation in which a lawyer is involved in my life.

"Are you at a place where you can talk?" There is a lot of commotion in the background.

"Yes, are you?" I let out a slight laugh.

"I am at the courthouse. They filed a fifty-two-page exhibit of evidence against you." Alex lets out a sigh. "The media is here."

"What?" Is all I can manage to express.

"Holly called a press conference. She said it was imperative for voters to know who they were voting for, and they are going to read all of the evidence against you at twelve-thirty."

"What evidence?" I scan my mind for any transgressions I have ever made that would be considered evidence to not vote for me.

"I don't know. They haven't uploaded the evidence yet—they are waiting for the gotcha at the press conference. I am not sure if you should come down here or if we should try and let it die in a hopeful silence." Alex coughs. "I am trying to file a motion to seal the case and stop the press conference, but the judge has not been receptive to my attempts."

"What should I do?" I flex my fingers. Why can't DaVile just let it go? This is unreal. He is truly doing everything in his power to sabotage the millimeter possibility that I could win this election. Why does he—? I stop myself, as I know why. Because like all narcissists, he won't let it go. I have harmed him by letting him go. He has a narcissistic injury. I have to feel his pain. Not because he is in pain. But because he feels as if I have caused him harm. By not wanting to be with an abuser. My insides squeeze to the point of almost completely passing out.

"Stay put. Focus on talking to everyone you can. This is a ground game. You know a lot of people will have already voted. And the ones that haven't are probably at work and not watching the news." He laughs. "This isn't funny, but it is completely unreal. Mia, this is only to get under your skin. There is no way they have fifty-two items of evidence against you. If they did, you would have zero custody of Schatzi."

I nod. This is true. If there had been anything of substance, "*Satan*" definitely would have used it against me. He did everything he could to strip me of any visitation of Schatzi.

"Okay, I believe you." I press my lips together as if I can seal this belief into facts and not just a string of hope made out of dandelion seeds. I know that I haven't done any real wrongs in life, but the doubt that runs through me is still too strong to shake.

"Mia, it will be okay. Go win this election. I will handle this legal battle. The press conference is to throw you off. Heck, it might not even happen." Alex's voice is strong. The energy is real. I roll my head in a circle and move my shoulders.

"Right … but please let me know what happens at the press conference."

"Of course. Talk to you soon." The dial tone rings in my ear. I shiver for a second and make my way out of the car.

I stride into the restaurant. I'm not bothered. This is okay. It's just a farce. It's fake. It's his typical MO. The big fake. To make me freak out and not know which way is up or down. With a deep, long breath, I inhale and exhale. I am unbothered.

The restaurant is a family setting. Chairs with faded cushions and Formica tabletops. The walls are painted with the Adriatic Sea and a TB plays a repeat tour of the Mediterranean highlights.

Ginger is at the table with Greg. Both have smiles of satisfaction on their faces. We have crossed over the halfway point of the election date, but we don't have the data yet. I'm not sure why or how they can be happy. I'm in a crux of fear and uncertainty. And that was before the call with Alex. I know we have to put everything into the day of the election, but maybe I could do more. Guilt rises in my skin as I sink into the seat. Should I even take a break to eat?

Almost as if she can read my mind, Ginger interrupts my internal monologue. "Mia, you know you have to eat, right? Like, you can't pass out at the polls. You are having lunch, not at lunchtime, but in the midst of the afternoon, when people, for the most part, are back at work. It's totally fine. Right, Greg?" She glances at her man. Their eyes meet, and there is this connection of love and support that I admire. Not jealousy but appreciation. And I'm thankful she has this type of love. Ginger deserves this, and Greg is a good man.

"Yes, of course. Mia, you can't be a leader if you pass out at the finish line." He pushes the plate of hummus and pita chips toward me. And I am not going to bypass hummus. Not now or ever.

"Okay, I am not trying to pass out. Thank you for your support. I just want to make sure that I do everything possible to win." I scoop up a nice helping of humus and take a bite. Heaven. So delicious. There are certain types of food that I could eat more than once a week. Mediterranean, sushi, Thai, Mexican, Persian, okay ... I get it, I just like food. No shocker there.

"Beyond the Sea" comes on the radio, and I'm all in. If only I was at sea right now and not in this time bomb of a countdown. Of course, if I were to mention the notion of sea in any capacity, then people would say, "Blue wave, blue wave." Right, maybe, but maybe not. It's interesting the way the tides move. In our inner circles, we see things a certain way, but is that majority? It's difficult to really be able to see the big picture and to realize the way the tide moves and how fast or slow things circulate. There was talk of the big blue wave and how it was going to come and crash down on Texas. The red spot in the center of the US. Could this be possible? It was yet to be determined. Or maybe it was only the start. Like the trickle of rain that begins before a major storm. Everything seems like it's okay. Like with Hurricane Harvey. There were all these warnings. "Buy Gas," "Get an extra battery," "Get out while you can," and then it was too late.

It was hard to see the big picture through the minimalistic moments of a soft rain falling. It was difficult to understand the reality of what was going to happen and how much devastation it would cause. It was a slight soft rain until it didn't stop, and then the reservoirs were released and people's houses were flooded out. Everything was gone, and yet it happened in a moment that no one thought would ever occur. Much like an election where you flip a seat that no one thought would flip anytime soon.

"I hate to bring this up, but I think you would be bothered if I didn't."

Ginger's eyes widen with fear. She knows me too well.

"Good God Almighty, what has '*Satan*' done now?" Her nostrils flare. Greg pats her hand.

"Alex called and said that Holly, the squeaky trash can that doesn't seem to dissipate, has called for a press conference today at twelve-thirty to release fifty-two pieces of evidence of me not being a good person and one that people should not vote for." I grab my Diet Pepsi and take a long swallow.

"Wow, it just keeps getting better." Ginger glances at Greg. "The audacity. Let's go to this press conference. I am ready to speak on it." She stands with her hands in fists.

"Ginger, I think we would better help to Mia at the polls, making last-minute calls to her identified voters." Greg grabs her hand and guides her back to sit down. "Also, hopefully, it's already over. If it even happened." He taps his phone to show her the time.

Her head shakes and red locks fall over her scrubs.

"I am sorry to be the bearer of bad news, but I know you would want to know." I grab my purse.

"Of course, we need to know, Mia. But the bad news bearer is not you, it's him. It's always him." She blows out through her teeth.

"I've got to get back out there." I glance at Ginger. "Are you able to join?" I swallow. I try not to ask anything of Ginger. She already gives so much that I don't want to ask for anything. But today is different. I need and want her to be with me at this moment. Whether it's a W or an L, our lives will forever be changed today. I will be listed in history as being on the ballot, and I will always treasure Ginger's support through it all.

"Mia, I told you I would, and I am." Ginger nods and rises from the table. "You got this, babe?" With zero hesitation, she leans down and kisses Greg.

"Of course. Go get them votes." Greg laughs. "GOTV. Right?"

I nod and smile. "Yes, GOTV … that's what we have to do. "I notice the numbers on my Fitbit. "We have less than three hours."

"Well, let's get out of here. What are you waiting for, Mia? There are votes to get and a seat to flip. Let's do this." She squeezes me in close, and I laugh.

This is how it's meant to be. I am filled with happiness and comfort of my best friend, my life partner, per our chosen labels, in this fight. Yes. I'm ready.

"All right, I'm ready. Which spot should we go to first?" I pull up the voting location map on my phone and show it to her.

"Let's go to the one-off of Kingsland, chat for a few minutes, and then hit up another spot. I think we can hit another few more spots before six, and then close it out at Cypress. That's the biggest location."

I nod in agreement and slide into the car. Ginger pulls out her phone and leans toward me. "Quickie voter-pursuit selfie."

I lean in, and we both give our "let's get those votes" look.

Laughter ensues, per usual, and I navigate us to the spot of our first joint voting location. Time to work the crowd. I am ready to flip some votes. I see the woman that has her red "MAGA" hat on … no doubt her side. I have my stack of lit in hand.

"Ma'am, can I tell you about Dick Mikelson? He is going to lower our taxes and fight for Texas schools." She tries to hand me some of my opponent's lit. She doesn't recognize me, and I don't mean in the "who I am" sense, but I have already worked the polls with her.

"No, thanks, I'm good, and, also, that's not accurate. He voted against public school finance reform. Even went against his party with this." I raise my eyebrows.

"Oh, you're that Mia whatever, right?" She squints at me.

"Yes, I'm Mia Verita … and I'm actually in this race to fight for the things that you say he fought for—you should check his voting record."

Ginger shakes her head at me." Come on, let's go to another spot. The energy here is not good with all that red."

I scan the lot; it is not that busy. "Yeah, that's a good idea." We drive to the next spot, which has an actual line of people.

"See." Ginger points at the line.

I move toward the front of the entrance in an attempt to catch some of the undecided voters. There is a hundred feet cutoff for how close you can get to the door. Sometimes there are poll watchers who police the distance. They take their job quite seriously. I wouldn't cross the line regardless of their presence or not. I do not want to harass voters. I appreciate that they are exercising their voice.

Another MAGA woman rushes up to cut in front of a couple en route to the door. I let her spew her inaccuracies about Mikelson. As they get closer to me, I take a deep breath and approach them.

"Hi … I'm Mia. I'm running for X … Could I talk to you about some of the issues I'm going to fight for?"

The woman and man glance at me. "Honey, you had our vote before we got here … but the red hat sold us when she said she was here for your opponent."

"Thank you so much. I appreciate your support." I shake their hands and glance back at a different MAGA. She has dropped some of her lit. It is scattered around her in the dark of the parking lot. The scene is disarray, much like the man that she has garnered her support.

Ginger's hands are in motion as she points to the entrance. Oddly, the lights have all begun to turn off, even though people are still voting.

My watch says it's a matter of minutes and the polls close. Not close in that the people in line will still be able to vote, but they do a "last call" in the line. Kind of similar to a bar. Last call to make your voices heard. Do not drink for a little enjoyment at the end of your night. No, this is your voice in the Texas House for the next two years. Do you want to bail on your chance to utilize your voice and vote for democracy, or stand a bit longer to push a few buttons? Until you get to the last big red button that says submit ballot.

And just like that, the clock hits 8 p.m. The parking lot is dark. The only glow is from inside the school. The last voters have been let in, and I stand on the outside. It's over. What's done is done. Either we've won or it was a good run.

My lungs are like two small balloons that have been overfilled. I sigh. Acknowledgment of the end is surreal. I have been doing a countdown for so long that it is odd to have the buzzer pressed. It's over. All the work. All the doors. All the phone calls. All the fundraisers. All the hands that I have shaken. Everything was put on the line. My chest is pumped and deflated simultaneously. The anxiety of the unknown begins to run various scenarios through my mind. Numbers upon numbers. Precincts and percentages. All will come to the final number. So much depends on a mathematical equation that will divide the votes between a group of people to determine how things will affect their lives for the next two years. The tally begins now.

Chapter Fifteen
"Numbers on the line, but sometimes it's a matter of time."

Ginger has not looked up from her phone since we got in the car. People are still en route to their vehicles. Her silence is too loud. It screams bad news. My chest is tight. The air has left my lungs. And tears are in my eyes. I am afraid to ask. I am afraid to hear. I knew this fear could become a reality. I knew that I might give it my all, and the answer would still be a no. The people might say, "No, thank you." Even if a group of people said yes, it wouldn't matter if more said no. People that chose to exercise their civic duty, might have decided that I was not their choice. For any number of reasons. If they talked to "*Satan*" or showed up at the press conference today, they would have at least fifty-two reasons to cast their vote in a different direction. No matter how hard we worked, it could be all for naught. I let a drop slide down my face. Ginger grabs my hand.

"Hey, no tears. We just got off the field. We have the entire night ahead of us." Ginger taps her phone. "Early voting is not always a sign of how a race will go." She forces a smile. I know it's forced because she has a puddle of merged lines on the sides of her mouth. It is about as unnatural as possible.

"How bad is it?" I stare directly into her eyes.

"Well, it's not great." She breaks my stare. "It's, well, you're down right now. But, hey, you've been down before in life, and look where you are at now!"

"Losing my first election?" I flicker my lashes. It's true. Things are not good. We gave it our all and we are behind. All those doors we knocked on. All the mail we sent. All the phone calls we made. All the texts I typed. All of it. All my friends and family helped. I swallow but can't get past the huge lump in my throat. How could this have happened? We did everything we were supposed to. I am stunned.

"It's okay, Mia. Let's go to the watch party and see if these people come to their senses." She puts the car in gear and pulls out of the dark parking lot.

"No, I don't want to go." I grab her arm. "Ginger, I can't. I can't be around anyone right now. I need to go home." I can visualize my closet and Schatzi. Who is not with me, since it's a Tuesday night? I wonder if *he* watched to see where the numbers are. I wish I had her with me. It would be so nice to hug her right now. I sigh.

"Mia, you have to go. Part of being a leader is showing up in difficult moments. You can't desert your supporters tonight of all nights. If it doesn't go as planned, you have the rest of the week to breathe." She squeezes my hand. "Tonight, you have to put on the happy face and be thankful to everyone who did everything they could to get you elected, whether that happens or not."

I nod. She is right. I have to go. I don't want to. There is not an ounce of desire in my body to go to this event. But I have to. I have to for the people. I got in the race for them, and I'm not going to leave them if I don't win. That's not the kind of person I am. My pride is being crushed, literally by the second with each vote that is counted. Each number that pops up on the screen. But Ginger is right. I can't cower and sit alone when all these people show up for me. Maybe the numbers won't get better, but we tried. We gave it our all. And though the pain of a loss is horrible. The mission does not stop because of an L.

Ginger pulls up outside of Little Woodrow's. Our team had reserved a big area to celebrate. Celebrate. I can't. We aren't going to celebrate. We are down. The numbers are bad. I walk into the bar, and people recognize me as I make my way to the table that is sectioned off for us. I force a smile. "Thank you, all … We might not have done it this time, but we gave it our all, and I just want to thank all of you." I hug Beverly.

She and her partner worked the polls every day for me, proudly adorned in Mia shirts and signs.

"Oh, baby, we did our best. Let's wait and see." She squeezes me in close. It's people like Beverly who can take a difficult moment and bring you up to move forward with confidence and happiness.

I pat her back. "Thank you so much for working so hard." I lean back so I can let her know how sincere I am.

"Baby, we would do it all over again. Now, let's focus on the possibility—the night is still young, like you!"

We both laugh. Beverly has a few decades on me. This "young" statement makes sense at this moment. I let a bit of the laughter fill me. I can siphon this energy in bits to make it slowly through the night. Regardless of the corner booth that is trying to woo me to it. I will not cower in the corner.

I pull up my lady britches and work the room as if it were a fundraising event, except it's the complete opposite. This is the event where everyone is supposed to see the rewards of what they bought into. Me winning. I glance at the big screen hanging from the ceiling. The numbers are scrolling in. My race is one of many in Harris County. And thus, it takes a good three minutes of the scroll before they flash my name. Still behind.

I let my eyes drift toward the ground and catch a glimmer of blue across the room. There he is, Maxwell Graham. I'm a bit surprised he showed up. I nod in his direction. That's good enough of an acknowledgment. We still haven't spoken since his wine delivery. I have been too busy, and my plate does not have space available for any more drama. That is one thing that I have a surplus of.

He makes his way towards me.

213

"Hey, Mia. It's going to be good." He grabs the sides of my shoulders and squeezes them firmly but not too hard. "I promise." His eyes are focused on mine, and for a quick moment, I am not in a room of despair. I am in a place of comfort. I blink and swallow. I hope and wish he is right. But the uncomfortableness of him is too much to consider on top of the tally of numbers. How can he be the right hand of "*Satan*" and then also show up at my watch party? It doesn't make sense.

A million scenes run through my mind, some are good and some are not. Maxwell is not the equation I want to solve right now. The only math I can focus on is the numbers and percentages on the TV screen.

The numbers on the screen barely move. The system to count votes must be completely archaic. Dinosaurs are probably in the room with their short arms, which is obviously the reason for the ice age movement.

"Thanks for coming out," I say with as much calmness as I can present.

His hands drop from my arms along with his smile. "I wore blue for you."

I laugh. "For me? What, like a conciliatory ribbon?"

Maxwell tips up my chin with his thumb. "Mia, you deserve more than a conciliatory anything. Good things are coming your way, with or without a win."

My chest tightens, as the only win he could be referring to is the one that ended very badly for me.

"Sure." Mary, the Democratic club president, is several feet behind him, and I nod in her direction. "Excuse me."

I march towards her. Despite the numbers, I need to have more of a battle face right now. Mary is known for her downer mentality and speeches. You would think the point of her offer of words was to make people depressed.

"Hey, Mary, thanks for coming." I offer a hug.

"Oh, Mia, it's okay. I'm sorry it didn't turn out, but you have grown so much as a person through this entire process." She rubs my arm.

"Ah, thank you ... but the election is only thirty-four percent in ... still lots of votes to be counted." I nudge my head at the TV. Fifty percent of the votes are in, and we are still behind. Well, maybe Mary is right.

I glance down and then back up. I have to put on my game face regardless. I can go cry in the closet afterward. Right now, I have to be strong for my team and supporters.

"Well, anyway, I've got to thank some more people." I force the sides of my mouth into a smile and walk toward the back of the room. As I swirl through the hopes and despairs of the crowd, the clock continues to tick as the ballot count grows but not in our favor. At almost ninety percent of ballots in, things have not improved for us.

Ginger taps my shoulder. "You did good, Mia."

"We're losing."

"Not really. You came out of nowhere and gave them a good fight. You have nothing to put your head down about. This is all good." She hugs me. "But you've got to give a speech, and then we can leave. It's getting late, and you know these people have to get to work in the morning."

"Okay." I grab the mic we brought and gather the room of people who are clearly there for us with their Mia shirts.

"Thank you, everyone, for coming out tonight. Thank you for supporting our race with your time, your talent, and your treasure. Oh, I need to give special thanks to TLA Pac for their last-minute investment in our campaign. Your investment gave us that final push to help us get over the hurdle in getting our voters to the polls, so I want to thank you specifically. And to everyone else, I know things are not looking as we had hoped. We will continue to keep the faith until our race is called, but I want to thank you from the bottom of my heart for believing in me and what we could do together. Thank you so much."

The crowd of course properly cheers, and I make my way toward Ginger. I see one of the board members of TLA,"Oh, Mr. Gates, thank you for the investment from TLA Pac. We really appreciate it. I hope it will turn out in our favor and the investment was well worth it."

He laughs. "Oh, it was worth it either way. We can't stand Mikelson, but I'm not the one you should express any direct gratitude to." He nods at Maxwell, who is by the exit.

"What do you mean?" I wipe some hair off my face.

"Maxwell Graham is our president and decision maker. Not me." He pats my shoulder. "Good luck, Mia."

I jerk my head back. What? Did Maxwell invest in the campaign? That's wild.

I eye the exit door. He is gone. Like so many other things. I somehow manage to gather my things and the tiniest bit of self-respect and exit. Ginger drops me off at my door. She knows not to walk me in. It's straight to my closet scene. I can't and don't have to hold it in any longer. Every part of me is shattering. I make my way into my house and pop open a bottle of cab. I bought a bottle of wine and a mini bottle of prosecco in case the numbers were different. I had really thought they would be different. I didn't expect a landslide, but I really thought we had a chance. I really thought that with the work we put in and all of the horrible legislation that the current representative had filed and voted for, we would flip this seat. I really did. My vision is blurred as the warm sadness flows down my face. The red drops of cabernet turn into a puddle of emptiness. The depth of the wine is not really there. I didn't splurge on anything impressive. But it was supposed to be better than my tried-and-true box wine. Yet, this wine is like a forgotten shoe left in the bar after midnight. Vinegar and bitterness swirl through the glass. It is the epitome of low dollars, and it screams of defeat. I pour it down the drain and cut the lights.

Chapter Sixteen
"Numbers can make the difference, but what is behind them that matters."

The pressure behind my eyes is like a hurricane filled with heavy thunder. I press the sides of my temples for any amount of relief I can withdraw from my skin. I normally don't get headaches from wine. The depression and sadness from last night's results could be the main cause. But either way, I am never going to get that type of wine again.

The sheets are crumpled up in a ball at the end of my bed. Like they formed into a fetal position. I want to fold them up and cover my head. To try and hide myself from the reality of the results of yet another battle that I lost.

I had told Jose that regardless of the results I would not be in right away. I look at the time on my Fitbit. It's 9 a.m. Crap. I move my hand around my nightstand in an attempt to connect with my phone. I make contact and glance at the battery notification. There is only one percent, of course. I swipe to my messages. *YOU WON! ANSWER YOUR DAMN PHONE*! is glaring back at me from Ginger. What?

I shake my head and tap my phone again to read the message. The phone shows the circle message, then shuts off. Are you kidding me? At this moment? My phone is dead ... wow. Of all times. I scramble around the room trying to find a charger. I push it into the wall and run to my computer. Thankfully, my computer is powered on. I pull up a browser window and type my name. All the PETA and lawsuit information fills the page with results. The news link is highlighted at the top. I click on it and my name has its article with my race. What is the actual what? What am I reading? The news article is from the *NY Times*. Surely, they wouldn't print anything erroneous and not about a Texas State House race? Further down the page, there are more articles. More news reports with my name and the word "won" are accompanied by it. What? For some reason, some people seem to think I won? What? I can't breathe. I push myself away from the computer and take in a deep, long breath. The blood underneath my skin is in a rapid pulsation beat. Too fast to keep up. I inhale and exhale slowly. *Be cool, Mia, be cool.* I grab my phone. It still won't turn on. *Come on, iPhone ... get this charge going.* I hit new email on my account and type to Ginger.

Phone is dead. I can email for the moment. What am I reading on the news?!?!?!??! I hit send. My email pings an automatic response from Ginger.

YOU WON!! !!!!

Those two words are so hard to read and understand them to be true. How is this possible? We went to the watch party. The numbers were in black and white. The lead was not in our favor from when the early voting numbers were first reported until the end of the news segment. I gave a thank you speech. Which was not a speech in which I spoke about what I was going to Austin to help accomplish. It was a conciliatory speech in that the fight was not over, but I appreciated everyone's efforts in this round. The clock alerted us it was late and a Tuesday night. People needed to get home since almost everyone had work today.

We left the watch party with our numbers down, way down. After the nasty swig of whatever wine that was, I went to bed with the numbers being down. How could it have changed overnight? Is this even real? Everything doesn't seem as if I am in the moment in which I am in.

I pinch myself. A pinch is not enough to bring a sensation to weigh over this cloud of doubt and confusion that fills the room. My only connection to the outside world is via the internet. All the possibilities of inaccuracy and fake news appear to be more of a possibility than the alternative in that I did win. I have to wake myself into this existence and push past all of my insecurities. I need to know that I am actually awake and this moment is truly real. The pinch is notable. Redness forms over my skin. I click through all the searchable possibilities of the election. Each one I scroll down through shows my name as the winner.

The winner.

My phone buzzes and buzzes and continues to buzz. It's back on and the texts and voicemails are in in full motion, as if a lot of people had attempted to contact me. I can't even hit the phone app to call Ginger due to the flow of messages. I take a deep breath and type Ginger back.

> *Please try and call me right now, I think it might work.*

Her smiley face pic blinks on my phone screen, and I slide the green banner and answer.

"Tell me it's real."

Ginger lets out a scream. "Yaaaaaaaaas, B, you did it. You literally won your first damn election!"

"How do we know for sure?" I pace in my apartment. Gosh, I wish Schatzi was with me. This is the perfect moment for a run to clear my mind or a snuggle. She has the softest ears. Her head cuddles up beneath mine when I hold her and rub her tummy. I swallow. It's going to be okay.

"Okay, don't with that rigged election bit. You won by a small margin, but it doesn't matter. The only numbers that matter are your voters being more than his. It's simple math. You

222

won. The votes have been counted, and you beat him. Mia. You won."

I scratch my scalp and run my fingers through my hair. Is this true? I glance at my computer and see my name listed as the winner. But what if there is a recount? Technically, the votes haven't been certified yet. This means the current Harris County Elections Clerk has to wave his magic wand over the ballots and say, "Bibidi babidi boo, these are legit." It might be a little bit more professional than that. Either way, we still have to wait for that to happen.

My lips press together, and I let out a deep blow between my teeth. "I can't believe it."

"Believe, Mia. Believe it. Believe in yourself. The constituents of Texas House District 193 do."

My heart flutters. The constituents believed in me. Me. Little old me who came from nothing. Who was in her closet with a bucket of tears two years ago. Little old me who wasn't sure how she was going to pull herself out of despair and sadness. Little old me who had two jobs to try and make ends meet. Little old me in a one-bedroom apartment all alone was able to earn enough votes to take out a two-term Republican in a safe Republican seat for decades. The first woman ever about to be able to hold the seat. My chest tightens, and I let out a slow breath. My dad would be so proud.

The buzz from my phone goes off again. "I have to return some of these calls. I will call you back."

"Sounds good, Representative-Elect Verita"

I shake my head in surprise. "Wow, that does sound good."

"Yes, but not as good as when we drop the 'elect.' Handle your business, I'll be over in a few."

The dial tone sounds in my ear. My phone continues its buzz orchestra, and I decide which texts and calls to respond to.

Trent Christopherson, the Democratic House Caucus Chair, left a voicemail and text. I read his message: *Congratulations, Representative-Elect Verita! Call me as soon as you can. We are having a caucus meeting today in Austin—we need you to be there.*

Wow. This is official. A caucus meeting. I have to go to Austin. Am I supposed to stay over? What should I bring? But more importantly, what is a caucus meeting?

I call Chairman Christopherson. "Hi, Chairman."

"Representative-Elect Verita, congratulations. Or maybe I should call you Landslide Verita." He lets out a hearty chuckle.

I can't help but laugh back. With glee. I am giddy. This is incredible. The sound of his voice makes it all seem truer.

We talk for a few minutes and recount the day. He lays out the necessity of the caucus meeting. We flipped twelve seats, but we are still in the minority party. Though we can still have a say in the Speaker of the House race. There are already six Republicans who have announced for this position. Even though the Republicans have the majority, they have split their votes, which allows us to have a say in the Speaker race, versus if all the Republicans voted together. It's important that we lock arms and vote as a block.

Six of the members who announced their run for Speaker, did so before the general election to get a head start on whipping their votes. A few did not publicly announce but still began their calls. Trades of favors and political coin began before they had even secured their re-election. Technically, no favors can be made in exchange for a vote for a Speaker of the House position. However, if you believe that favors and trades

225

don't happen, then I have some beachfront property to sell you in Arizona.

The reality is that even though only Republicans and one Democrat have filed to be the Speaker of the House, all seven members have been reaching out across the aisle to garner votes. In this position, Republicans do want to obtain Democrats for support, but they can't have too many Democrats on their side, or they will be seen as not a true Republican, or they are going to be more fair to Democrats than their party and its "values." People will call them a "RINO," meaning Republican in Name Only. They will be ostracized as being too friendly with the Democrats. Social media campaigns will be run against them and local talk show and podcast pundits will slander them. It becomes a twisted tightrope dance in the extreme sport of political balance. How much support you pull from Democrats and how much support you can have from your party.

It's also telling how much support you have from the extremists of the Republican House members, especially from the oxy-moron named caucus, the Freedom Caucus. This caucus couldn't be further from the idea of freedom than the thoughts and prayers for mass shootings can actually prevent the next monstrosity.

My phone is going to be filled with messages and phone calls for my vote as well. The unease of the situation flickers in my mind as I realize how many tough decisions I will now have to make, even before I am sworn into office.

The drive to Austin is about two hours. My phone rings on and off with congratulatory messages and what Ginger keeps referring to as "early requests."

I hang up the phone. I can't help but laugh.

"Another one?" Ginger glances at me. Her dark brow is raised.

I nod. "Yes."

"What was it this time? Someone wants a road named after their mom as a gift?" She cackles.

I press my eyes together and shake my head. "Honestly, that is pretty close. This guy wants to know if we can rename one of the buildings on a state school campus."

"Not even sworn in and they are filling up your inbox with this nonsense. Did he upset his mom or something?" Ginger shakes her head.

"No, it's actually for him." I shrug.

"Him? Wow, that's rich. Actually, wait, no, if he were rich, he could just make an endowment to the school and get it." Ginger growls. "Don't tell me he gave to your campaign?"

I purse my lips. "Yes, I think it was like twenty-five dollars or something."

"Twenty-five dollars and he wants a building named after him?" Ginger wails. "These people are unreal. But why does he have your number?"

"I don't know. Seems like a lot of people do." I press my eyes together. It's almost one. I don't want to be late for my first caucus meeting.

Almost as if Ginger and the car can read my thoughts, the pink dome appears over the hill. There it is.

In unison, we say, "Wow."

"Ha, you owe me a Coke. No, wait, make it a glass of wine." Ginger grabs my arm. "You have an office in the Capitol!!!!"

I squeal. I can't help it, this is too much excitement not to squeal.

We rush up the steps and Ginger waits outside of the caucus meeting. Only members are allowed in, not even staff.

All the new members are introduced and given an opportunity to speak. Chairman Christopherson eyes me. I am last.

"And we left the last new representative-elect to be our final speaker. She officially goes by Landslide Verita." He motions for me to join him at the podium. An actual podium that I could grasp onto for life support if need be. Yet, I am not nervous in this room. These are my peers. We were all elected equally, even though I won by the least amount of votes.

Everyone laughs at the introduction as they all know the numbers in my election and the challenge that still exists. Dick Mickelson still hasn't acknowledged his defeat.

"Ha, thank you, Chairman. It's so nice to be in a room with all of you. Some of you I have met on the trail and some I have admired from afar. I appreciate the paths that you helped to forge to make it possible for me to join you here. I look forward to working with you this session and doing everything we can do to make Texas a place for everyone to be safe, successful, and have equal rights."

I tap on my legs as the room claps for me. I am not sure if the applause is out of appreciation for my quasi-speech or that the speeches are now over. Maybe a little of both, leaning more toward the latter. At least that's probably how I would feel if I heard the last of at least fifteen speeches. Some of which were longer than others. But I won't name any names this time.

George approaches me as the run begins to dissipate. "Good job, I'm proud of you. And also, I am thankful that I won't have to see Dick's face on the floor this session. Honestly, there are a lot of Republicans who are thankful for that as well." He taps my shoulder. "Use that to your advantage."

I laugh. "Sure, thank you."

"I'm serious. We are going to check in to our offices and grab an early dinner. You should join us."

"That would be great. Text me the time and place and we'll be there." I glance down. "Is it all right if my best friend joins?"

"Absolutely." He nods and grabs the shoulder of another new member as I leave the room.

Ginger is on the bench outside of the room on her phone. "Yes, she did. I know." Our

229

eyes meet. "Oh, got to go, the representative-elect is ready for me, you know you can't leave them waiting." She laughs and pops out of her seat.

We hug. It's almost as if it's been a month since we have seen each other.

"I still can't believe it," I whisper into her ear.

"It's true." She steps back and squeezes my arm. "Even the *New York Times* has reported it." The sides of her lips pull up into the largest smile I think I have ever seen on her, other than when she got married.

Ginger leans in and gives me another hug. The transference of so much pain and emotions that we have been through together to now have this elated moment of joy is surreal. Will it always be like this, or will I be able to slide into a normalcy of being elected by the people for the people?

Chapter Seventeen
"Familiarity does not exist, just because they know your face."

"Representative-Elect Verita, congratulations." A man in a navy suit nods at me.

"Thank you, good evening." I give a slight wave and immediately my cheeks are warm. I have to work on these impromptu greetings.

We make our way to the car. "That was wild." Ginger starts the car. "I get you being recognized in your district, especially with that last push of mail you were able to get out ... but here ... I mean ... already?" Her eyelashes flutter.

I let my shoulders rise and fall almost like the tide that rolls in with confidence and uncertainty. Much like today. It was filled with so many high moments and then these little ones where I question the reality of the situation.

"I know ... it's weird. But George told me that lobbyists have an app with your picture and bio, they know how to approach you." I rub my lips together. I am going to need to remember this when happy faces come a calling.

"An app?!?" Ginger shakes her head. "Gosh, that seems so wrong but yet also brilliant." She breathes through her teeth.

"Yeah, like you want to hate it but also appreciate the mind fuckery behind it." I laugh and then gulp. "Wait, it's not so great realizing that it's to play me though." I bite the inside of my cheek.

"You'll be okay." Ginger stops the car. "Remember, you have me in your corner and I think there are some other good ones …" She rubs her lips like she wants to say something else.

I nod. The silence is thick. So many more words to share. I take in a deep breath.

"There is so much to do. The caucus said we will have a training for the new members. But I have to start the hunt for all of my staff. I don't even know where to begin. I have to find an office in the district. I have to figure out my work. I have to figure out Schatzi." I sigh.

"Whoa, slow down, Rep. There is time, and you have people that can help you with that. Remember all the volunteers you had on your team? Remember the members that have reached out?"

I nod.

"Right, you are not alone. It's going to be okay." She reaches for her purse in the backseat. "Here, pull out my notepad and a pen. Let's make a list."

I can't help but grin. Typical Ginger, with her lists and priorities. She always knows how to get things done.

"Okay, first I should get a Chief of Staff, except I can't pay them as a Chief until I am sworn into office. Can you believe that?" I shake my head.

"That's wild but also not totally abnormal. Since, technically, you are not in office until then, right?"

"Yeah, but I have to get them to help me before I am sworn in and I have to pay them."

"And that's what the campaign funds are for … which adds to your list you need to have another fundraiser in Austin. I was talking to some of the staffers about it while you were in your meeting."

I jot down hire a Chief of Staff, schedule fundraisers, and all the other items I need to do. I still feel like there is not enough time to do all of it. But this is what I signed up for, that and the thick skin. I roll my eyes.

I glance at the time on her car as we pull in through the gates of my apartment. It's past nine. I have kept her all day. I have to be a good friend to her at this moment.

"Thank you for everything. I know you need to get home to Greg." My heart warms and yet a bit of sadness pulls at the tapers of the bottom of it. Yet, this is the right thing to do.

Ginger nods and leans in for a hug. How many hugs have we had today? If hugs counted toward my steps, I bet I would have run through at least three hundred today.

Once inside, I lock my door and slide up against it. I glance at my texts.

One of the texts I had yet to open was from Maxwell. I was afraid to open it earlier, and now I might need a little liquid courage. I pour myself a glass of wine from a gift I picked up in Austin. One of the perks of being elected is lots of gifts.

The message pops up on my screen. *Congratulations, Mia ... I apologize ... Congratulations, Representative-Elect, let me know if you need any help with the transition et al. —Maxwell*

I let out a deep breath as I read it again. Is it too late to type back? It's only 9:15. I probably wouldn't type a professional colleague past nine. But today is a different day. I haven't even made it through all of the text messages and voicemails. I read his message again.

It's a nice message, but at what level? Is his offer merely on a professional level? Does he qualify as only a professional colleague? I still haven't thanked him for the large last-minute donation from his organization. Of course, I mailed a thank you to the group. But he deserves something more than a handwritten note. Like a high-five or something. I laugh. My level of giddiness has not calmed down since the caucus meeting. I glance at his message again.

Is it possible that he could be a decent person but just paired up with a bad client? I don't know. The last thing I want to think about right now is "*Satan.*" I don't even care if he knows that

I won. Of course, he probably does. He probably worked the polls himself with more vengeful lies in an attempt to turn any swayable voters. I shake my head. *Move on, Mia.*

I pick my phone back up and type: *I apologize for the delayed response ... today was a bit hectic, but I would be interested in finishing up our convo from the other night ... I might even consider giving you a few extra words.* Should I add a wink or "Haha"? Nah. I hit send as is. It's time to be me, as I am.

The text bubble flashes with three little circles.

I didn't realize you still talked to us little people.

I laugh. *Well, I would prefer to talk in person to people ... you in general. But I know it's late.* I am rather bold with this election win.

Are you still in Texas?

I squint my eyes. *Of course.*

Well, then you're never too far away.

Hmm. I wonder, though, and type back. *What if I was in Austin?*

It's only a couple of hours, are you there right now?

I smile. Austin. *No.*

Are you at your home?

Yes, if you want to call it that. I glance around my small abode.

I do, see you in ten.

Chapter Eighteen
"Castling does not involve the queen."

New-found truth: lobby-gifted wine tastes divine. I am too amped up to lay my head on my pillow. Jose was one of the messages that I did respond to this morning. He assured me that we would discuss work options tomorrow. I, in turn, assured him I would be back at work on Thursday as well. Despite the win, I need this job to have a livable income. Yes, there is a per diem while in session. But that does not cover much, let alone your life still exists outside of Austin. Granted, I only have an apartment, but I have to still account for it and my other expenses.

My gosh, I am going to have to figure out my custody schedule for Schatzi. Maxwell has never been inside my tiny apartment. I tap the sides of my legs and begin to pace. The place seems semi-okay. No clothes out. No dishes in the sink. I grab another wine glass from the cupboard. It is not a big leap of assumptions to think that Maxwell will want to have a glass of wine with me. Granted, he had brought over a bottle the other night, when he left it on my doorstep.

Is it bad that I am having "*Satan*'s" lawyer over? Arg. I bite my lip. I am going to hope for the best, in that he is hopefully a nice person. I don't want to go out nor do I have anyone to really go out and see. It's a Wednesday night. The idea of a good conversation is what I need right now. This is okay. Nothing wrong. I am an adult. He is an adult. Just two adults going to talk about the biggest upset in this election cycle. My race! The numbers have registered but still seems like a possible dream that I have overextended.

The knock from the door interrupts one more round of self-doubt. I peek through the hole in the door. Maxwell is dressed in a pressed suit. Does he ever wear casual clothes? I open the door.

"Hi there." My face is flushed. The warmth in my cheeks is a dead giveaway.

Be chill, Mia. This is no big deal.

"Congratulations!" Maxwell opens his arms. "Is it all right if I give the representative-elect a congratulatory hug?"

I laugh. "Yes, of course." Of course? Who am I? I don't know in this moment. And his arms are around me. He is so much taller, and I am enclosed in his warmth. I'm in a warm forest filled with coffee and, what is that, cardamom, like a spicy tea? Mmm.

I sniff and take a step back.

Pull yourself together, Mia.

"Can I offer you a glass of wine?" I make my way toward the kitchen, which is about five steps from the front door.

"Please. Here, I got this for you. We don't have to drink it, it's just for you." He hands me a chilled bottle of Perrier Jouet Champagne.

"Oh, wow. Um, would you prefer champagne over a cabernet?" I glance at him. His chilled bottle screams, "Open me now, you didn't get to celebrate with bubbles on election night. Now is your time."

"It's purely up to you, Representative-Elect Verita."

I laugh. "That's a mouthful. I bet you are looking forward to dropping the 'elect' part."

"Indeed. So, champagne then?" He peels back the gold foil.

"If you insist." I pull out my two champagne flutes, the only two I have. I found them on sale at a Thrift Store. I paid $2.50 for both. I think the glasses are real crystal.

"Nice." He nods at the flutes and pops open the champagne without the cork being soared into the ceiling. I need to learn that trick.

The flutes are filled with a light shade of a diamond-like sparkle. The bubbles are like whipped cream on top of this presentation.

"To winning your first election. Congratulations."

We clink glasses. The bubbles circle my tongue like a fruit basket filled with grapefruit, green pears, apples, and what is that, vanilla?

"By the way." I take another sip. "I didn't get to properly thank you. The donation from TLA Pac really helped us get the vote out. You claim this win as much as the rest of us." I tap my glass against his.

His eyes sparkle a darker blue. His gaze meets mine, and I glance back at my glass.

"Yes, of course. But, Mia, this race was all you. Your story. Your hard work. Your persistence. I can't wait to see what you do in Austin." He lifts his glass and takes a sip.

I nod. "Thank you, I appreciate that, but this race was won by the people, for the people."

Maxwell laughs. "Not even twenty-four hours since being elected and you already sound like the perfect politician." He laughs again. "If that can even exist."

I swat his arm. "Hey."

"I'm sorry, I am only kidding." Maxwell lifts his glance again. "Or am I?"

"You better be. And please don't make me doubt you." My eyes meet the floor. Maybe this was a bad idea. Maybe I messed up again and misread the room and a person's intention.

"Hey." Maxwell lifts my chin. "I'm sorry. I won't make you doubt me. I should have been more sensitive."

I rub my lips together, but I am not sure.

"Oh, did Alex fill you in on the fifty-two bad reasons press conference?"

I pull back. "How did you know about that? Did you go?"

"Not exactly, you know Holly is still in my law firm for the moment. Anyway, someone from our office alerted me to it. Apparently, PETA was alerted to it as well." He takes a sip from his flute. "As it seems, as soon as Holly began to speak, PETA rushed the stage with their signs and completely drowned out Holly. It was a funny sight to see. The news did a highlight reel on it."

I rub my eyebrow. "Who would have thought PETA was like my guardian angel? Well, I mean, I guess it's really Schatzi." I wish she were here right now. I glance up at Maxwell. We both know why she isn't and it has to do with him. Regardless of how you cut it—and I am cut, the wound might not be bleeding out, but it is not entirely sealed. How could it be? Schatzi was mine. I still have to share her with "*Satan*." I swallow as if I could make all the bad memories disappear into a void of empty air.

"By the way, since you are now elected, we can file a Stay on the custody suit."

My eyes squint. "What do you mean a Stay?"

"Among other things that you get to benefit from as a legislator, any lawsuits against you are put on a Stay until after the session. If you were a lawyer, you could also Stay any of your cases. Meaning, nothing can happen. They just sit in the atmosphere until the session is over." Maxwell pours more of the champagne into each of our glasses.

"That's a long time. Maybe he will move on?" I take a sip of my glass and almost spit it out as I try to hold back laughter.

"Yeah, I wouldn't suspect it. And not to bring any more of a downer into the situation, but he might have even more help this round, or did when he came after you for the second time." Maxwell hands me a towel from the counter.

"Help from who? Isn't his evil treachery enough?" I shiver.

"One would think, but, unfortunately, to balance out some of the benefits of being elected, you are also now a prime target for the opposition. They are going to look for any way to make your life more difficult." He runs his large fingers through his dark brown hair (one might call it chestnut).

"More difficult?" Apparently, this guy still doesn't know how much trauma his client put me through.

"I'm sure people warned you about how difficult politics can be before you decided to run?" His eyebrows raise.

"Yeah, there were the standard comments about 'I hope you have thick skin' and 'politics is dirty,' etc." I take a long swallow from my flute. I had thought about these things. But I

243

also didn't really consider them a threat, as I knew the possibility that I would win was low. My focus had never been on what happened after I won. It was more of how to get to the finish line and work as hard as I could to secure the win. Plan for the aftermath afterward.

"Well, I am a bit of a novice myself about politics, but I know things are going to get more difficult. I can only imagine the target they have put on your back. You took out a safe seat. They will be doing everything they can to take it back." Maxwell puts his hand on my arm and lightly rubs it. "I'm sorry, I am not trying to upset you. I guess I, uh, just started to think about the reality of it myself."

"Right, it's fine. It will be fine. I think I have already gone through hell and back, and here I sit in my living room with '*Satan*'s' assistant." I raise my glass. "Either I am a pure idiot, or maybe I am stronger than we both realize." I laugh and let the cool liquid settle on my tongue. The bottle has maybe two more pours in it.

Maxwell has his eyes on me. They are clearer than when he arrived like a moment of boldness has begun to dissipate. His brow is furrowed. He nods. "We both know it's the latter."

My lungs fill with air as the words form in my mind. I have to talk to him. And how I feel about Maxwell and the concept of anything more than whatever it has been up to this point.

"Speaking of strength … it's taken a lot for me to be around you."

Maxwell pulls back and the right side of his mouth forms into a smirk.

I shake my head. "No, not like that."

His shoulders slightly sink.

"I mean … I appreciate all the help you gave to the campaign and the whole jail situation … but it's difficult for me to see you outside of the courtroom situation with "*Satan*.""

"*Satan*?"

I press my eyelids shut. "Sorry, with my ex-husband, your client, Mike DaVile. Um … that was really traumatic for me, and I know I did not win in any matter in the court system or with my arrangement with Schatzi."

Maxwell nods. "Yes, that was definitely not in your favor. And I understand your hesitation to not want to be around me." He rubs the bottom of his chin. "I can't change the past. I can only focus on the now. I wish I had stronger words for this moment. Perhaps, actions will speak louder and help change the way you feel. Time will only tell. Unless you feel differently?"

"I'm not sure." I pour the last of the bottle into our flutes. "Thank you for the champagne and conversation." I swallow back the rest of the remnants in my glass. "I have to be at work at my regular time tomorrow."

Maxwell swallows the last of his champagne and walks toward the door. "Regular, now that is funny." He opens the door. "Mia, nothing in your life is ever going to be regular again." He raises a finger and then drops it back at his side. "Have a good evening."

What was that about? I shiver as I close the door. Never going to be regular again. I guess. But then again, when was my life ever regular? What was regular about my quasi-marriage? What was regular about the joint custody of my dog? What was regular about winning my first election?

Nothing. Nothing has ever been regular about me. Some things have not been great. Especially the non-regular aspect of things. But maybe not all the non-regular things are bad. Maybe that's not so bad. Maybe things not ever being regular is just how things are supposed to be for me. Or maybe not being regular is my regular.

I put the glasses in the sink. Once again, I wish Schatzi were with me. I know she would look up at me with her big brown eyes that are topped with caramel-colored eyebrows. She has this look that she gives me that puts me at ease. Like she gets me. Better than I get myself that's for sure. Today is one for the books, but tonight is a riddle that I still need to solve.

Chapter Nineteen
"A queen knows her worth."

Several bouquets and balloons are scattered over my desk. My face warms. A tingle sweeps over the back of my neck. Why am I embarrassed about this outpour of support and congratulatory messages? One of the notecards pops up from cornflowers and Mexican bush sage. This person truly got the Texan flower in-season assignment. I grab the card, wow. It's from the president at my alma mater.

"Congratulations, Representative-Elect Verita! We are so proud of you. Thank you for making a great representation of St. Edward's University."

My eyes fill with a watery substance that is obviously not salty at all. Nope, not me. I blink to clear them. That's right—clear eyes, full heart, and I didn't lose! I laugh.

"Something funny?"

I jump.

"Oh, sorry, didn't mean to startle you." Jose raises a cup that reads *Vote, Your Life Depends on It.*

I laugh. "No, you didn't, it's cool. I was surprised to receive congratulations from the president of my alma mater."

"I don't know a lot about politics, but I can say with full confidence that anyone who

247

knows you even a little bit is going to be coming out of the woodwork to congratulate you, and then they are going to come and ask for favors."

My head nods in motion, and the realization of this makes me a little sad. The reality of being in a position of power and that people would seek you out, not because of a desire to have a real friendship or relationship but rather to have you as a token of power in their black book of numbers.

I sigh. It is what it is. I know I signed up for all of it when I put my name on the line. It doesn't matter about the behavior of others. This is not why I got in the race.

"Well, don't worry about us here at X. We will not be asking for favors, but we do need to discuss how the next six months or so will go. I know the legislature is in session from January to May. Are you wanting to take a leave of absence?" His brown eyes peer into mine as if he can read my inner thoughts. If that were the case, he would see a frenzy of little messages with exclamations.

I let out a laugh that can only be described as uncomfortable. "Well, I can't actually take a leave of absence … and, honestly, I wouldn't want to. I really like working here, and to be frank … I need the income. I was hoping I could work remotely during the session and anything that couldn't be handled remotely, I could attend to on the weekends?" It's my turn to read his eyes and facial expressions. Is Jose going to be okay with a remote employee even though this position was not ever described as remote? There are too many companies that still are bothered with the idea of remote work, even though, technically, it is entirely feasible.

Jose cocks his head to the side and then to the other, almost like when Schatzi is not sure if she is okay with what I am saying.

Before Jose can say anything, Mallory walks in and screeches. "Mia! Congratulations! Can I hug you?" Her arms are wide open, and then she drops them to her sides. "Wait, I'm sorry, Representative-Elect … would you be okay with a congratulatory hug? If not, no big deal." Her blue eyes are sparkling. This is definitely someone genuinely happy about the news.

"Ha, of course. Thank you." Our arms embrace, and it is such a nice, warm hug. I needed a hug this morning. That is something about waking up alone that is not the best. No one to hug. No one to wish you good morning. At least on the mornings that I have Schatzi I can hug her and talk to her. She enjoys my morning banter and my rush to get out the door. I can't help but smile. My mouth is going to need some serious moisturizer from this level of chagrin.

"We are so proud of you," Mallory states as she pulls back with two firm grips on the sides of my arms. She glances at Jose. "What are we going to do without her? Can't we figure something out?"

Jose laughs. "Mia is two steps ahead of us. She wants to work remotely."

"Yes!" Marjorie pulls back and high-fives Jose. "Wait, will that be too much for you though?"

I shake my head. "No, definitely not. I normally don't like to brag about my capabilities, but I think this situation is just. When I was finishing my degree, I was working full-time and I had to take care of my ex-brother-in-law's newborn. It's a long story. But the Cliff Notes version is that I was able to juggle all of it and still graduate Summa Cum Laude." I cringe internally. Why did I share that? *I don't want to brag—BS ... Arg.* I should have kept my mouth shut. I could have just said, "Hey I will be able to handle this because of a variety of reasons," but, no, Mia and her lack of filter. Ginger would be disappointed.

"Wow, well, we knew you were something special when we interviewed you. Then the election ... this ... I am on board for it. How about you, Jose?" Her attention leaves my face and moves to Jose. He takes a sip from his mug.

"No te canse' ahora ..." He raises his mug and makes eye contact with me. "Que esto solo empieza."

"Jose, I do appreciate your Spanish, and without translation, I am going to take that as a yes. Let's meet later today to work out the logistics." Mallory squeezes my shoulder and leaves my office.

I nod at Marjorie while I silently die inside. It's almost as if I can see the ashes of my

250

remains being swept off into the wind. If I hadn't listened to the song on repeat and didn't know each and every lyric by heart, I most likely would not have picked up on what Jose said. His Spanish is much better than mine. He is clearly a native speaker, and the exact lyrics that he chose couldn't have been better except for the fact that I have no other reason to believe that he chose them because he did see my Danza Kuduro dance. The dance of shame and horror was what one could describe as at least PG-13 and ended in a Rated R for blood and a hospital. Good lord. Catch me before I fall into a faint of humility.

My fingers move repetitively along the sides of my legs. The fabric of my dress is soft. I take comfort in it, and I barely let my eyes meet Jose's. They are full and bright with a hint of mischief. Yup. He saw.

"Congratulations, again." Jose taps the desk and walks out.

I slump down into my desk chair. Thank goodness my face of red is covered by the wall of bouquets. Is it too late to crawl into a cave, or is my newly elected status against this conjecture?

My destination of cave life is interrupted by the buzz of my phone. I am not sure if I even want to answer it. Cave life has its appeal. But then again, I didn't knock on over ten thousand doors to ignore my constituents or colleagues. Ginger's pic is on my phone as it rattles from side to side.

"Mia's Cave—how can I help you?"

"What?! Cave? You've only been elected for a little over twenty-four hours, how can you already be in a cave?" Ginger lets out a hard laugh. It is not the normal laugh, it is forced. She must think something politically motivated has already happened to hurt me when in reality it was me. I hurt myself with my stupidity. I sigh and glance at the clock. It's 11:30.

"Is there any way you can meet for lunch today?" I hate to ask for yet another lunch date this week, but I really need to discuss this in person.

"For my state representative 'elect' for the next thirty-plus days? Absolutely. It's Wednesday, how about Aka Sushi at 12:15?" There is a *tick, tick* on the phone, which means Ginger is most likely in the process of securing a reservation for us.

"Sushi for the win. I'll see you there." I put my finger over the red and let it make a touchdown. Can I wait to discuss this until then?

My phone buzzes again, and it is as if the universe has decided to keep my mind busy. The number is not one logged in my phone, but given the amount of calls I have had over the last two days, I have been answering them blind.

"Hello?"

"Representative-Elect Verita?" A cheery voice like a car salesman asks.

"Yes."

"This is Representative Mark Jones. Our districts share borders."

"Yes, indeed." I force myself to sound happy. I know who this is now. We share borders, but he is not exactly a kind person in regard to the votes he has taken. Not as bad as the guy I beat, but quite close.

"We are hosting a fundraiser for Speaker-Elect Don Balles. The entire Harris County congregation is going to be listed as sponsors for the invitation, and I need to know if you will be a host as well?"

Speaker-Elect? I know this guy has been able to round up the votes, but he is not the speaker until we take the vote, which happens to be the first vote, once we are officially sworn into office, into our position. But the entire Harris County delegation? That's interesting, given the delegation has more Democrats than Republicans. But further, why is he calling me, a Democrat? So many questions.

"By sponsor, do you mean to donate to the fundraiser?" I do my best to hold back any laughter because if the answer is yes, it's an automatic no for me. I have zero dollars to give, let alone even if I did, I would not be sending them to a Republican. Talk about a Dino. (Democrat in name only.)

Mark laughs. "No, sponsor with your name. Your name now holds more value than your actual money." He laughs again.

My shoulders tense. I get his sentiment, but it is so wrong in so many different ways.

"Right, well, I will get back to you later today about this if that's okay?" I bite my tongue from any offers of why I need the time. Because he doesn't need to know my whys. Those are internal reasons that do not need to be given. *No* is a full sentence, and I am not ready to give any answer right now.

"Yes, that's good. We print the invites tomorrow. You are going to want to have your name on the list. Speaker Balles takes these things personally, as most would."

I let out a small, polite laugh. "Good to know. I will talk to you later today." I let the phone hang up without any more of a long drawn-out goodbye.

There should be a book about politicking that has nothing to do with getting elected but rather staying elected, and the ins and outs of how to deal with situations such as these. I know that my county is very much against Speaker Balles. He has made numerous racist and sexist statements over the years. My name on his fundraiser will definitely cause issues. But if I don't put my name on the list, that will cause issues for all of my bills and my reason for the hard work of being there in the first place.

This is a moment when I wish I had done more research on the inner workings of politics instead of just policy and how it affects the everyday person. For the past several years I combed through various legislation and the aftermath of it. This caused me to want to run. But the actual politicking of it ... I was clueless. However, thankfully, the Democratic caucus had assigned everyone a mentor and mine was pure gold. I scroll through my favorites on my screen and hit the newest addition to the list.

"Hi, George, I have a quick question."

"I'm all ears."

"Are you going to have your name on the fundraiser for Speaker-Elect Balles?"

"Yes, but you don't have to."

"Representative Jones said that the entire Harris County delegation is going to have their names on the list." I glance at the clock on my computer. I need to wrap this up.

"That's correct. But if you are on the list, the activists will be upset. Just keep that in mind. It's your decision." He clicks his mouth.

"What would you do?" I need real guidance here. This seems like a bad spot to end up with my party or with being able to get things done.

"Given it's Speaker Balles we're talking about, I would have my name on the list. He holds grudges, and he is more than petty."

"Good to know. Thank you." Such a quality leader. I can look forward to being able to work with, if that's even possible, given the numbers of our party. I sigh.

"Anytime, talk to you later." The phone's dial tone rings in my ear and it's a reminder of a dead zone. One I am about to enter with another decision that will not put me in a good spot no matter what I do.

Arg. I haven't even been sworn in yet and I am overwhelmed with my name being on an invitation. An invitation, a few words, my name, how bad could it be? I grimace.

My purse is on my shoulder as I lean to lock my computer. A pop-up message bings.

Don't forget we have an all-hands-on-deck meeting at 1:30! It's Jennifer. I'm surprised she hasn't come by my office. It was pretty regular for her to swing by on her way to get coffee.

Thanks, see you there. I send my message and a bright yellow envelope beams at me from a bouquet of lavender flowers. The message is written in bright, big, bubbly pink ink.

Mia! Congratulations. I am so proud of you and happy for our state. You will be incredible. Let me know if I can help in any way here at work or elsewhere. —Jennifer

Oh my gosh, here I am with a mini-pity party about no congratulations and Jennifer delivered a bouquet of deliciously scented flowers and a sweet message. And despite my lack of appreciation, she still cared enough to remind me about the meeting. I need to get it together. I haven't opened all the cards on my desk. I am going to have to schedule these things. If I had staff, they could assist with this. However, I need to figure out who will be on my staff. For the capitol and my district office.

Focus, Mia.

I need some help. If I start to let things slip between the cracks, people are going to be upset, and that is one thing I can do my best to prevent.

If that is possible.

There is a tiny prickle that runs over my hairline, and I am aware of the reality of the idea that not everyone will be happy with me. To be a people pleaser in the world of politics is completely impossible. With a background of an abusive relationship and always trying to second guess the next problem to avoid a fight. To achieve the goal of wherever the new posts had been placed makes it really difficult to sit in the notion that fake situations of one person cannot be compared to the real situations of groups of people. The reality is that in this system, you will never be able to make everyone happy. Even though I really don't like this concept, it's too painfully true. Laws affect people's lives. There is legislation that can help people, and there is legislation that can really hurt people. The latter is the one that hits hard.

Politics is a tough road. So many people said to me, "*You better have tough skin.*" This is the concept of being able to take criticism. Which can be difficult. Yet, I think it is more important to be able to compartmentalize and realize that you will make hard choices and sometimes those decisions will come back to haunt you, whether it's in your sleep or the light of day.

I text Representative Jones: *Yes, you can add my name to the hosting committee.*

Chapter Twenty
"The prick of time continues to trickle in."

Ginger is already at the booth with a glass of wine and some edamame. She must not be on-call. I wave as I make my way through the restaurant.

"Hello, Representative-Elect Verita." An elderly man raises his glass to me as I walk by.

"Hello." I make a small wave and pass quickly.

Is this my new normal? Being recognized in public? Am I ready for this?

I lean in and give a hug to Ginger.

"Oh, wow. Did I just get an intense hug from my state representative?" She wiggles her shoulders and winks at me. Her energy is contagious.

"Indeed. Are you not on-call?"

"Don't worry, Representative, I would never." She lifts her glass and takes a sip. "It's my off week. I took the week off." She takes another sip as if she intentionally cut herself off.

I nod. She didn't think I was going to win, so she took off the whole week to take care of me. If that isn't true friendship I don't know what is, and I am also a little sad that she thought I would lose. But then again, no one really thought I would win, so she was with the majority of her speculation.

"Hey, I took the week off regardless. Either way, I knew this week would be a lot, and I wanted to be there for you." She takes a sip of the clear liquid. It's pure and clean like her intentions. "Besides, I have so much vacation, it only made sense." A small laugh releases from her mouth.

I shake my head. "You are too much." A glass of prosecco is placed in front of me. "Oh, I don't know if I should have any." I glance at Ginger, and then at the waiter, who has already left.

"Mia, one glass is okay. Besides, we haven't had a chance to really celebrate. I mean, this is not the real celebration. But, seriously, a baby glass of bubbles, it's nothing."

I take a sip and out of the corner of my eye, the elderly man nods at me. I put the glass down. "I don't know. Don't look, but the guy over there knew my name. I don't want to have any issues."

Ginger laughs. But this time it is a real laugh. Her normal laugh, not the hard or small ones she has given the last few days. "Mia, if you didn't think you were going to have issues or be recognized, then running for office was a bad idea." She laughs again. Almost like she has held in this level of laughter and reality that has collectively been kept tight inside.

The sides of my mouth pull up into a grin because who can't smile at someone who is almost hysterically in tears for nothing?

I nod. "Okay, are you all right?"

Ginger nods and then shakes her head. "No. I think I am still in shock and awe for you. But, seriously, the prosecco is fine. What is the drama that you needed to tell me about?" Her pensive glare is back. She has returned to her problem-solution-centered gaze.

My eyes roll back inside my lids, as I too am back in the realism of my world. I press my lips together and let out a deep sigh. "Remember the interview I had with my company that ended not so great?"

"Um, I would say it ended incredibly— hello, you got the job." Ginger laughs.

"Right, that part was good, but remember the part where I ended up in the hospital?" I raise my eyebrows.

"Of course, I am reminded of that one a lot."

I swallow. "I'm—"

"Don't say it. I didn't mean about that bill. I mean just the whole event."

I take in a deep breath. "Okay, but the part about the dance, remember that?"

Ginger's eyes are wider than I have ever seen. "No."

I nod.

"No." Ginger shakes her head like she is a contestant in a contest of head nodding. The motion does not stop. I shudder. This is as bad as I had imagined. Ginger is not able to hide her shock with the shakes and overuse of the word *no* in response to my continual admittance.

Seconds, maybe minutes have gone by for far too long with the repeated question answer of *no* and my response of *yes* and the shake of her head. I am dizzy and my head is not the one in this repetitive motion.

"How do you know?"

I let my eyes meet the floor. The table has a white cloth. Can I fit under it? I glance around the restaurant and the elderly man has his eyes on me again. Or have they ever left? That answers my question about the utilization of the table for a quick exit of my demise. I most assuredly cannot do that in front of this stranger who knows my name and who I am. Is that even a thing? It doesn't matter.

"Jose said some of the words from the song to me today."

"What? What does that mean?" Ginger's eyes are scrunched up, and if it weren't for her perfect non-wrinkled skin, I am sure I would be able to read her future on her forehead.

"He responded to a question by speaking a verse from the song that I was dancing to." I let my head drop forward.

"Hmm … I don't know. What was the lyric?" Mia gets out her phone. Her fingers are in motion as she searches for the translation of the song. I know she knows it, but Spanish is not her strong point.

Tingles run along my scalp in their private anxiety-filled dance, courtesy of this situation. "He said 'No te canse' ahora' … then he

261

raised his mug at me and said 'Que esto solo empieza.'"

Ginger is like a mad hatter as she punches into her phone. "Hold on, say it again but slower." Her focus is only on her phone.

"Ginger, it means 'don't get tired now,' and the second part he said was 'this is just the beginning.'" I flutter my eyelashes. The reality of the words and how he said them could not have been a coincidence.

"Woah. Okay … that is a lot to unravel." Ginger glances back at her phone. "I don't think we have enough time right now for this. How about after work?"

It's my turn to check the time. She is correct. I need to get back to the office. Regardless of the embarrassment. "Okay, are you sure you can meet after work? It's been a lot lately. Is Greg okay with it?"

Ginger laughs. "Please, he is thrilled for you, and he understands that we are going to need to make up for all the time we are going to miss when the Session begins." Her lips form a full pout.

My chest tightens. I know this is real, but all these little things that I didn't spend any of my focus on keep being brought up. The idea of not being able to see Ginger regularly for five months will be hard.

I nod.

"Hey, it's going to be okay. Austin is not that far. Just a quickie flight or road trip." Ginger squeezes my hand. "Come on, let's get you back to your current office, and we can figure out a plan after five for how to move forward."

"Thank you."

Ginger shakes her head. "I am going to petition one of the other representatives to file a bill to make you limit the amount of thank yous to   me."

It's my turn to laugh. "Not a chance!"

I make my way to my car and stop as I reach the lot. There sits my car in the spot where I left it, but not in the same condition. This must be a joke. Not again. I check out the front wheel. There it is, bright as day. A shiny nail embedded into the black thick tire. I literally just got a new tire a couple of months ago. This can't be a coincidence. I think I have had up to twelve nails in the last two years. I know the roads here are not great, but this has to be some sort of record. Ginger's car pulls up behind me. She unrolls the window from the passenger side.

"Everything all right?"

"Not exactly. I have another nail in my tire. It's flat." I glance at my phone. I really need to get back to work. "Is there any way you can drop me off and I can handle this after work?"

"Get in. Oh, wait, take a pic of the tire, and let's see if there are any video cameras with a view of your car. Maybe we can catch the culprit in action this time!" Ginger scans the building.

"There is one! We might have lucked out finally!"

263

I laugh. "I doubt it. It was probably put in by my office. Oh, wait, there is a camera there as well."

"I will contact the restaurant after I drop you off, and see if I can view the video."

Ginger maneuvers the car out of the lot and onto the main throughway.

"I just don't understand if it is him, why he can't just leave me alone." I shake my head.

"You know why." Ginger pulls into the lot of my work. "Narcissistic injury."

Chapter Twenty-One
*"A piece can't play both sides of the
board."*

The hits keep on. Smack. Hit. Pounce.
Every which way I turn there is some new person
that has popped up on social media to announce
how much they don't like me, and my ideas, and
to proclaim what a bad job I am doing. Even
though I haven't even been sworn into office yet.

The most recent is from a selected group
of activists. As stated, they were not happy about
my name being listed on the Speaker Fundraiser
invitation. There were talks of betrayal and
statements of desire to primary me. Threats of me
being primaried by another Democrat in the next
election. But they didn't care; they saw it as an
incredible offense. Like I had committed political
suicide. And people wonder out loud why we
don't have more "normal" folks who run for
office. We know that the other side is going to
attack, but your team attacks too. They are
relentless. We had someone post a picture of
themselves at a costume party, where they chose
to wear a petticoat. The activists showed up at her
house with signs and bullhorns. For what they
considered a fashionable offense. Cut against the
grain and focus on the cause, regardless of your
attire. The politicking of it all. Have thick skin.
My lips press together, as I can see a seal of my

fate: to be silent or to move forward—a constant theme going forward.

Clothes are funny in politics. Men are supposed to wear a button-down shirt, slacks, and maybe, sometimes, depending on the party, a full-on suit. Whereas women are critiqued on the cost of the attire to the appropriateness of it. After I won, I was counseled by some women-led groups that insisted that I invest in some scarves to wear on the House Floor. Scarves? What? No. I was not going to wear scarves, I was not accessorizing for a winter photo scene. Granted, I do believe there should be a certain level of decorum for the House Floor, like not flip-flops. Open-toed heels, okay that's fine, but flip-flops? We should show the House Floor a bit more respect.

When I finally hired my chief of staff, he had his opinions about my attire as well and questioned if I owned any pantsuits. I couldn't help but laugh and remind him I was not going to wear a political power suit from the '90s to prove my prowess. I could do it in a dress just fine.

Chief of staff almost seems like a misnomer, as they are constantly in motion to halt their elected boss from everything and anything that they think might put the office at risk. Kevin has been a constant red stop sign that blares at me on the daily, more like hourly, I might even say by the minute. I get it. I only won by a handful of votes, and we don't want to upset any of them. Like the list that continues to grow of my fanbase of disappointment for the position that has not even begun yet. Technically, my chief cannot officially begin working as my COS until I am sworn into office. That's the way the state of Texas works. No one gets to work until we have been sworn in. Of course, the reality is that all the representatives who are not freshman can begin to file bills before we are sworn in, since their previous term is not up. Along with their staff.

The incoming class has to decide how to handle so many disadvantages before our hands are even raised in the air to take our oath. I reached out to my mentor, who advised that I should make the hire immediately for my COS since good COSs go fast. But I would need to supplement his salary with my campaign account funds. Which I had a good laugh about. What campaign money? This is when I was introduced for a second discussion with FTM and how he handled business and issues where problems needed solutions.

The three letters were right there. I am not sure why I was hesitant to hit the call button. I won and with his help. This should be easy. But I was also advised to be careful around FTM. By various people.

"He holds a grudge," one member mentioned.

"He can be petty," another one spoke up. We were at a small dinner after the election.

"Never cross him," was the big one.

Though I had no intention of doing any of those things, the idea of the necessity to tiptoe over shattered glass when around FTM was a bit of a concern. This was not a conversation I was

267

excited about. My vitamin B dropper was in my hand regardless. I suctioned two healthy droppers full of the red liquid and let it settle into a puddle under my tongue. I counted out the thirty seconds before I let it run down the back of my throat. Yuck. Not the best taste. Was it helpful? Maybe? I was able to go forward and my anxiety was a little less on the fringe of frantic. I was calm. Not smooth but calm.

"Hello, Representative Morales This is Mia Verita."

"Mia, how is my favorite bet this cycle?" FTM laughs with a deep baritone.

"Oh, that's nice to hear. Thank you. I was hoping you might be able to offer some advice?" I did my best to make my voice sound as smooth and confident as his. Maybe if I had been in the political game as long as he has I would be. Or maybe he was just born with confidence. That is definitely the energy he emotes.

"Always. This is about campaign funds, yes?" FTM clicked his tongue.

My eyes squinted. Who could have told him? Or maybe he is the one we all go to for this type of advice. He has a history of offers that donors and allies have been unable to refuse. He had decided to run for another elected position and had to give up his seat. When his campaign did not end with success, he decided he wanted his old seat back. Rumor is, that FTM asked for assistance from political allies who had supported him in the past, but they refused. Their reasoning was not to support a challenger to a representative that was doing a good job. FTM did not take the no well. He went on to win his seat back on his own. Then he made calls to remind the allies of the lack of support he received. A promise was made along the lines of "If these allies wanted to see any of their bills for that upcoming session make it out of, Committees or pass on the House Floor, they would need to make reparations for the decline of support to FTM in his election." Rumor has it that all allies had to donate more than double to his campaign before the session began. That's the kicker—you can only raise money when not in session. We had a limited amount of time to raise money from November to January. Why do we need to raise money? You have to be able to support yourself in Austin outside of the measly per diem and state pay. Most people who run for office are independently wealthy or have a spouse to support them. Whereas I had neither.

Further, how was I going to pay for Kevin's salary from November to January with the slim pickings of a campaign account that I had left after the election? I had been advised to spend everything I could and leave nothing on the table to win the election.

"Yes, I took it to heart with spending everything I had to win and, well, I did." I let out a heavy sigh.

"Hey." FTM laughs. "We wouldn't be having this conversation if you hadn't. That was a wise move. Now it's time to get the people that didn't make as many wise decisions to come to their senses."

I nod as if what he said is a simple solution that I hadn't thought of. I laugh.

"Right, but how do I do that?" I hope my self-doubt is not too loud on the other end of the phone.

"All right, I'm going to send you some numbers, and I will co-host a fundraiser for you at the Austin Club."

"Oh, wow, thank you. That's really great. What   day?"

"It's got to be next Thursday, after that, I will be out of pocket for the holidays."

"Okay, perfect, great."

"You call and personally invite everyone that I send you. You tell them that FTM asked you to call. Tell them you are calling in some favors. Then you go down Mikelson's campaign finance report and you invite all of them as well. Remember you are in the power seat now, and if they want to talk to you, they need to show you how much they want to support you."

The sides of my mouth raise. The way he magically intertwines words to not say the part that he is really saying out loud is truly a work of art.

Could I be this level of an artist of words to inspire these organizations and donors to kick into my campaign? I had barely raised any money on my own. The major contributions had been from HTLA and that was because of Maxwell.

I eye my phone. We hadn't seen each other since he came over after the election. There had been a few texts here and there and missed phone calls if you want to call them that. I hadn't exactly put forth the effort to pick up when I saw the green circle with his name slide over my screen. It was an unsettled situation. He seemed like a good person, but I am not sure that I can get over the part of him being "*Satan*'s" ex-attorney. It is almost like I have PTSD from that entire court interaction.

My shoulders slump, and I am deflated from the inside. I can sit and wallow or not. I roll my shoulders as my lungs fill with air. I need to use this kick of energy to make the phone calls. Not to Maxwell. He is a situationship that I need to work through a bit more mentally before I can see him again. Now is not the time to take on a mental health Rubik's Cube of questions and feelings that I don't have the time or space for. This possibility of anything will need to be boxed for now. The only box my focus should be on is the bank. I need to fill up my account and figure out how I am going to find my place in Austin.

My phone vibrates in my hand, and I jump. It's my friend Briona. We kept in contact during the election cycle. Her numbers came in first, and I had called her with so much happiness for her. It has been nice to have a friend before my arrival in Austin.

"Representative-Elect, have you found a place yet?"

I laugh. "I'm actually doing call time right now, to be able to get a place. My fundraiser is next week, and I am not sure if I will even have enough people to fill the small room."

"With FTM on the bill? You know those players will roll up with their wallets open."

"I hope, I need to be able to pay for my chief over the holiday."

"I hear you. Same, Representative-Elect, same. You should get a place near me—they have another unit that opened up."

My eyes blink. "Really, that would be so cool to be by you. How much is it?"

"It's a really good deal—I negotiated them down to $4K."

"For the whole session?"

Briona laughs. "Stop it. No, per month—where in Austin are we going to be able to stay for $4K for the whole session?"

"Uh, hopefully somewhere …" Oh my God. I knew Austin prices were high, but $4K a month was nowhere near what I had budgeted for. This fundraiser was going to need to be super successful.

"Hey, listen, if you want it, let me know by next week. They are holding it for me as a favor."

"Okay, will do." Another favor. Maybe it was time to call in the favors.

I worked my way down FTM's list and Mikelson's campaign report. Call time was not my favorite time of the day, but it had to be done. It was almost 8 p.m. Time to call it a day.

I poured myself a glass of wine when a text message popped up on my phone.

I can only imagine how difficult it will be to get in touch with you once you are in office.

Another text popped up with a sad panda emoji. Wow.

I just finished calling 80 million people for my fundraiser next week. Can I put you down for a solid $10K? I let out a little laugh as I hit send.

Seems like a high rate for a text exchange ... Can we lower it to $5K and a dinner?

Hmm. Dinner. I don't know. I literally just did the mental workout of this being put into a box. But I am hungry and so is my campaign bank account. Arg. Decisions under distress should not ever be made. I haven't had anything to eat since breakfast. Almost as if on scripted cue, my stomach growls. You have got to be kidding me. Even my body is in betrayal over my thought-out decisions to wait and process.

I'll up the ante and bring you dinner if you don't want to go out.

Oh my gosh ... this guy. I glance down at my outfit. I am in my yoga pants and campaign shirt as if I have been out canvassing all day, which, theoretically, I have been in pursuit of donors, which can be compared to the procurement of voters. Regardless if we go out or stay in, I am going to have to change.

Okay, we can have dinner. But I need to get out of my apartment. I feel like a prisoner from being trapped here all day.

I'll see you in fifteen.

I need to figure out where he lives or if he is an extremely fast driver. Fifteen minutes is barely enough time for me to change clothes. I rush to my closet, which is not that far, given my apartment is only six hundred square feet in size. I throw on a simple black dress that I had recently acquired at my local GWs. It probably cost over a hundred dollars for the original owner, but I bought this pretty baby for under a ten spot. That's what I call a proper steal. My chest tightens. Steal. Theft. All things that happened with the finality of my divorce. Could I really ignore all of that and move forward with the possibility of something outside of the courtroom with Maxwell?

The knock on my door interrupts my cycle of courtroom versus possibility. I need to make a decision on this tonight on which way I want to go. Sure, he has been nice, but am I betraying myself and Schatzi to even entertain the concept of a relationship with Maxwell?

Schatzi begins to bark, as always. She barks whether it is a welcomed visitor or not. Don't all dogs?

"It's okay, Schatzi, let me see who it is." I peer through the peek hole to make sure it is a welcomed visitor. Through the glass is a suit that I would most likely recognize in any line-up, and a bouquet. I squeeze my eyes together. Though I have received more flowers than I have ever in my life these last few weeks, this is still a surprise.

I open the door and Schatzi continues to bark while she simultaneously wags her tail. Okay, this is good. There is no growl.

"Hello." Maxwell raises a floral arrangement and offers me the dog bone first.

"Um, I thought you said you wanted to take me to dinner?" I raise the bone in question.

"Ha, touché, I was hoping that Schatzi might like that while we were out." He rubs his thumb against the edge of his chin.

I can't help but smile. "Very kind of you." I gaze down at her. "Schatzi, would you like this doggie bone?"

Her mouth is almost in a full smile back at me despite the quick lick of her lips. This reminds me that I need to get more dog bones for future moments of reward for any time that we miss each other.

I go into the kitchen and cut the plastic off the bone and offer it to her. Maxwell is at my side and hands me the bouquet. "These are for you. I got them earlier today, so they have been out of water for a bit and, thus, might be thirstier than me." His eyes are dark as if he is hungry for more than a drink.

"Thank you." I squint my eyes and grab a vase from under the sink. After the water is poured, I grab my purse. The energy is off in the room. I haven't had a man alone with Schatzi here ever.

"You ready?" Maxwell must sense this, or he is actually thirsty as well.

"Indeed. Hold down the fort." I rub Schatzi's head. She barely acknowledges me as she is too busy with her new bone.

The car ride is quick and quiet. Sometimes it seems best to save the heavy conversations for real face time instead of a dark car on a dark road headed on a path of uncertainty.

As we make our way to the table. A few people nod at me. I am not sure if this is a mere greeting or a recognition of who I am. Or rather what I am about to be sworn into. The office to represent them.

"You look lovely tonight." Maxwell grabs my fingers and squeezes my palm.

A shot of blood surges through my veins. *I am okay. This is okay.* I warn myself.

"Thank you. I would clarify my compliment to you, but you always look nice in your suits … Do you have any casual wear?" I laugh.

"Of course. Maybe someday I will let you see it." He smirks at me. Like he has an inside joke for an upcoming moment.

"It was nice of you to bring Schatzi a bone." I rub my lips together. I want to bring up a difficult topic, but I also don't want to.

"It's the least I could do. I knew it was your day." His eyes meet mine, and I let my stare break first.

"On that … I want to be honest with you." I rub my fingers along the white table cloth, in an effort to smooth out wrinkles that do not

276

exist. "I am not sure what this is that we are doing?"

Maxwell nods. "Ah, yes, well, this is a restaurant, and we are about to have a nice meal." He waves his hand around the room for me to take in the scene.

"Right, I mean—"

"I know, I apologize. I was trying to make light of a not-so-light situation." Maxwell's chest and shoulders rise. "I never saw myself in a situation like this. I don't have a game plan or map or any type of guidance for how this should go." He takes a turn on smoothing out the cloth. "I wish our initial meeting had been under different circumstances. I know that your divorce and pre-curser to it caused you a lot of pain. I can see that. I can almost feel it sometimes when I see the sadness in your eyes." He grabs my hand.

I let him hold it, but only lightly. Like a beginning discussion of a possibility.

"I don't know if I can get past our … how we met," I say in a quiet voice, loud enough for both of us to hear and loud enough for me to process it.

"I know. I understand that." Maxwell takes my palm and circles his index finger around the lines. "We can go at whatever pace you need or not, it's your choice."

"Are y'all ready to order?" A tall woman with bright blue eyes and a crisp white shirt peers down at us. I might have waited a moment if I were the waiter, but I guess some people don't know how to read the room.

"Could you please give us a few minutes?" Maxwell offers the most assertive grin I think I have ever witnessed.

I bite the inside of my lip after she leaves.

"You don't have to answer tonight. The only thing you have to decide is what you want to eat." Maxwell offers me a menu full of choices.

I nod and scan the options. "I'm going to opt for spicy and get the Chakalaka."

Maxwell grins. "I will switch things up and go totally opposite of that and get the Gugulethu Espetada." He bites his lip.

"Definitely, different from mine, but alas, both dishes are from South Africa." I clear my throat after the server leaves our table. "I talked to my office to see if I could get any video from the last week of my car."

"Oh, what happened?"

My eyelids press together and a vision of all the nails in my tires over the last year flashes through my mind on a loop. All the bills I had to pay to fix my car. All the time I tried to find out if it was by accident or by malice. All of this and Maxwell didn't know this. There was no reason to tell him I thought his client was vandalizing my car. I had no proof. All I had was a theory and that is as good as a wish on a star in an empty dark sky.

"I had another nail in my tire. Which caused me to have a flat tire, yet again."

"Again, how many flat tires have you had?" Maxwell crinkles the tablecloth on his side of the table.

"Hmph … too many to count. I think we are on twelve or thirteen." My throat is dry and little beads of nerves creep up on the back of my neck. This sense of doom from the reality of not being truly safe. Not when I have nails in my tires and constant threats of taking my dog. When will it end?

"When did this start? Have you gone to the police?"

My mouth is formed into two straight lines. "There is nothing to do with the police, as I can't prove anything." I shrug. "They will just say something about the city having bad roads and construction."

"But you haven't ever contacted them? It's important to have a record. Once we find the culprit, then you can tie them to all of the nails."

I sigh. "Okay, well, I have the dates and the amounts of money I have had to pay for each incident."

"That's good. Have you received any threats or have any idea who would do this?"

My eyes burn, and I feel like they are about to pop out of my head. "Are you serious? Any idea? Like you don't know?"

Maxwell rubs his thumb along the bottom of his jaw. "Of course, there is the usual suspect, but do you think it could be campaign-related?"

"No, this is part of his MO. He has been tampering with my car before I even filed for divorce." An image of Christmas Eve morning and not being able to start my car blasts in my mind. It was only later that day that DaVile told me he had unplugged the wires in my car. My lungs squeeze together. I take in a deep breath. *Breathe ... you are safe; it's okay.*

Maxwell takes a swig from his glass before continuing. "Well, that MO ends now. What did your work say? Were they able to get any footage?"

I shake my head. "Nope, apparently the video auto-deletes after seventy-two hours to save space."

"I'll talk to my PI and see what options we have to end this."

I blink a few times as if to wake myself up and realize this is not a fantasy. Maxwell is actually trying to help me and end this constant threat.

"What about Schatzi and the motion he filed for full custody?"

"Well, everyone is entitled to their day in court, but now that you are a representative-elect, we can put the case on hold until after the session, per the Texas Constitution."

The server returns with our meals, momentarily pausing our conversation. Maxwell's meat is hanging from a metal skewer, it's several rounds of beef resembling beads on a necklace. Whereas my Chakala is in a small bowl and the curry scents are intense.

As soon as the server drops off our plates, I pick up where we left off. "I didn't know that. Do we need to file something to pause the case?"

Maxwell raises his fork. "Already done and granted."

"But what about my visitation with Schatzi—will he actually be able to get full custody?" Fear and pain flip-flop in my head … with a level of dread I did not think was possible.

"I can't make promises, it's unlikely, however. Better yet, we might be able to get you more time with her." He reaches for my hand and squeezes it. "It will definitely be different this time around."

"More time with Schatzi, that would be like winning the lotto!" I am suddenly switched from sadness to anticipation of good things to come in my future.

Chapter Twenty-Two
"You can't catch anything, unless you learn how to play."

Today was going to be what some members call "Numbers Day." After the returning members who have seniority in the House choose their capitol office, desk on the House Floor, and parking spot, the new members get their chance to find where they will be. To me a seat was a seat, and in the capitol, no less! In each session, the head ranking Capitol staff decides what will be the method to determine the rank of each new member. This session was done by drawing a ping pong ball out of a box in order of your district number. Meaning if you were House District 1, you would get to pull from the balls first for your house ranking. Whatever number you chose would be your rank in your freshman class. I was one of the last members to go in accordance with my district number. There were three balls left in the box to choose from. The one ball, the two ball, and the twenty-two ball. I bet you can guess which one I got.

I eyed the ball, yes as fate would have it, I was not number one or number two. But I still was about to choose my office in the Capitol. I push open the door to find Kevin on the other side. I am sure he is going to be a bit disappointed.

"Hey," I greet him.

"What number did you get?" He glances at my hand as I show him the ball.

"Twenty-two … that's almost the very last spot."

I nod. "Yep. But we still have an office in the Capitol, so I think it's going to be okay."

We walk down the corridor and through the stairs. The selection room is on the second floor. The Capitol has had some renovations over the years but it is by no means updated. The carpets are faded maroon some have marks that need to be tended to. This is all done with seniority as well. If a freshman has an office with a tear in their rug and a senior ranking member has a doorknob that they would like to have reinstalled a million times. That door knob is going to be replaced a million times before the rug is addressed.

"I'll probably get a million steps walking these halls during the session." I glance at my Fitbit app to see how many steps I have made today.

"Definitely, we will probably be in the basement." Kevin's eyebrows furrow.

He is quite a bit younger than me. I get the disappointment, but we are in the Capitol. Most staffers are young; they are new to the working world and can make do with roommate situations and budgeting in a way that older staffers wouldn't or couldn't. Especially once they begin to have families or want to buy a home. The whole concept of being a staffer in the

Capitol is a springboard for many careers making triple if not more than their current salaries.

I turn the knob and open the door to the selection room. There are two easels with maps of the building. Another poster board is on a chalkboard with a drawing of the House Floor and numbered desks. And in the back of the room is a layout of the parking garage, which I feel is like driving into the Bat Cave. You go down underneath the Capitol to park.

"Representative-Elect Verita, you can check out the office spaces, the rest have been chosen, these are your options." The head staffer points at the map.

Capitol staff returns year after year unless the Speaker decides to change things up. Yet, the Speaker won't officially be determined until after we are sworn into office. After we take our oaths, we take our first vote on the House Floor, which is to elect the Speaker, who has only ever been a man. In fact, if you had a Texas Capitol reunion of any woman alive or dead, and asked them to sit in any seat in the House or Senate, we wouldn't have enough women to fill the seats ... still.

Kevin and I check out the map. There are two different offices to choose from. One is on a Republican-heavy floor and the other is on a floor with my border mate and classmate, Roger Schmidt. I chose that spot and signed my name for the location. Next, Kevin is given a booklet for us to choose our furniture. All the furniture is solid wood and the chairs are high-quality leather, all made by Texas prisoners for zero dollars. That's right, unpaid labor, does that sound familiar?

"When do I get to pick my office?" A loud voice calls out from the front of the room.

Kevin and I focus our attention on the man. I shake my head. I wish I had restraint and did not show any signs of acknowledgment. Dick Mickelson is staring at me.

"All right, Representative-Elect Verita, we can choose your desk over here."

I follow behind the staffer and keep my back toward Mickelson.

"Here ya go, these are the available desks." The staffer points out a few desks.

"Uh, I don't know if you want to be by the press desks." Kevin taps on the desk near the row of press seats.

"Hmm … yes, but the ladies' room is right there. I think that makes the most sense." I tap on the available spot. "Besides, how could being by the press be problematic?" I laugh.

Kevin's eyes widen but he refrains from speaking.

"Alright then, sign up to be by the press." The staffer offers the paper for me to sign for my desk. I sign my name, Representative-Elect…until January, then I can drop the "elect".

"And finally, you need to choose your parking spot." The staffer points to the parking garage map. There are lots of red Xs and a few open spots. I squint to review which one is closest to the elevator. There is plenty of Capitol security, but something about this change in my life makes me more nervous than normal.

"Don't I get to pick out my seat this time?" Mikelson bellows from behind. A few Republican men pat him on the back and laugh. "You'll be back soon enough."

The audacity. I ignore this the best I can and pick my spot. The staffer gives me the keys to my capitol office. *My* capitol office.

Kevin and I avoid any interaction with Mikelson and head toward our office, which is in the basement.

The place is empty. I hadn't even thought about needing things to put on the walls and decorations. More things to add to my to-do list.

"We've got to hurry and get to the fundraiser. Probably should take a lift, the parking is bad on 9th street." Kevin grabs his file folder.

"Yeah, I'll order one."

It takes us almost five minutes to make it through the basement and back to one of the Capitol entrances. We rush to the Lyft. Thankfully, the fundraiser is not far from the Capitol. By design, most members have their Austin fundraisers at The Austin Club. It's a historic building and the history that has unfolded inside those doors is even more impressive than the large crystal chandeliers and tall white pillars out front.

TFM gave me his list of donors to call as promised. I also called the list of Mikelson's campaign donors. The place is packed, but they are not all here for me. I am sharing the room with Roger Schmidt, which I don't mind since we are now also hallmates per our new office choices. It also cuts down on the cost of renting the room. Which makes the most sense/cents given I am here to raise money not spend it.

Roger and I are supposed to keep to different sides of the room to not interfere with any relationship-building with lobbyists. Yes, a room full of lobbyists similar to being in a chummed water and sharks have been released into the area. I am okay. It's funny dealing with lobbyists over regular donors. Lobbyists are paid by multiple groups or a specific company to represent them and their issues in the Capitol. Which seems counterintuitive if you consider that is what we were elected to do.

Yet, money always talks. Money ensures that you might come back for another session. Or maybe you can afford to pay your campaign staff. Smaller groups that lobby with their mouth but not financially can sometimes move the needles. Yet, in the last few decades, it has appeared that the financial lobbyists are the ones who are moving the needle or blocking the progress. This is one of the foundational reasons I chose to run for office. I really want to represent the people of my district.

I have to do this part though too. I have to have fundraisers. I have to meet with lobbyists and I have to listen to what the groups or companies that they represent have to say. I do want to hear their concerns. Some are even good.

As the groups mingle some are obvious about their intention. They are not interested in building a relationship. They are dutifully there to say hello, drop a check or envelope, and bounce. Others are slower movers, they want to chat, they want to do a Q&A & a. But all of it feels similar to cattle being herded into a corral, not knowing if they are going to be slaughtered or fed.

"Well now, I'm surprised to see you. I heard they weren't sure if you won." An older white man in a faded yellow suit points at me.

I smile. "Indeed, I did. How are you?" is all I can offer. The tension could not be cut with a knife, it would break.

"Well, still surprised, but I guess we will just have to see how things go this session."

The guy to his right nods. "Representative-Elect, I'm John Dunns and this is Brian McCarty, we are with the Houston IAL Pac."

I offer my hand. "Nice to meet you. I'll be interested to see which legislation you are concerned with this session."

"Oh, you'll definitely be hearing from us. And this is your Chief?"

"Yes, I'm Kevin, good to meet you." Kevin offers his hand and Brian puts the envelope in it.

"Make sure that goes to something good." He nods at us and leaves the room.

More people move in and have similar interactions offering a level of surprise that I won or scrutiny that maybe I didn't. The sensation of voter fraud over the last few elections has caused so many people to doubt the legitimacy of an election when it turns out opposite of their hoped outcome.

"There she is!" A guy comes from the front of the room toward our table. He has a blond woman at his side.

"Representative-Elect Verita, you have no idea how happy we were that you won."

"Thank you, I appreciate that." My somewhat deflated ego begins to fill back up a bit.

The blond woman nods. "Really, you have no idea. We could not stand your predecessor! Good luck this session."

The guy hands me an envelope.

"Thank you."

I turn toward Kevin once they're out of earshot. "Well, that was finally someone that was happy."

Kevin shakes his head. "There are a lot of people that are happy you are here instead of Mikelson, including staffers."

Chapter Twenty-Three
"Hand on the 19th, eyes focused, and a full heart."

The royal blue satin hangs on my hips. It was the perfect length. Hits right at my knees and rests over my curves with enough room not to see any lines from underneath the material. Despite my disdain toward the idea of scarves on the House Floor, today, I put on the silk scarf Ginger had given me as a joke. She had to hear me complain more than once about the audacity of the scarf instruction from the unsolicited appearance session. This scarf was different, though, it spells out "Resist" in Morse Code. Calvin Klein might not agree with the look, but I knew this was the perfect political message for me to be sworn into office.

A string ran against my calf. No. Not today. I let a groan slide from my throat. The hem has fallen. Of all days to not have it together.

"Hey, no worries. I've got this!" Ginger rushes to her purse and whips out a small sewing kit.

"Are you serious? You keep a sewing kit in your purse? Wow." I laugh. "This is next-level Ginger. You have really outdone yourself today."

"So have you." Ginger glances up at me as she works the needle like the true surgeon she is. "I am so proud of you."

I nod. "I couldn't have done it without you." My lips press together as I nod. This is the moment. Right here. In a makeshift fashion fix with my best friend, my life partner, and I am about to be sworn into office. Her red locks cascade over her shoulders. Her dress is a bright green. She said it was a reminder that people should have kicked in more to my campaign. I think some of the FTM stories have gotten to her.

"And I wouldn't let you. But this is your win. Now, you need to take your oath and get to work for the people." Her head bounces as she jumps up. "There you are, good to go."

"Ginger, seriously, you are the best." I hug her.

"Mia, today is not about me. We are celebrating this incredible moment and you."

I slide into my desk chair in my capitol office. That's right, I have an office in the Capitol. The Texas Capitol! My cheeks warm and my chest tightens. It's almost too good to be true. I take in a deep breath and smooth out the non-existent lines on the desk. My office is barren. I need to get some pictures to put up on the walls and fill the bookshelves that we picked out.

A tap on the door calls my attention away from the empty walls and minimalistic design of my four walls. Maxwell is in a navy blue suit with a light blue tie. His eyes pierce in my direction. I take a deep breath. It is almost as if the oxygen has been removed from the room.

"Hey there." His smile moves from his lips to the lines near his eyes. A bit of a twinkle.

"Hi, Maxwell, how are you?" Ginger gives him a light hug.

"Good, would you mind if I have a quick moment with Mia alone?" His hand is on the door.

Ginger jerks her head back and glances at me. "Okay, sure." She mouths *Call me right after* me as she closes the door behind her.

"I'm sorry about that. I just wanted to have a moment with you before you are officially sworn in. I hope that's okay?"

"Okay." My heart is on ultra-drive. What is going on here? We have barely talked in the last few weeks. It was almost as if we had been left on read after our dinner. He went away for Christmas, some preplanned trip to see his family. I wasn't really sure how to think about him, and with the numerous calls and texts about everything under the sun from my staff, other representatives, media, and the list goes on, I haven't had a chance to sit in my feelings and decipher if there was anything between the two of us.

"I know your world is about to become super busy and you might not have time for me, but I will be here for you. Whatever you need. Whenever you need it. I am here." He pulls out a small box from his coat pocket. It is small. Is this? No. He wouldn't. It's too soon. That doesn't make sense. Also, doesn't seem like his style. But maybe because it's my inauguration? I don't know. My mind is an absolute mess.

He puts the box in my hand. I slowly open it and a silver necklace is laid neatly in the box. Little tiny diamonds form a crown over the body of a queen chess piece. It's perfect. Wow.

"This is beautiful, Maxwell." I unhook the clasp and give it to him.

He takes it and places it over my neck. "Just like you. You are the queen, remember you can move in any spot that you want to, and I have you covered. I have blocked every attempt to come at you. I will always guard you and keep you safe." He snaps the clasp and kisses my neck.

I turn and our lips meet, his arms are at my waist as he pulls me in closer to him. He smells of tobacco and a warm summer rain. His lips run over mine and his tongue swirls in a circle as my tongue meets his. A deep tango twist moves in a melodic beat as he lets me relax into the moment, and I am overrun with pleasure. He takes my head into his hands and pulls his head back.

"My queen, it's time for you to be adorned."

I laugh. "You're funny, but I agree, it's time."

I grab my constitution from Ben and we make our way to the House Floor. I kiss Maxwell briefly and wave goodbye as Ginger and I find my seat. You are only allowed to have two people with you on the Floor. I obviously chose Ginger and a framed photo of Schatzi.

The Speaker calls us to order and all the representative-elects stand to be sworn in. I search the galley for Maxwell. Our eyes meet. I touch my necklace, and he nods.

My constitution is open to the 19th Amendment. I place my left hand over it and raise my right hand. The House Floor is packed. It's warm and bright. Silence fills the room. So many people have stood in my same spot and made a promise to uphold our values and laws. I scan the crowd of people. Full of happy faces. Some people are using their programs as fans. Little kids have their focus on the exit. It's easy to see they are bored out of their minds and have been asked to be quiet. The Speaker stands in front of the microphone on the Dias.

"Members, repeat after me."

"In the name and by the authority of the state of Texas I, Mia Verita, do solemnly swear, that I will faithfully execute the duties of the Office House of Representatives of the State of Texas, and will to the best of my ability preserve, protect, and defend the Constitution and laws of the United States and of this State, so help me God."

The End.

AUTHOR'S NOTE

Thank you for reading FFS: Politically Correct. If you enjoyed it, please consider leaving a review or recommending to a friend.

Thank you to my friends, my family, and colleagues that listened, read, or discussed the various ways this book could and should go. The list includes A, K, MM, V, S, B, J, S, TG, and many more.

ABOUT THE AUTHOR

Gia Stone is an author of steamy romances and fictitious novels. Faulted characters, misguided motives, and misconnections are at the heart of her books. She loves to collect passport stamps, savory memories, and race medals.

Gia's favorite quote is "The gem cannot be polished without friction, nor a person perfected without trials."